GOING, GOING, GONE

JACK WOMACK

GROVE PRESS
New York

First published in 2000 by *Voyager,* an imprint of HarperCollins*Publishers*, London, England

Published simultaneously in Canada
Printed in the United States of America

FIRST AMERICAN EDITION

Library of Congress Cataloging-in-Publication Data

Womack, Jack.
  Going, going, gone / Jack Womack.
    p. cm.
  ISBN 0-8021-1685-X
  1. Presidents—United States—Election—Fiction. 2. New York (N.Y.)—
Fiction. 3. Time travel—Fiction. I. Title.

PS3573.O575 G65 2001
813'.54—dc21   00-064368

Grove Press
841 Broadway
New York, NY 10003

01 02 03 04   10 9 8 7 6 5 4 3 2 1

For everyone whose eyes I saw,
above the mask

So where did we go wrong? Well, I figure the wrong-
ness was always there ... So many terrible scenes
with – forget it, deactivate it, let it go, it is only in
your memory now, remove it. You have the power
to do it.

—William S. Burroughs
May 12, 1997

ONE

Soon as I spiked I turned my eyes inside. Setting old snakehead on cruise control always pleases, no matter how quick the trip. I looked out the window for a minute or an hour or so, listening to stoplights click off blue, orange, blue. Meteor showers of Maryland-bound cars shot past down there on Connecticut Avenue and I made wishes on their long swirly trails. It pissed me bigtime that my innkeepers liked the guests to suffer silence, and I made a note to bring along a hi-fi next go-round. I thought I felt Metroliner vibes four hundred feet below me, steady as a motel vibrabed, but it was nothing but blood doing a sprint up my legs, trying to get to my heart before it was too late.

I'd just started examining the pattern of the tooled holes in my wingtips – circles inside of stars, looked downright masonic if you ask me – when I heard those jingle bells ring. In my mildly altered condition it never would have occurred to me that Martin would never blitz his own battleground, so I jumped. Only natural considering my iffy relationship with DC's boys in blue. Luckily enough, before I could make for the john and drown my bagged cat I realized I was only hearing the phone, and so I restashed my stash. Usually I unplug the ringer at check-in, but this time it had slipped my mind. You

1

always risk clipping a good buzz in mid-hum, when you sign on for a twenty-four-hour shift. Goes with the territory.

'Morning,' I shouted at the receiver, trying to remember which end was which.

'Evening,' Bennett said. 'Can't you tell the difference?'

'Six of one, half dozen of the other.'

'Are you drunk?'

'Dog's on the leash,' I assured him.

'You finish the distribution?'

'Hold on.' My hand was getting numb. I'd put a tourniquet round my arm with the phone cord somehow and thought I'd better unwrap it before I could spontaneously amputate. 'You were saying?'

'Was there anything left to distribute?'

From afar Bennett came on like a Harvard Dillinger, but up close you knew he was just another dental hygienist. On his evolutionary scale I topped out around Fishhead level – try as he might, he never cottoned to watching his boss treat me like Future Man. Too bad for Benny but Martin and I went back many moons, plus we had more in common than old Ivy League ever would with either of us. 'Cut the j'accuse,' I said. 'Produce reached the market.'

'Speak English.'

'Speaking.'

'What about it, then?'

'About what, my brother?'

'Don't brother me.'

'Not to offend. I mean only in the broader sense.'

'When'll the wolves start howling?'

'English, Bennett. Please.'

'When should the roundup start?'

I reviewed my own experience. 'Body phase lasts maybe twenty minutes. Then it calms down a little and you think everything's square. All of a sudden chemistry takes the wheel and you park yourself in Mars orbit for nine hours

2

or so, depending on whether or not you ate beforehand. DuPont boys be able to handle that?'

'They're capable men.'

'You say so. Motto of a park ranger's be prepared.'

'Oh, hell –'

Help.

Without warning I found myself listening in counterpoint. Side effect? Could be, but Bennett was a prankster. 'You going stereo on me?'

'What are you talking about?'

Help.

Whoever was shouting help was broadcasting through a separate channel. He wasn't in the phone but didn't seem to be in my head either. I gave the room the onceover but I was the only one on duty. Whoever he was he sounded like he'd been sealed up in an oil drum. Possibly an unfortunate who'd run afoul of one of Bennett's less restrained subcontractors.

Help.

'That's not you, is it?'

'What are you on now?' Bennett's words popped out of the receiver; they were purple, and diamond-shape. Amazing how long the effects last sometime.

Help.

'Help you what?' I asked. 'Who's out there?'

'Walter!!'

'What?' I thought it best not to go into a lot more detail; things like this kind of disturbed Bennett's peace of mind. 'Must be hearing things, compadre. Nothing to write home about.'

He hissed like a stabbed tire. 'I've got a message. Think you'll remember?'

'Try me.'

'Mister Rollins says they want to meet you again tomorrow morning for breakfast. It's essential that you reconsider the offer.'

3

'Can't oblige,' I said.

'Essential, I said.'

'I heard you the first time.'

'Essential.'

I knew my limits. He'd be putting the needle down again and again till I finally got up and changed the record. 'All right, but tell 'em I got to charge a full day rate.'

'Understood,' he said. 'Meet them in the Willard coffee shop, nine sharp. The Willard Hotel. It's a hotel. Know the place?'

'Warren G. Harding shot his niece there, didn't he?'

'Nine sharp. Willard Hotel. We'll be waiting. Think you'll need any help waking up?'

'Not yours.'

Bennett skipped the gracious goodbye pages when he took his Emily Post lessons. Once he hung up I savoured the sound of blood rushing past my ears. The seller goes where the market calls but these assignments in DC were always a trial. Nothing like a trip to the land of the two-headed men to remind you why they dumped all that marble in a swamp. Nowhere else will you get the lingering miasma and rotting vegetables that sustain sound government. On a regular schedule the fen's trolls burn off excess gas. The glow attracts fools and children. The stench overcomes them, the gas hits the blood like carbon monoxide, the bog sucks them under. They're done for. Stay out of politics, my brothers, there's no keeping clean.

Bennett's call had rung down the curtain on my mind's nightly adventure. Even though I considered taking it from the top I noticed it was midnight, and since I'd been hit with this unforeseen breakfast subpoena I decided I'd better take the sensible road and toddle off to snoozeville. While shedding my outerwear I let myself go blank. Listened to walls creak as they eased their weary stones, heard the wind tickle the ivy's dry threads. I was stashed in the usual drawer, an N Street townhouse with 1850 skin and 1965 guts. Claims adjusters infested the ground floor offices but the apartments were available for government transients. I don't know who crashed in my suite when I wasn't in town. Martin didn't say, I didn't ask. The joint must have been classville in buggywhip days but the trolls had been hard at work since. On a five-star scale I'd give the leftovers a negative four. A junkman wouldn't take the furniture if you paid him. Turn on the faucets and take bets on what colour the water'd be. Cockroaches big as chihuahuas and just as quiet. Every morning rats raced through the groundcover out front to the point where even a dead sober man would think the yard was trying to sneak away from the house. Well, it was never more than a couple nights' flop to me and after all, I've done time in places that made this look like the Savoy-Plaza. I'd just started kissing the sheets when my unseen friend returned.

Help.

Definitely not Bennett this time. I tried hauling myself up but it wasn't easy.

Help.

Where was that boy? Somewhere on my left, maybe? Don't believe the yarns, there's not much to be gained when you start hearing people who aren't there. 'Yo boyo, your signal's coming in clear. Show yourself.'

Help me.

'No need to be shy,' I called out, thinking I'd pinned him down on radar. I tiptoed to the bathroom and pushed at the door. 'Hey Livingstone. Stanley here.' No answer, so I flipped on the brights and peeked in. 'Anybody?' Nobody. Now if I'd stayed horizontal I could have probably convinced myself that the evening's entertainment simply intensified those bad DC vibes, but once up my reptile brain couldn't be rubed. Maybe I landed in the middle of one of those CIA campfire tales you always hear. Those necrophiliacs had no need to unscrew my bulbs, but they wouldn't have cared. This was probably the kind of fun they had when they weren't out shooting Nixon.

Help.

I did a Norman's mother. Nobody in the shower so I checked under the sink. Bug city; ten thousand long-term leasees but none of them were talking. Men of science test all theories, so I stared down into the toilet bowl. In heightened states the sight of running water calms me down, and the longer I looked in the better I felt. Nothing but an unexpected side effect, I told myself. No telling what'll bob up when the mind starts simmering. In my more adventurous days I once dropped a little blue tab, supposedly some derivative extracted from San Pedro cactus buds. Maybe so, but all it did was make me sneeze uncontrollably for fourteen hours.

Please help.

I looked up and I saw them standing there. Almost there, I'd better say. This was the first time I could eyeball somebody's front and glim their back simultaneously, but that wasn't the real mindbender. It was hard getting a fix on them because half the time they were turning colours and half the time, shifting into black and white. Made me want to shout focus at the projection booth. He wore what looked like a Bellevue suit, except the arms didn't have those fashionable belts and buckles. Just as well because if they had he couldn't've lugged the doll. His honey lay in his arms like a swoonstruck bobbysoxer. She gave every indication of being out on a heavy nod. Under the circumstances, mind you, I'd hesitate to say either one would have bled if you cut them. From what I could tell he'd had it hard wherever he'd had it, and she looked like she'd been dragged by a truck from Cleveland way past Detroit.

Please help us.

Neither of them were flapping gums when the words came through, but I heard him stone clear. The shakes hit me where I stood and that's a side effect I never get from that evening's particular family of chemicals. Closing my eyes, I tried to think of something to say. When I raised my shades once more my new pals were starting to fade. They didn't seem to notice, but I didn't think they were too conscious of anything, to tell the truth. Going, going, gone – and that was that for them.

Somehow it was worse having them gone. I rolled back into bed and listened hard. Even though I didn't hear him anymore it still took time before I could start copping Zs. What with all the excitement I'd worked myself into a tizzy. I couldn't shake the notion somebody was hotfooting over my grave. Seeing ghosts will do that, I suppose, and that's the way I finally chalked it up. Axe-murdered in this room years ago, probably, and the walls couldn't hold back on what they'd seen any longer. Fortean phenomena, the logical explanation. Nothing weird about it until it happens to you. Just one of those strange things happening every day, like green snow or a frogstorm, or buses showing up in threes.

I couldn't wait to get back to New York. Of course I didn't foresee I'd have guests along for the ride.

I cooled on my slab till roostertime, then rose and soaked my head in sunshine. No distressing afterburn, I was pleased to note – no neckache, no blurry vision, no need to brush one-handed while propping myself up with the unused paw. While scrubbing I decided to show up extra sharp for these boys. I shaved close, played coathanger for my priciest suit. Sparkled like a diamond in the rhinestone counter when I got there. The Williard Hotel's slavemasters weren't big on face control, and the coffee shop was almost one hundred percent DC riffraff. Most looked nitrogen-poisoned, stumbling around blind with walking bends, good for nothing but taking fingerprints or filing them. I breezed through their midst and ignored the looks the secretaries shot me. Martin and Bennett held court at a booth in the rear. Most of the dregs on hand favoured official federal government style.

7

But my boys were men of taste, and put on a Washington style show. Seven-layer silk ties, trifold linen squares, cuffs overloaded with silver and gold; suits thick as overcoats and shoes shiny enough to scare away the schoolgirls.

'Everything went exactly as you predicted, Walter,' Martin told me. 'Congratulations are in order.' My boss came on like he always did, the head man in Statuary Hall. Bennett looked like he'd sat on a pickle and couldn't get it out. He eyed me as if I were some evil bird swooping down to bag his waffles.

'Muchas thankas.' Taking a load off, I signalled the waiter.

'Sleep well?' Bennett asked.

'Slept better.'

'Too much on your mind, perhaps –'

I lit into the mocha java the second Pierre set it down in front of me, but that was a serious mistake. Gave my tongue third degree burns and for a second I thought my throat was going to seal up

'Hot?' Bennett asked.

'*Beelzebub*,' I said. 'Like drinking the sun.'

'You remember our associates,' said Martin, stretching out his hand like he was introducing the dog act. 'Mister Hamilton. Mister Frye.'

'Morning, my brothers.'

The co-conspirators nodded and winked and I returned the favour. Hamilton was silver-haired, silver-tongued and slippery as wet glass. I don't think he was a mammal. Old mellifluous knew anything he served up had to drip with syrup, otherwise it'd never slide down. His sidekick Frye seemed content with the job of vestigial twin. If you taught a ferret how to walk on its back feet and put it in a three-hundred-dollar suit, you'd have Frye. He sat there emitting a series of sinister chuckles. Those two were kingsize trolls but it was never clear to me what precise realm of the swamp they oversaw, and they seemed the

8

sort who'd like to keep it that way. Martin screwed a Lucky into his holder. Bennett almost fell out of his chair, offering his lighter.

'You get it?' he asked. Martin fired up and shot one smoke ring through another.

'The Willard used to be such a magnificent hotel,' Hamilton proclaimed, oozing the grease of sociability. He knew if he came on like Uncle Bob he'd get an invite to any Friday dinner. 'Sad, how much it's changed over the years. You're not old enough to remember what this was, before it was a coffee shop.' I'd have guessed nobody was. 'It was a corner of the grand ballroom. The ceiling and those walls are false, you see. My friend Donald Cook's graduation party was given here in 1926. Donald was the son of Senator Cook, he died on the *Brittannica*.' I was starting to wish I had. 'An unforgettable evening. We kept our flasks at the ready, filled with hooch. Whenever the chaperones turned their heads we'd have a snort. I danced with Sally Patterson half the night.' He went all cow-eyed, recalling the scent of long-lost fur. 'Fifty beautiful young men and women, learning the ways of the world.' I suspected he placed himself pretty high on the beauty scale. 'The stage was there.' He pointed at the steam table, where two Japs stood slinging hash. 'Seven smoke musicians. Real hot poppas from New Orleans, as we used to say.' He burst out in soft song. '*If the man in the moon was a coon, coon, coon –*'

Hambone pursed his lips like he was spitting out water-melon seeds. Frye made with the chucks: *hmnf hmnf hmnf.* Bennett sighed; he probably spent half his life hearing about parties he wasn't invited to. Martin, like me, played icecube.

'I did some stepping out back in Cambridge myself,' Bennett said, at the same time eyeballing me. 'Not very good at it, though. Two left feet.'

'I suspect you underestimate yourself,' Hamilton said.

'Surely I wouldn't have held a candle to you, sir.' Bennett

kissed most people's feet because he was too short to reach their ass.

'Sweet memory is all that lingers once the ball is over, gentlemen,' said the old codger. 'So soon we forget.'

If this went on much longer he was going to drag out the uke and start yodelling. After he tossed off that little lyric from the hit parade I was in no mood to foxtrot. 'I've forgotten why you asked me here, actually,' I said. 'Not to cut you short, my brothers, but I've got a train to catch.'

'Mister Smith,' Hamilton said, speaking in my direction, as if he'd been struck blind but suspected I had a quarter. (My legal given is Bullitt, by the by, but I use a more forgettable monicker for piece work.) 'I want to offer you the opportunity to reconsider our proposal. We think you're our man for the job.'

'I don't even know what your proposal is,' I said. I'd turned them down simply because I hadn't liked their looks; you get to my level and you can start getting away with that, sometimes. 'Told you I like to see the sandwich before I bite down.'

'Son, your qualms are understandable,' Hamilton said. 'Ordinarily we'd have already enlightened you, but I fear a certain restraint was and is called for in this situation.'

'Restraint's my middle name.'

'So Martin has told me. And Bennett, as well.' Little mongoose glared at me with beady blue eyes. 'All the same your talents are such that we're willing to make allowances for your, uh, personal style.'

'I appreciate your appreciation,' I said. 'Need more than that, though.'

'In the fullness of time you'll be provided with all necessary information.'

'Time's filled up. Spill or I'm walking.'

'*Walter!*' Martin looked ready to come down hard, but I fired back my own daggers and he eased off on playing up

10

the Great White Father bit. Hamilton didn't look any more or less upset than he had when I'd said no, two days earlier. There was something about this I hadn't liked from the start. Since I wasn't officially on the payroll, and wouldn't have been one of Martin's Bennetts even if I had been, I wasn't covered with the kind of insurance you have to have when you get too far out in the jungle.

'Hear Hamilton out, Walter,' Martin said. 'It's a very simple proposition. Once you have all the details I'm sure you'll change your mind.'

'OK, so let's play catch. You going to tell me, or am I going to have to guess?' Our waiter slunk back to top off the percolations, but I shooed him away.

'I always appreciate forthrightness.' Hamilton's eyebrows hopped like caterpillars doing a mating dance. 'What would you guess, if you guessed?'

'This have anything to do with pharmaceuticals?' I asked.

'That's to be decided.'

'Will I be playing the old sucker game?'

'Could be.'

'Sowing the seeds of disarray?'

Hamilton dipped a shard of toast into a pool of yolk. 'Do you read the newspaper, son?' he asked, leaning over so far I could count his fillings.

'How else do I know what I've been up to?'

Hamilton hooted. *Hmnf hmnf hmnf,* said Frye. They were in on somebody's joke, that was for sure. 'Surely an intelligent man such as yourself,' said the Grand Codger, 'understands that at moments *sotto voce* is preferable to *fortissimo.* You understand the broader problems with which we constantly grapple –'

'We who?' I asked.

'Is that a question, Walter?'

'Who are you, anyway?' I asked. 'Can't quite put my finger on it.'

11

'Walter –' Martin started to say.

'You don't have J. Edgar's thumbprint on you,' I said, thinking I'd better start sharpening the pencils. 'Since you're out in daylight and aren't moist, I can rule out CIA.' *Hmf hmf hmf.* 'You're about as military as I am. My man Martin generally doesn't let on who pays for the groceries long as I make the delivery. Usually, I don't care. But truly, my brothers, all this incognito cum laude is making my mind start to wander. Feel like I'm in a tryout for Skull and Bones.'

'You're thinking of Yale, Walter,' said Bennett. 'We look like Yalies?'

Martin glared like an icy road. For a minute I gave them the benefit of the doubt, thinking they simply feared being taped al fresco. In truth there's no better place to talk trouble than out in the out and about. Every time Martin and I faced off to swap tales we took to the ozone, and hit the bricks. An old trick, never fails to keep nosy parkers from tuning in on the party line. It's a subtle concept for the layman to grasp, and these two clowns were no laymen. Just as I was starting to give in the old gringo flipped me such a death's head that I realized he was doing the Miss Priss bit purely for entertainment value. I got the notion he didn't care who heard what he said, since he never exactly said it.

'Walter, are you aware of what happens this November?' Hamilton asked.

'This is February.' *Hmnf hmnf hmnf,* said Frye.

'Good things take time,' Bennett said.

'There's an election this November,' said Hamilton. 'You'll be voting?'

'Never,' I said. ''99 bottles of beer on the wall. I don't sing along.'

Hamilton made with the tut-tuts. 'Possibly we're not as cynical as you are.'

'Try me.'

'Are you familiar with the field of candidates? Does anyone in particular come to mind?'

He had me there, but I wasn't going to let on. Thinking for a second, the obvious name popped into my head. 'President Lodge.'

'Thought we were going to have to cue you, Walter,' Bennett said.

'What about on the Democratic side?' Hamilton asked.

'Usual suspects, I suppose. Johnson, Humphrey. Pritchard. You think it'll matter?'

'You are cynical, son.'

'Call me son once I'm in the will,' I said. 'If I had to guess I'd say Lodge'll be re-elected. Incumbents always are.' Hamilton eyed me like I was a puppy who wet the rug. 'No?'

'We'll be clear on that by the end of next month, Mister Smith,' he said. 'But that's no concern of yours.'

'There's a name you've forgotten, Walter,' Bennett said. 'Among possible candidates. Who do you think you've forgotten?'

I shrugged. 'Gimme a phone book.'

'An old family name,' Martin said.

'But not that old.' The shift in Hamilton's vocalese as he purred his way into a growl made me appreciate the ease with which this old coot could hop from his wheelchair and whip out the shiv. Takes practice to glint like Jehovah when you're wearing a Brooks Brothers suit, but he had it down pat. 'The Kennedys –'

'Them?'

'Walter, hear us out.'

'Not a chance. I'm no steeplejack. I work the ground floor and mezzanine and I want to keep it that way. 'Not a chance –'

Hamilton lobbed his dentures my way and flashed those big blue peepers. 'This would entail your serving in the traditional *agent provocateur* position, Walter.'

'Walter, you could do it in your sleep,' Martin said.

'Probably done it in your sleep,' said Bennett.

'There's nothing to it –'

All signs on this eightball pointed to no. Number one swoon tune in DC was Never Waltz With A Kennedy. Once you involved yourself, even with a third cousin of a third cousin, it was only a question of time till Old Black Joe, reliable as napalm, caught you and dipped you in his deep-fryer. Giving his public rap sheet the onceover could crack your mind like a bullwhip, and nobody knew scratch about the deals that strayed from the path en route to Grandma's. His five boys couldn't match him except in pawing frails, try as they might and by all indications they tried. Nature herself had taken the girls out of the competition, there were five of them but every one strangled themselves in the womb to keep from coming out. Every spring through the thirties the Kennedy Curse struck anew. Once between the cartoon and part six of *Perils of Nyoka* I caught a glimpse of the gang in the 'Ten Years Ago Today' segment of *The March of Time*, filmed just before they went to London in 39'. They'd lost another one, the last. The boys wore black tie, Rose shrouded her weeds. Old Joe pried the top off the blarney jar and told the reporters Willa God, boys, all's jake but you got to watch Willa. She'll get you every time.

'Not a chance, not one in a million.'

'Walter, you need to hear specifically,' Hamilton started to say, but I wasn't listening. I heard something else.

Help.

Like I needed to see old brother Jell-O and his snoozy moll just then. They hung out by the cash register as if intending to clean out the till while a crony caused a distraction.

Help us.

Without signalling, my ghosts took the off-ramp and faded. I told myself I'd kicked back too long in the tub last night and was still pruny. But I wasn't kidding anyone, the luck of genes makes my system flush like a storm drain. Possible, though, that this new product was time-release. That could bring any number of complications about on down the line. Might mean all kinds of trouble uptown as well but the Dupont Circle boys could find out on their own without a park ranger. Even now their slammerful of potential perps were probably tearing the roof off the drunk tank, ripping out the porcelain, shitting on the ceiling, standing there franks in hand and howling for the bastards to turn the northern lights back on.

'What's so funny, Walter?' I heard Bennett say.

'Is he having a stroke?' Hamilton said.

'Just weighing the odds against the house,' I testified, coming out of my stew, laying both hands near but not on the Big Book. 'Pardon the trance.'

'No question you're the man for the job,' Martin said, and then demonstrated the folly of total self-assurance. 'You're Irish as they are, why wouldn't it work?'

Fortean ghosts were hard enough to bear but this took first prize in the Stupid awards. Something must have short-circuited in Martin's head, or else he was feeling more comfy around these characters than he had any right to be. He was no more tater tot than I was, and he knew that as well as I did. Now neither of us played the rules according to Hoyle, and while no VIP players who might suspect ever admitted seeing us deal with our spades hidden, we knew they always kept their guns on the table. Couldn't speak for my boss but I had no yen to scope scenic Guatemala and the deeper south unless I had a return ticket tight in my hand. It especially made me sweat buckets when his idle comment provoked Frye into burping up something other than chucks.

'Black Irish, maybe.'

Bad, bad news. No question his superior snagged it, but old Methuselah didn't return fire. Martin's mask slipped enough to show me he knew he'd been bugging too frantic on the canyon's lip. 'If you would hear us out, Mister Smith, you'd understand what a valuable opportunity this could prove to be for you,' Hamilton said, steepling his hands as if to pray to himself. *'Carpe diem.* A new world hitherto unimaginable to you will either open or close, depending upon your decision. May I continue?'

His picnic basket was starting to sit heavy on my grave. 'Pass the mustard,' I said.

'What?'

'Need to spread it on those fat slabs of spamola you're slicing off.'

'Now, Mister Smith –'

'I'm passing. Thanks anyway.' Easing myself up slowly, I aimed a finger at the timepiece hanging on the wall. 'Got to roll, I fear, New York's waiting.'

'You strike me as an infinitely adaptable fellow of subtle resources,' Hamilton said. The smile he gave me would have shamed a wax museum. 'Martin knows you're the man for the job. Perhaps we should agree to leave the matter open. It seems to me you should be considerably more interested in hearing us out than you've yet understood.'

I understood he could probably corner the market in nasty if he wanted, but I didn't want to wait around and find out. 'Tally ho, my brothers, that train's at the gate.'

'I'll be calling you,' Martin said.

Didn't look back as I strolled but I knew they kept me in the crosshairs. Took the long way out through the lobby, to tell the world I was in no rush. Soon as I was out of range I let my feet do their business. Had the admiral outside whistle up a cab, and two minutes later I was cruising up Connecticut en route to DuPont Circle. Neglecting to stop by the stationhouse to give the gang my regards I bounded down the escalator and hopped the noon express. Settling into a crowded car I switched off the seat's radio and settled back, trying to put breakfast, that song, those ghosts, everything out of mind. In two hours I'd pipeline straight into Penn

Station's warm marble barn and then it'd be hello, New York. I couldn't wait.

Once I was back in the free world I wasted no time heading for my castle. No sooner did I get there, though, than I realized I might as well have left the drawbridge down. My greeting committee floated above the corner of the living room, near the window and to the left of the hi-fi.

Help.

What really made my bag rise this time was my quietude in the face of this species of unnatural. Bad pennies are forever turning up but not being surprised when you find them is another matter indeed. There was only one thing left to try. Hair of a different dog taken in ideal conditions proves an unfailing remedy in most cases of aftershock, and I could see no reason it wouldn't work here. I have to be truthful and say I don't know how hard I looked. Unplugging the phone, I greased and papered my Victrola's spinner and slid a new needle in the tone arm. Thumbed through the C shelf until I spotted the right man. Lay down the shellac, grooved the point and let it spin. No crime in listening. Never was.

'Pastafazoola, Tallullah –'

No crime in singing along, though the neighbours might disagree.

'Pass me a pancake, Mandrake –'

No doubt about it, *these* palefaces weren't hep to the jive. My two ghosts took the hint and condensed. Suspected they'd be back but that was then and this was now.

Alone again I stashed the cash Martin'd slipped me for my efforts in the strongbox, then pulled down my humidor to keep a date with Mary Jane. Dressed her in something tight and kissed her down to her toes. Got a Pepsi out of the fridge and lent Cab my ears. Though I don't teetotal I'm not one for putting on the boozebag. Body trips leave me too full of that old ennui. The ideal agents as I see it are the ones

17

that take your head off and let you hold it awhile. I cooped inside, content, till delirious night came creeping through the streets. Then, after a quick rinse and shave, I snatched up my wrapper and ankled downstairs.

Two blocks west on the slum end of Park was my crib away from crib. Those up on their long-gone New York know the tale of McGurk's Suicide Hall, famed Bowery hotspot of the gay nineties, a most favoured lure for the addled and unsavoury, whilom HQ of the fearsome Coney Boys. If you soaked McGurk's in cheap black and Chinese red you'd get Max's. All the ambience of an opium den full of Dada girls, though louder. El perfecto, in the vernacular. No Packards lined the curb two deep so I suspected the night's talent didn't attract the riffraff. When I checked the marquee I saw that I was right. WELCOME THE VELVET UNDERGROUND AND NICO TO MAX'S KANSAS CITY. I'd head upstairs to revel after I perambulated the lower depths to see who was where. Before I could go in I noted out of the corner of one eye some character in a Rogers Peet suit, passing out flyers at the corner. He had a small table set up and a sign hung on the front. MAX YOUR PO INSTEAD, Some kind of anti-war gig I figured, and headed inside.

Smoke of all notions hit me like perfume as I stepped out of the ozone into the pressure chamber. Once my peepers adjusted for night vision I made out the personnel on board. In the far distance Warhola's full moon hair beamed through the night. Candy and Jackie had been bookending him but now they got up and were making for the stairs. Judging from the pudding bowls at the far end of the bar I reckoned Mancusian talent passing through town had dropped by to judge the competition. Closer still huddled the usual gaggle of Brooklyn tomatoes and Bronx bagel babies, decked out in their slickest Serendipity flash. If you didn't choke on hayseeds those farmgirl charms could warm the coolest heart. In the middle of the action were my two most usual suspects, and I gladhanded cheer all around.

18

'What's happening, hepcats?' I asked, doffing my homburg, and calling for the drink that hits the spot.

'Walter,' Trish said. 'Where've you been hiding?'

'Here there everywhere,' I said. We pecked cheek and did the vertical rub. Trish and I were hard on the sheets not that long ago but when she showed too much interest in how, exactly, I harvested my cabbage, I took to the fields. Knowledge is danger, knoweth the man, and I doubted she'd have approved of my every escapade. Even so we remained tasty pals. She was wanton that night, a flame-haired vixen, smoky and dazzling, total Gernreich on the hoof. As I eased my paw down her treacherous rear slope I found myself as always sliding across a Lothrop and Stoddard unitock. Trish had spent her heedless youth in a stately Wayne Manor out on the Philly main line, and the domestication clung. 'What's with the girdle, Myrtle?' I said. 'I'll need brushes to keep the beat on this tom-tom.' Our compadre Borden lounged close by, swilling with a smile, his fedora's awning hanging low. As usual he rode out in standard Fourteenth Street undertaker drapes. Good to see he'd regrown his chin shrub, made him look like a top shrink doing field work. Over time I'd clipped my own hedge down to its most nefarious essential. Kittens purr like mad when you brush their fur with the old pussy tickler.

'How deep's the scene, my brother?'

'Subcutaneous,' he said, a man of select words.

'You've been missed,' Trish said, playing bumpercars with my hip.

'Just a weekend cruise,' I said. 'Felt like a month.' A sudden flood of would-be cognoscenti streaming in threatened to do a Johnstown on us. Felt like I was taking the Sea Beach Express on the fourth of July. We started sliding our feet to the rear of the bus, trying to miss the wave.

'Care to divulge?' she asked.

'Lips, ships,' I said, shaking my head. Realized, scanning the room, that I half-expected to spot my silent Cals floating

19

somewhere over the backbar, trying to find space before coming in for a landing. Wished I'd upped the dosage on my nerve tonic. 'I earn my gold stars. You?'

'Mother's pearl,' she said. 'You have to ask?'

'When's showtime?' No sooner did I wonder than I felt the vibes ripple through the floor, and saw the lamps start to shake.

'Shortly. Let's move,' said Trish, and with Borden we carved a path through the wall of superfluous flesh, making for the ascent. 'I've been on tiptoes all day looking forward to this. They're so fabulous.'

'Utmost,' said Borden, playing jungle guide as he led us off. 'Utmost fabulousity.'

Hard to slouch walking up stairs, but he pulled it off. 'After you,' I said to the beauteous one, keen to see what lay under that doily she'd wrapped around her waist, but my chivalry went begging.

'My turn to take the scenic route,' she said, pointing upwards. 'Scamper.'

I did. Once we topped out we parked ourselves next to sweet Candy and ever-charmless Ondine, near the front. The band kicked off *Venus In Furs* and we let our heads fill up. The usual goofball light show was in progress, the band looked as if it were being attacked by yellow amoebas. Sterling stood there strumming away, Cale did his Bob Wills on Seconal bit, crazy Angus wandered back and forth whacking that Tibetan oildrum and weaselly Lou glowered like a nine-year-old looking to get spanked. Blondie sat off in the corner slapping her tambourine and making with the teutonics. I was just starting to settle in for a long decadent night when I heard Trish shouting at Borden.

'New girls in town, must be.'

'Tres wild,' Borden shouted back. 'Canadian?'

'Hardly,' Candy said; even though she tried to whisper, her voice always carried. I turned in what had become an unexpectedly popular direction. That was it, listeners. I saw them, and I was sunk.

'Check the ensembles,' Trish told Candy. 'These girls can shop.'

The little one – five four, near as I could tell – was severely mod, and radiated cuteness. Hair Sassooned, eyes raccooned. The white go-gos were strictly 1967 but I wasn't going to argue with the Nancy Sinatra look. Her mini kept riding up over the shoreline but that gave her something to do with her hands. Most inviting indeed, but that night it was hard not to savour the lure of the economy size. At first I thought Little Mod's gal Friday was tall as Sterling, maybe six four. Then I realized she was taller.

'What's that on her hip?' Borden asked.

'Looks like a whip,' Trish said. 'Gerard's understudy?'

'Nobody told me,' Candy said.

Big Girl's queenly strut distracted the audience and even the band, but they kept playing. As she and Little Mod crossed stage front Lou swallowed his lines but recovered nicely and nobody really noticed. For the first time in her life Nico demonstrated a facial expression. I guided my mouth towards charming Miss Darling's ear. 'Candy, my brother sister. Is that a him?'

She shouted into my own receiver. 'Goodness, no. She's real.'

'Seriously?'

'The hands,' she said, glancing at her own, frowning.

'Muchas thankas, my angel.'

Where she wasn't black, Big Girl was blonde. She drew her crowning glory up in thick golden ropes tied in a topknot. Over her birthday buxotica she wore beatgirl tights, though hers covered arms as well as legs. She hid her hands in fingerless gloves and her stems in boots of shiny shiny leather. No question she was blessed in the torso department. The plastic shell she'd squeezed herself into clung to her soft centre like frozen chocolate. Knobs big as desk erasers tipped her rocket launchers. Sunnyside up, she was unsinkable, and miraculous to behold, but I favour mine over easy. When Little Mod aimed for the stairs, Big Girl followed and I caught the full rear view in Cinerama. You could stack a week's dishes on that shelf.

'My brothers. My sisters,' I mumbled, feeling that the window for action was a narrow one indeed. 'The pink ray's nailed me. Please excuse.'

'Don't waste valuable resources, Walter,' Trish said.

'Rugmuffins,' Borden muttered, giving them the fisheye as they headed downstairs. 'Tag team, I'd guess.'

'You'll be sorry if you try,' she said. 'Those praying mantises will bite your head off.'

'Tiny tiny,' I shouted as I left. 'Tiny whips of leather.' Once I'd barrelled back down to the first floor I swivelled in every direction, trying to pick them out in the crowd until I caught them in my beam. Wasn't hard to spot the big one, archons willing. The ladies looked like they were still fishing, and hadn't seen that I was ready to take the bait. I was just circling in for the thrill when some Long Island desk jockey who'd mistaken the place for an Automat came out of nowhere and made a move on Little Mod.

'You got a pencil?' I heard him ask her. She shook her head. 'I need to write down your phone number.'

The little one looked at him like he was a dead cat. For the first time I noticed she was packing some kind of transistor in her hand. New model, I supposed, all black and shiny as Big Girl's boots. She had turned around to see what delayed her little friend. El Dopo, figuring out that he wasn't getting anywhere with his original target, now turned his attentions to the secondary, with as much charm and success. 'How's the weather up there?'

I was close enough now to hear the full script. 'Exit,' the big one told him. She had the voice of an eight-year-old but the lung power of a nursery. 'Presence undesired.'

'Excuse me?' he said, pulling a Bennett and going all smirky.

Just as I was ready to cut in on this dance my gut told me I should hesitate, and I did.

'Fly the coop,' Little Mod said. 'Offer service elsewhere.'

'You're the ones look like you're selling,' I heard him say, obviously taking the wrong turnoff. 'What is this, sugar? Only dykes need apply?'

Big Girl raised her little voice. Half the room turned to look, and then the same half of the room turned deaf mute. 'Motherfuck you,' she broadcast. I looked around for Max's bouncers, but they'd evidently taken the hen's teeth route. The would-be charmer deflated, somewhat, but he puffed back up in no time at all. That was his mistake. He put his paws on Big Girl's knobs as if wanting to tune in the ballgame. 'Look, honey,' he said, pinching them, 'you come prancing around like this and you might as well put a sign on your ass saying, for sale –'

Big Girl clicked her elbows against her sides as if getting ready to have her posture checked. Two small metal umbrellas suddenly appeared on the backs of the wiseguy's hands and snapped open. Looked like it was a carnival trick until I saw the blood start to run down onto his cuffs. Big Girl licked her lips. His knees buckled, but he was held in place. Maybe he wanted to scream; maybe he couldn't feel it, yet. My own interest in the ladies was fading fast, and I thought I'd better get out while the getting was good. I nearly had but as her would-be inamorata's knees started buckling, my personal interest faded like ink in the sun. I'd nearly sneaked by them when Little Mod spotted fresh prey. Looking in my direction, she tapped her moll's arm.

'Him,' I heard her say, staring directly at me. Big Girl made with the elbows again; Casanova came loose and hit the floor. Only then did he let out with a wail that would have deafened a banshee. Onlookers gave him the Kitty Genovese treatment, and pretended to sleep standing up. Before I could get any closer to the door Big Girl had put me in her vice, and no matter how hard you run, you can't get traction on air.

23

'Pacify,' she said, hauling me up like a side of beef. 'Presence essentialled, comprendo?'

'Klaatu barada nikto,' I stuttered, unable to elaborate.

'Your place,' said Little Mod, leading the way. 'Let's go.'

TWO

Time was if the census man came rapping on my door to do the rundown and happened to ask how I preferred to spend nighttime in my blue heaven, I'd have said working the dusk-to-dawn shift, being held in a lovelock by a brace of pussycats. Nothing like experience to set you straight. Let me be truthful, my brothers, and pass along some useful advice: theory beats practice when it comes to tag-team action, take my word for it.

Nobody tried to stop us when we busted out of Max's. Didn't know how Casanova was dealing with his new stigmata but figured somebody was giving him aid and comfort. 'Ease up, sugarplum,' I pleaded. 'Pretty please?'

Big Girl showed me no mercy; just snarled like a werewolf and kept me snared in a full nelson till we'd passed under the Third Avenue El. Not fifteen minutes earlier I'd fancied going to the mat with her two falls out of three but that was before I knew I'd be wriggling with Gorgeous George. She gripped me like an industrial press.

'Shorty, please, let me out on parole,' I bleated to Little Mod, but she pulled a Helen Keller on me and didn't stop the parade, rolling those hips like she was a state champ baton twirler. 'Uncle,' I cried. 'Aunt. Cousin. *Hey –*'

Eyeing our retinue a rheumy-eyed coot out for an evening stroll gave us a headshake. '*Kids*,' he muttered. 'Wait till you're drafted.'

'Mute yourself,' Big Girl growled. Even under these outré circumstances I wasn't going to say her high-pitched howl didn't possess a certain unique appeal. 'Submit identifiers.'

'Smith's the name,' I swore. 'One of the Smith boys. You picked the wrong man out of the lineup, girls.'

'Truth us!' she roared. Sounded like Shirley Temple with rabies.

'I'm truthin'!' But she wasn't buying it, and tied that anaconda tight. Big Girl could have strangled a dray horse one-handed. Unpleasant feeling to know the street was somewhere underfoot, but try as you might you couldn't reach it. '*Ixnay*. Lungs. Need 'em.'

'Where's your padding?' Little Mod asked me, still eyes front. 'Pad, meant. Where do you pad?'

I gurgled and burbled like it was titty time for mother's angel and that finally caught her ear. Way her eyes bugged when she turned and saw me made me guess my face was blue as new dungarees. 'Chlojo!! *Nya!!*' she shouted. Soon as Little Mod made with the kibosh, Big Girl let the choke out. She shouldered me hard with those concrete blocks she swung and kept me in the express lane as we hit Second Avenue.

'*Qua?*' said Big Girl.

'Don't rip him,' said Little Mod, circling round as she stepped, shooting daggers at her pal. 'Keep viable. Briskfoot yourself.' I'd always considered myself a lingo major but I might as well have been from Fiji for all I could decipher of their frisky banter. 'Your address?' the wee one asked. 'Specify.'

'275 East 18th. Number 8.' The ongoing shortage of oxygen I suffered sent me into bendsville, and made me think tapping the molasses would work. 'Ladies,' I said, 'your beauty steals my senses. If you'd –'

Big Girl put the airlift on me. *'Mute!'*

'Stop already with the clobberin' time,' I choked out as she continued girlhandling my poor frame. 'Give me a break –'

'This it?' Little Mod inquired, bouncing up the stoop of my abode. I nodded, flashing a goonpuss. Big Girl finally let loose of me long enough that I could catch my breath, step forward and part the waters.

'Come up and see the etchings,' I said, seeing nowhere to go but upstairs. They let me lead, keeping me from making a break for it. My shack was a standard walkup the landlord redid in the late forties, after they ferreted out the last of the Gashouse Gang in order to cram in a few more cash-heavy Europeans. Ten years later I lucked out, and found the place two weeks after first setting foot in NY. Came here straight from Seattle, trying to make my way to Morocco while it was still paradise, but of course everybody knows *that* unhappy ending. Never caught the Marrakesh train but breaks come and breaks go, and it wasn't long after when I overcame my disappointment when I happened upon my natural metier, that is to say, pharmaceutical improvisation. As I threw open my door that evening, giving these ladies full entree to wonderland, I tried to guess how long before I'd know if the breaks I'd get that night would be metaphorical or actual.

'Here's the castle,' I said. 'Make yourself at home. Not that I've got much sayso.' After the rehab the kitchen was still meet and greet central, and the first room you stepped into. The bathtub, thankfully, was long ago banished to the far end of the flat and therefore no longer pulled double duty as dish drainer. The hens gave my place the deadpan, looking like cotillion debs at an Irish wake. 'Squalored,' said Little Mod.

'Squaloriffic. One ten a month, can you beat it?'

Big Girl filled the place like it was a dollhouse. A one-woman mystery spot, she somehow took up twice the space than would have seemed natural. After a fumble or two at the wall I found the overhead. In Max's my guests had profiled perfect, but landlord halos tend not to bestow a Hollywood glow. Little Mod took on five or six years between blinks, and it surprised me to see how dark pint-size was – Greek or maybe even Arab, probably, but in the wrong states that wouldn't cut enough slack to get served. A northerner, no doubt, or from the great west. As for Big Girl, once I got up close her looks and her demeanour made me sure she'd spent more than *one* summer in the Ladies' Cooler over on Tenth Street. She plastered on the warpaint but it couldn't hide the scars. Poor girl had an express line running along her neck and her face practically in HO scale. Shanked in the shower, no doubt, by a short, jealous lifer.

'Forgive impolitesse,' Little Mod said, throwing me a half smile like she wanted me to catch it. 'Haste wastes.'

'What doesn't?' Once they stopped trying to hurt me I started feeling those manly tingles they aroused in me anew. 'Let's get comfy.'

'Where's your public space?' she asked, seeing the single kitchen chair.

'Baby, once I'm across the threshold it's *all* off-limits to the declassé.' Big Girl elbowed me, not accidentally. 'I'll lead on.'

We criss-crossed my crib, which was in its usual state of dishabille. In the frontest of the two front rooms I kept my books, a couch, a lamp, the standard domestic accoutrements. The other room was sanctumville, where I housed my shellac. These old walls may have worn plaster couture but the frillies underneath were nothing but chicken wire. I'd spent big moolah having solid oak shelves fitted to the brick underlay so as to avoid collapse. Even so, whenever I came home with a new find I feared the new disc would tip over the line, and my little blue heaven would sink down to China.

'Weight load's borderlined,' said Little Mod, eyeing my warehouse.

'Six thousand, three hundred and four. All 78s.'

'78 what?' Big Girl said, seizing a prize. There aren't many on the ball these days when it comes to America's priceless heritage, but that's not news. It wasn't her ignorance of the once well-known that made me break out with nervous tics, but the way her baby-voiced peeps counterpointed the sound of a dry branch underfoot. Definitely didn't please me to see her suddenly giving the onceover to the black half-moons in her paws. She held them like a two-fisted pie eater.

'Babycakes, you got to use silk when you're shining up the master's voice.' I relieved her of her burden, fearful to see what she'd sent to the hangman. My luck held, though. Bennie Moten's Kansas City Orchestra, *She's Sweeter Than Sugar*. One copy down, press-fresh at that, but I'd laid away three more in stock in event of April showers bringing tears in May. In this case it was still a heartbreak. Didn't matter how many copies of the record there might be, Bennie wasn't going to come up out of the ground with anything new.

'Unintentioned,' said Big Girl. 'Classify.'

'Museumwear, Chlo. Populacra,' Little Mod said. 'Records.'

When she said *records* she might as well have been saying *polly want a cracker*. Strange to say but somehow I just knew in my bones that until she actually saw my prizes, wax platters had been nothing but some philosophical concept she'd needed to read about in college. Of course nobody pays attention to 78s anymore except for those in the know, and you know who *you* are.

'Soundbites?' Big Girl asked. Before I could suggest that she shouldn't, Eulie nabbed one from the shelf and slid it loose. She petted the disc like it was her favourite kitten. I turned on the deathray but didn't blow, not until I saw the label. Then I lunged, and managed to wrestle it from her grip before she started playing pattycake.

'Ladies, ladies,' I said. 'Toss me around, but not these.'

I let out one king-size sigh when I realized how terminal

the damage might have been. Black Pattis are scarcer than dodos these days but this beauty was ne plus ultra. Matrix number 8045, Hightower's Night Hawks, *Boar Hog Blues* backing *Squeeze Me*. Sounds like it was recorded underwater but nobody kissed a cornet like Willie Hightower, and this was all that was left of him. Snatching a shammy and a bottle of cleaner I started lifting Little Mod's prints. The gals gaped in my direction, fixated, as if I were pulling diamond rings out of my sleeve.

'Purpose?' Big Girl asked, almost broadsiding me with her veranda as she swooped down for the kill. Ordinarily, I wouldn't have minded tumbling into that great divide but the task of maintenance required focus. I emerged from her shadow and checked the surface – clean as a bald head.

'Hand oil clogs the grooves,' I said. 'Eats into the wax. Dig, I'm not just a packrat but a *preservationist*. Just call this place Preservation Hall.'

I never saw two grown women look so stupefied and so annoyed at the same time, but I was rolling, and kept up the spiel. 'Libraries toss these babies out with the bathwater. Orphans in the storm till those with a heart take 'em in. History in the hand, only place it won't get away. These aren't like LPs, these bleed. Scratch 'em and you cut out their tongue. Break 'em and one more gets thrown over the side.'

My audience seemed to get my drift, so I segued before the yawns started. 'Well, seat yourself, my dears. Let me tender some perky libations.' They both stepped into the living room and unsherpaed, putting their black bags on the floor. Big Girl plumped down on a chair my grandmother left me and her big keister smashed right through the rattan. She started wiggling but it looked like a no go situation. I was wondering what to tell the rescue squad when the chair frame cracked open like a pecan, and she hit the floor with a powerful thump.

'Hurt?' asked Little Mod. Big Girl hauled herself up, frowned and kicked the two halves of the chair straight through the apartment into the kitchen. Didn't want anyone to trip over them, I supposed. I didn't so much appreciate her thoughtfulness as I did the fact that she hadn't aimed the pieces at me.

'Accidents happen,' I said. 'Let's try the divan.'

Both of them sat down on the sofa. It moaned but didn't take the gas pipe. 'Let's make with the labels, why don't we?' I asked. 'How do yours read?' They gave me a stare as if I was a chinaman and they were the new white slaves. Downright unsettling to see molls like these two showing the whim-whams. 'Call me Walter. Walter Bullitt. What do they call you?'

'Eulalia. Call me Eulie,' she said. 'Walter.'

'Euphonious indeed,' I said, and, still standing, bowed low to Big Girl. Didn't imagine she'd let me kiss her hand. 'My petit-four?'

'Chlojo,' she rumbled.

'Pardon?'

'Chlo for Chloe,' Eulie said. 'Jo for Josephine.' They gave each other a look, and nodded. 'Chlojo.'

'Music to my ears,' I said, judging that Eulie wasn't the only one showing tell-tale traces of the woodpile. When it came to the colourbar Chlojo had hardly any coffee in the cream; but there was another story being told when it came to the super-structure. Impressed me that they seemed to feel so fancy free when it came to coming and going as they pleased. 'Gals, my cat's on its last life. You'd better fill me in on something . . .'

'What?' Eulie asked.

'Look, let me pledge my allegiance first. I'm no Royboy, there's no tattletales here. The skin game leaves me cold and my sheets stay on the bed. But I can't help but wonder about the bloodline I'm picking up on here. Tell me Big Momma, what boat'd Bigger Momma come over on?'

31

Chlojo fisheyed me; then grinned, clam-happy to read the book without using the dictionary. Her teeth looked false but they also looked like they could bite through the Brooklyn phone book. 'Jadish,' she said.

'What?'

'Swedish and Jamaican,' Little Mod explained.

'Nice grouping,' I said; I can always spot the spots. Of course this was a talent anyone born to the colours knew in their bones: it was tricky to function in the modern world unless you could tell at first look how black white might really be. 'I'm cool. Want to make sure you know you're not the only ones with your hand in the tar.' They gave each other a quick corner look and then turned their gaze back to the main attraction. 'You two on a diplomatic gig?'

'Diplomatic?' Eulie asked.

'I'd like to see the hotel clerk tell her no dogs need apply,' I said, pointing at Chlojo. She didn't pick up my thread that time, though; she and Eulie just sat there staring at me like they were at a county fair and I was in a jar. Maybe I was off on the diplomatic guess; they didn't seem especially American but they didn't act like foreigners either, at least not from any of the countries I was familiar with.

'Well, fill me in, ladies,' I went on. 'Much as I like to let my imagination run wild I doubt you're here to brush up on your orgy skills. What *is* on the menu anyway? Is this the appetizer or are we already having dessert?'

'I'm sorry?' asked Eulie. 'We're dining?'

'Nya, Eulie,' Chlo said, her big marble eyes shining like black suns. 'Explicate presence. Detail.'

I winked at Chlo, who may have been somewhat antisocial but at least seemed hep to the jive. Sad to say she didn't wink back.

'Have you experienced hallucinations lately?' Eulie asked, pulling her drumsticks up on the sofa and spreading them

32

like she was keen to be stuffed. 'What you believed to be hallucinations?'

That was a difficult situation, my brothers. Try as I might to be gentlemanly, I couldn't help sneaking peeks down between her legs to see what they were wearing in Tierra del Fuego. 'Could be,' I said. 'Depends on the produce.'

She shook her head. 'What's meant?'

'Business-class tickets out of Bittersville,' I said. 'Mind masters only, got a cold war going with the bodybreakers. Can't stand cokey joes, speedsters, redheads. Only junky I ever saw handle the stuff was Old Bill –'

'Which drugs?' Eulie asked.

'Psychedillies. LSD-25, 34, 65,' I said, and ran through the repertoire. 'Mescaline and or peyote, fly agaric, ergine, ibogaine, yage, psyilocibin derivative and in the natural state, virola, so forth, so on. Then there're the government beasts I test-market prior to distribution, DMT, STP, BZ, THL, VMC –'

'Have you seen a specific vision?' she asked. 'Two people?'

'Stallion and mare?'

Eulie blinked, and then her bulb lit. 'Gendered accordingly, AO.'

'Who's asking?' An undesirable notion crept into my mind like a cat burglar and now it was my turn to shake with the whim-whams. What if Bennett was having a go at working the pimp side of the street? Could be he'd gone flakeola, and started up his own ops unbeknownst to Martin? That runaround always landed on the offbeat for somebody. Bennett couldn't get me to do anything I hadn't already done, but the way they lulled me into sociability made me tell these sisters in blood more than I ever wanted Bennett to hear. Entrapment, no doubt. B-boy looked in the files, found a pair who'd blown their cover, brought 'em into the office and gave them the opportunity to keep passing unhindered.

'Who we represent?' Eulie asked.

33

'You got it.'

Chlojo gave me a sly eye and chirped, 'Society for Psychical Research.'

I played back everything I'd squawked to them about. After running through it I realized I wasn't as in deep as I'd feared I was. That comment I made about having a hand in the tar might sound fishy to a fisherman, but something that vague could be talked away, especially if I called Martin on *his* hand. Back in the catbird seat: I decided to just act natural and lay off the code.

'That so?' I asked. 'So are they ghosts or Fortean phenomena?'

'Fortean?' Chlo asked. 'Define.'

'Paraworldly,' I said. 'The unlikely and unexpected, but with basis in fact. Lake monsters, abominable snowmen, poltergeists, fish falling from the sky –'

'Unusual coincidences, living pterodactyls, cows giving birth to sheep,' Eulie added, sharing a fast stare with Chlojo. 'Forteana.'

'Well? Which are they?'

'Uncertain,' she said. 'They aspect both. Investigation warrants.'

'Whatever they are, how'd you know I needed an exterminator?'

'We centred upon disturbances in the field,' Eulie said. 'Prompting interest.'

'What field?'

Ignorance being bliss, she kept me happy.

'So why do they want to give me their business?' I asked.

'Coincidence, undoubted,' she said. 'You've seen them here?'

'Today,' I said. 'First time I saw 'em though was last night, in DC. Then again this morning.'

'Washington, DC?'

'Know the place?'

Eulie looked less than slaphappy. Chlojo lifted her head like she wanted to give the ceiling a onceover. She had as many scars under her chin as she did on her face, and it struck me she'd been through major trauma. Car wreck? High-school chemistry experiment gone haywire? Crazy boyfriend? She was put back together pretty well, considering. Maybe she used to work as a lab rat for a Palm Springs nip and tuck man. Some scalpel jockey honing his blade on the riffraff before trimming the dowagers.

'Saw here when?' Eulie asked, leaning forward, legs apart.

'Oh,' I said, 'before I went to Max's. I spun some platters and they hightailed it.'

I subtly began to fold up in the middle, because my southern inflation was starting to become a little too obvious. I was damned every which way and up with these gals. Didn't matter if I tried not to go on beaver patrol with Eulie; I'd slide my eyes in the opposite direction and there I'd be, gazing deep into Chlojo's posturepedic couture. Their six of one and half dozen of the other was knocking me way past blueball into mood indigo. The worst of it was that no matter how much these two were giving me happy pants, not knowing who they really were or why they were really here made me feel like a cat in a bag listening to the riverboats getting louder.

'You see them now?' Eulie asked.

'Nowhere nohow,' I said. 'They weren't much for tunes.'

'We need to execute necessaried tests. Is that acceptable?'

'Sure,' I said, 'don't let me get in the way.'

She nodded to Chlojo and they started unloading their gear. I picked up her empty satchel thinking at first it was leather but finding out soon enough it wasn't leather or plastic. Whatever it was, it looked expensive, so I guessed the stuff was one of those new miracle space age things like Tang. Eulie positioned a set of twelve little black blocks on the floor and started tapping each of them in turn with a foot-long black rod. The tip of the gizmo was round and I couldn't help wondering if Trish had been right, and my unforgettable guests were little miss muffets after all. Sad story indeed if true but I thought I'd wait till all evidence was in before passing judgement. Eulie stroked the beast's sides in the expected manner as she tapped each box. The tip lit up with a pink glow like a car's cigarette lighter. She aimed her rod my way, and it was hard not to flinch.

'Chlojo, position in accordance.' She snatched up the boxes and laid them out in a semicircle on the hearth, in front of my bricked-up fireplace, on the hearth. 'We'll ready en momento.'

The little one was a charmer, no doubt; impressive as I might have thought Chlojo to be at the getgo, the longer I was around her the more I found myself developing a soft gooey centre for the wee missy. She had some trace of an accent; sounded familiar. 'You two New Yorkers?' I asked.

She shook her head. 'Jersey.'

Farmer's daughters going hogwild in the big city: that explained their fashion parade if not the goofball behaviour. You may take the girl out of Secaucus but you can't take Secaucus out of the girl. My nerves started doing that jingle-jangle-jingle; I knew if I was going to keep playing host with the most I was going to need relief.

'You ladies wouldn't drop your drawers if I fired up, would you?'

'What?' Eulie asked. Chlojo finished lining up the boxes and stood up. I took a pinch and a Bugler from the stash at hand and started up a one-hand Detroit roll.

'Herbifaction,' Chlojo said to Eulie.

'Of course.'

'Muchas thankas,' I said. After giving the bone a quick lick I flipped up the crystal on my Doxa Firelight and clicked the bottom stem; the fire flowered up from the face and I listened to the sweet music of popping seed. 'Pause that refreshes,' I mumbled, drawing south until the fume soaked the alveoli; then I let the north wind howl.

Chlojo gave me a loan shark's grin. Sticking her fist into her bodice she tugged out a change purse. Squeezed it open, and she extracted a bud the size of a bing cherry. She held up her treat as if expecting me to beg.

'Lovely one, I'm used to Manhattan grade,' I said, stepping over to be polite. 'No need to cop my muggles off eighth-grade hoods at the Nutley Dairy Queen –'

Live and learn. When I took a whiff of that bud of hers I blasted off through mere proximity. Before I knew what hit me I was one with the floor, overcome by g-force. My head felt like the Babe had knocked it into the upper deck, and even though my blinds were drawn I saw the saucers swooping down to get me. '*Valentine*,' I heard somebody say before realizing it was me. When I finally returned to the solid world, a minute or so later, I saw Chlojo flashing a truly sinister rictus. Eulie was holding my shoulders, and demonstrating far more concern than her duplicitous sidekick.

'What *is* that shit?' I asked, feigning a semblance of coherency. Clearly no playground was involved here. Only explanation I could figure was that these gals had big brothers in green overseas, and they loved their siblings dearly. 'Vietnamese?'

Chlojo sized me up as if deciding where to kick me next. 'Secaucus.'

The yen was on me; I somehow had to reserve acreage on this produce. 'Not bad,' I said, lifting my hand and seeing fourteen. 'Would you ladies care to share and share alike –?'

'Chlo,' Eulie shouted, passing her big buddy the rod, distracting us for the moment from considering profitable co-op schemes. 'Positioning. Formation ninety percent sure. Ready yourself.'

'AO,' Chlojo said, pointing the rod directly at the small boxes. The rod's tip began shining fire-engine red.

'What? What is it?' I asked.

'They're seeable, Walter?'

I shook my head, and realized I shouldn't have. It still didn't really feel attached to my neck. 'Nope.'

'Walter, how many hours since initial contact?'

'Uh, twenty hours?' As I drifted back and forth over the enhanced plane it struck me that I should be more candid about my state, the night before. 'First time I saw them I'd just dropped something vaguely psychoactive. Would that –?'

'You've known similar alteration during successive showings?' Eulie asked, extracting what I thought was a white business card out of a pocket I hadn't seen. When she held it in front of the boxes the card got bright pink spots all over as if it had chickenpox.

'No more than usual.'

'Conceivably facilitated,' she said. 'Wouldn't generate.'

'Eulie,' said Chlojo. 'There.'

Each little box started putting out a deep blue shine, looking like they were heating up, though since I wasn't dripping I could tell they weren't. After ten seconds or so the shine intensified and something like St. Elmo's fire outlined the fireplace mantle. There were two lamps on in the room and one in the record chamber and all of them suddenly started putting out black light. Our skin turned deep purple and the gals' teeth went all snowy. Place looked like some California head shop. When I touched the walls I felt static electricity giving me that doorknob in winter feel; an ozony perfume filled the air, the kind that comes up when a rainstorm suddenly ups the ante, and bolts start belting down from the lords above.

'This going to hurt the records –?'

'Are you sighting, Walter?' Eulie asked. I watched my ectoplasmic pals begin to gel in the far corner of the living room. 'Walter?'

'There she blows,' I said, pointing.

'Shield, Chlo.'

They both reached up into their dos as if primping for company. Eulie pulled out a small round box and popped it open. This evidently was just the moment for them to put in contact lenses. Now I've always been under the impression cheaters were glamorizers, but the look theirs gave them weren't so much Rita Hayworth as Lon Chaney. They were yellow, with spots and lines. Seemed impossible to see through but I guess they did.

'*Godness*,' said Chlojo. I think she'd met her match. The rod's knob shone like the headlight on the midnight express. Their geiger counter, or something, started clicking out a mambo beat.

'Walter!' Eulie said, sounding touchy. 'You recognize?'

'None other.'

My airy pair, as always, didn't seem to be up on the news that we were close at hand. They just hung there in the corner like a painting you could walk all the way around; looked sealed in lucite. I took advantage of their lassitude and gave them a closer one-two. I'd have put the dude at my age, thirty or so. From the look of him I guessed he'd been standing on Everest when somebody pulled it out from under him. The buttons on his jacket were gone, the lining hung down all raggedyass; his pants were wrinkled as Grandpa's kisser. The shoes didn't matter, they kept fading in and out. His dreamgirl was a goner, no wondering about that. Couldn't tell exactly what did her in but judging from the bruises I'd think somebody'd played xylophone on her with a pair of meat tenderizers. She'd been a luscious morsel once, though, and her face wasn't touched. Her eyes were shut. His weren't. I don't know what he saw but he didn't seem to like it.

'Scrolling?' Chlojo asked.

'AO,' Eulie said, putting her card underneath the end of that red-hot rod. 'Ratio coordinates verifying. Wave accessibility doubling, enter primary codes –'

39

No need to eavesdrop; I might as well have been putting the glom on Armenians. Impossible for the layman to get much of a grip on the wonders of science. Wished now I hadn't cut those paraphysics classes during the six months I cooled my heels at the U of Washington. Knowing the basics would have let me be more hep to *their* jive. They did their chores as if this was the kind of thing they did every morning before breakfast. I settled back in the purple gleam to soak in the zen of the moment. Just then the phone rang. The gals sprang hurdles when the jingle bells started clanging and the ghosts took off on a fade. Eulie and Chlojo glared at me; in my state of heightened enlightenment I wasn't too clear on what I was supposed to do. '*Answer!*' Chlojo shouted, starting toward me. I snatched up the receiver and bleated a hasty salute.

'What's shaking?' Trish's lovely dulcets charmed my ear in reply. La Fabulosa never fails to send me express, but on this evening, at that moment, I'd have been a lot happier if she'd gone to play stickball on somebody else's block. 'Cat got your tongue? Speak up.'

'Basta,' I said, going low-toned and sultry so she'd think I was in the midst of heavy loveseat action. Chlojo and Eulie were getting frantic with their machinery but the ghosts weren't sticking around. 'Not talking. Loose lips, ships.'

'Don't feed me that huggermugger.'

'Unavoidable, fabs.'

'You hotfooted it so fast out of Max's you beat the smoke out the door. Give me the dirt, handsome. You get anywhere trying to shift into babe-o-luscious or did those fair maidens put on the brakes and toss you out on the curb?'

'Ixnay on the usciouslay,' I chided.

'You mean they're still there?' The amazement in her voice annoyed me, but there was no need to get into it here. '*Both?*'

'The sixty-four thousand dollar question.'

'It's groovitudinous?' she asked.

'Maxima.'

'Mea maxima groovitudina.'

'Must run,' I said, knowing she rarely recognized hints when she heard them. 'Tally ho.'

'What's the protocol in this situation?' she asked. 'Draw straws?'

'Flip coins,' I said. 'Look, haste wastes. We'll chat anon, bet on it. I swear.'

'You're so sexigismal.' She whinnied a king-size horselaugh. 'Fill me in later. Don't need the liner notes but I got to see the cover.'

I clicked off and cradled.

'Sorry, sorry,' I told my house guests. Chlojo popped her contacts out and gave me a look that could fry eggs.

'Forgotten, forgiven,' Eulie said, shrugging. 'We've quantified theoreticals. Cease and rebag, Chlo.'

Big baby slung the satchel over her arm and dropped in the boxes like she was scooting along on cotton detail. Eulie slid the rod and her card back into her bag and pressed the top shut. 'You're rolling?' I asked.

A pause. 'Leaving, yes. We've questions still, but have basics.'

'Will you let me in on why these two have such a heavy jones for me?' I asked. 'This is my castle, after all, I'd like to know who keeps hopping over the moat.'

'You've nexused,' Chlojo said, stonepussed.

'I'm what?'

'You're centring the phenomenon,' Eulie said. 'Unexplainable, presently.'

'Lucky me.'

'We'll visit again. Possibly without notice. Acceptable?'

'We can work something out,' I said, sidling in closer so she could better appreciate my own charms. Maybe it was only Chlojo's wicked muggles in action but the notion stuck in my head that I'd never met any kitten with her kind of purr. It wasn't just the white boots; the pink ray shone on her with a vengeance and I was rocking with a steady roll. I was willing to cut her some slack even if she was one of Bennett's. 'When?'

'Depends on circumstance,' she said. 'Walter, I'm questioning. How do you work?'

'Whenever I need to but I don't make it a steady habit,' I said. 'Long as you keep your time in to a minimum the boys in the boat might keep you on the line but they'll never haul you in.'

'No, I'm confusing you,' she said. 'What is your job?'

Mighty peculiar line of inquiry if Bennett's goal was to find out something he didn't already know. Granted, he might not have filled her in on what my gig was even if she'd asked. 'Freelance work,' I said. 'For the government, mainly. Acts of chemical interference in the national interest.'

She stared at me. 'That's necessaried?'

'You'd be surprised,' I said. 'In return I get considerable leeway when it comes to how I spend my free time. Listen, there's something I got to ask.'

'What?'

'Let's say you're Greek, maybe Sicilian. Just for the sake of saying it.'

'AO,' she said, frowning. 'Why?'

'But Chlojo here *owns up* to being half Jamaican. How does she get by without constantly getting run down by the bloodboys?'

'Uncomprehended,' Chlojo said. 'Bloodboys?'

Eulie smiled like she'd finally gotten the punchline. 'Chlo,' Eulie said. 'Recollect preparatory briefings. Foreseeable dissimilitude.'

Chlo nodded. Neither of them answered my question. 'Walter, would you favour us?' Eulie asked.

'Love to,' I said. Couldn't beat these two when it came

to keeping mum. If they weren't Bennett's gals that was probably a plus. Truthfully I was getting to the stage where I'd start going not just out of the way for Eulie, but completely off the map. 'How so?'

'Would you demonstrate a record?'

'You mean you want me to play one?' Both of them gave me the go-ahead. 'Got any favourites?'

'Nada,' Eulie said. 'You select.'

Strolling casually to the wall I pondered the choices. Chick Webb or Charlie Christian? Barbecue Bob or Blind Lemon? Maybe put on the mountain boys to get a different kind of missing? Grayson and Whitter or Tom Karnes, in that case? Or go lightheaded and pick Ted Weems and his Orchestra? 'Nagasaki' as done by Billy Costello, the guy who did the voice of Popeye? Inspiration hit me and I slid out one of my faves. The gals circled me like buzzards, eyes wide, while I performed the rituals. After laying the disc on the papered plate I positioned the needle and let Geeshie Wiley spin.

If I die, if I die,
In the German War,
Pleeeeeeaaase take my body
Send it back to m' mother'n'law

Geeshie, like a lot of us, still had a certain freedom of movement back at the end of the twenties, on into Depression days. Geeshie was one of those angels who dropped down at the hotel where the music man was staying long enough to cut a few platters before sailing back into the sky. Left a better taste in your mouth to picture it that way, at least. In any event Geeshie disappeared on her own long before the bloodboys could take care of it for her. I had both her records, all four sides. Found one in the Seattle Salvation Army. Twenty years later found this one, the best, *Last Kind Word Blues*, in a junk shop on Allen Street. After that, no more Geeshie. No more

43

of any of them, only their records, and those marvellous labels: Grey Gull, Electradisk, Puretone, Resona, Columbia, Melotone, Radiex, American Odeon. My people preserved – sweet, black, and shiny.

During the third instrumental break Eulie spoke. 'It's familiared, I've heard.'

> *The Mississippi River,*
> *it's deep and it's wide*
> *IIIIIII can stand right here,*
> *See my face on the other side.*

'Who is it?' she asked when the song ended.

'Geeshie Wiley,' I said, lifting the disc up, reclothing and reshelving it with all the respect Geeshie deserved. 'Where'd you hear it? Wasn't ever on a comp, far as I know.'

'These are all like that?' she asked, gesturing at my wall of sound.

'Most aren't that good. Some are. A few better but not many.'

They started toward the kitchen. Eulie looked better to me then than she had all night, if only because she was getting ready to take off. Call me an idiot, it wouldn't be a new experience. These mantraps may have been hazardous as hungry tigers or Southern cops but she'd put enough of a hex on me that I was no longer fretting over it, at least not too much. 'We kind of got off on the wrong foot. You sure you got to rush off?'

'Presently,' she said. 'We'll return.'

'What about your phone number?'

I was really digging that goofball baffled look that her face took on so often. 'It's unlisted,' she said, after a second. 'I'll contact.'

'Got you.' Hadn't gotten her yet, but if I had any say in the matter I would.

'Walter, make note of when they return. Record how often you see them and where, and when.'

'*When* they return?' I asked. 'Not if?'

'When,' she repeated. 'We'll be touching, Walter.'

'In touch,' Chlojo muttered.

'I mean we'll be in touch.'

'Either way sounds good to me,' I said, and before I could say anything else they were out the door. 'Either or. Whatever.'

Even though I hotfooted it, by the time I got to the windows in the front they'd already disappeared. Hated to see such sweet delights hit the bricks, but if there wasn't pain in life the pleasure wouldn't count for shit. In lieu of carnal life I lay down on my sofa, feeling the imprints they'd left, and reached into my stash to roll up a nightcap. All the lamps still worked so I supposed the lightshow hadn't DCed the AC. Sad to say, the phone was also still working. After letting it go four or five rings I took a long drag and decided to see who was so persistent at that time of night.

'Been thinking about our offer?' Bennett, naturally. Privacy wasn't a concept he took much stock in.

'Don't be a worrywart, my brother. Wears away the stone.'

'No worries here, Walter,' he said. 'Any worries on your end?'

'Can't say there are –' Taking another draw, I realized I hadn't ascertained the provenance of Chlojo's supernatural produce. Hoped Bennett's phone call was merely one of the aftereffects.

'There will be,' he said, trying to do Bogart, failing miserably. 'You can't imagine. I can.'

'You got a licence to use that imagination?' I asked. 'By the way, what'd you send those cookies over to see me for?'

Silence. 'What the hell are you talking about?'

'Bennett, you'll get no Oscars playing the coy miss,' I said. 'There's no fooling a fooler, my brother.'

He sighed. Nothing I tried seemed to prompt him to hang up. 'The hell with you. Do what we ask or you'll be sorry.'

'What is it again I'm supposed to be doing? Refresh my memory. I get distracted when roller derby queens put the strongarm on me.'

'You're incoherent, you idiot.' No doubt about it, those babies weren't his. That lifted my happy heart a little higher. 'Get back on the wagon before it's too late. Remember what we talked about this morning? In Washington?' Another pause on his end. 'You remember being in Washington?'

'Haven't blacked it out yet but I'm trying,' I said. 'Bennett, I told you and Martin and those two nightcrawlers, I'm not having anything to do with the Potato Famine and I mean it. Bug off.'

He hung up. I laid the receiver in the cradle and panned the room. My two ghosts hadn't wasted any time; they'd come back for an encore now that the crowd had thinned out.

Help, he said, or at least I heard it being said. Remembered he'd kept the lid on while the girls were here but could be their gizmos put the quietus on him. Seemed like I was going to have to get used to these two moochers, but as long as their being around brought back the livelier pair, I could handle that. I'd started to take a final toke on the nubbin when he came up with a fresh line.

Walter, he said. *Help*.

THREE

Having old see-through tuning in on my *nom de guerre* and trying to make with the small talk like he'd cornered me at a party made me come down with one bad case of chicken pox, accent on the bird. Didn't think it'd set a good precedent if I started letting ghosts get the upper hand, so after the first time he called for Philip Morris I went all tastee freeze on him, suspecting that if I made any kind of move he'd really start with the chitchat. Seemed to me the only way to play this was by going easy on the shuck and jive; tried pulling a maitre'd act instead, acting like he was trying to crash the list.

'Whom do I have the pleasure of addressing?'

Walter.

'Must be some confusion. I'm one of the Smith boys.'

Help.

'Kind of losing my patience here,' I said, the challenges of ethereal plane communication seriously messing with my head. 'Who are you? You got a name? A handle? What'd your mom call you?'

Now he threw the Silent Sam treatment on me. Seemed to be giving me the beady eye but it was hard to say for sure. I tried tiptoeing a little to the left to see if his look followed but it didn't, he stared straight on like I was still there. I trotted behind him, and then popped up on the right. Not a glimmer of recognition in the boy.

Walter.

It came clear to me that even though he knew I was there and even had a grip on my monicker, the advantage was mine when it came to who knew where the other was hanging out. I leaned in a little closer to him but didn't notice anything I ever read about in the ghost stories – where he dangled wasn't colder than anywhere else in the place. I wasn't feeling any vibes that I didn't ordinarily feel; not a hair on my neck was even thinking about rising. Now that I had him under the microscope I saw he wasn't giving me the beady eye; what I couldn't see for sure was if he *had* eyes. Where they should have been there were just two black tunnels in his head that went somewhere you knew you wouldn't want to go. His comrade in arms still lay there in his arms, staying noncommittal. I imagined if she'd known, she'd have been just as happy to be out of it.

Help me.

'My brother, you got me at a disadvantage,' I said. 'If I'm going to scratch your back, you ought to least pretend to scratch mine.'

It was pretty obvious though that he wasn't in any shape to scratch anything. Giving up on the old college try I left him behind and walked into the kitchen, feeling the call of the gut – realized I hadn't chowed since I was on the train to NY. Before I opened the icebox I took a peek to my rear but they'd not left the front room. Nothing like breakfast at midnight; I turned on the radio and turned in WNEW while fixing myself Adam and Eve on a raft. Nightbird was clearly in a heavy Zombies mood but I could deal with it. As I put away the snacks I let my mind wander, not that it wasn't always a challenge to keep it leashed. Thought about those girls, especially peewee. Chlojo had those rococo qualities, but she was a moody miss and besides I never felt much at ease with ladies who looked like they'd as soon bust your lip as kiss it. Now that I'd had a chance to see both close up, Eulie was the one I'd –

Walter.

Train of thought skidded off the tracks again. He lounged in the doorway, striking the usual pose. Got bored in the front room, I supposed, and came to see what was doing out here. I offered them eggs, but they weren't buying. Just when I thought they were going to do their hang-dog act all night they started fading from the floor up, as if somebody was taking an eraser to him. Ten, fifteen seconds – no more – and they vamoosed.

Now I don't spend much rehearsal time on the Big Book but at least I know the lines. The BB tells us after you catch the last bus to tomorrowland you have to make a pit stop at demiurge central before they let you up on the high ground. The archons and fiends of this world know they can't keep you there forever, so they make you miserable as they can while they got the chance – it's their metier. I'd always had doubts about this theory, not being as much a believing man as my father was, but I had to admit once I got a gander at my ghosts I was willing to buy it. Judging from the looks of those two I wondered if the demiurges hadn't figured out a way to hold onto passers-through indefinitely.

'Hello, out there,' I hollered. Nothing. Decided to taper off on my theological meanderings, and went to dump my dish in the sink. I noticed something on the counter, near the breadbox. *Bless her heart.* Chlojo left me a present; a forest-green bud about the size of a shooter waited for me, probably the one she'd done me in with earlier. I slid my paw into a kitchen mitt before plucking that june bug. Considering how scent alone produced a DMT-like rocket launch I could only imagine how high I'd fly if I actually touched the bud; dropping it into a baggie I smiled, knowing I'd never have to smoke it to go sailing – *perma-pot!* you couldn't beat it with a stick. Before snapping the bag shut I couldn't resist taking one quick huff. When I came to, next morning, I saw two empty boxes of Betty Crocker cake mix and a used batter bowl, but no evidence that I'd baked.

'Tell me,' she said, 'tell me tell me tell me –'

Trish beseeched me all that day, wanting the dirt on how my evening went. Finally the little voyeur wore me out and I hoisted the white flag.

'Uncle,' I said. 'Where you want to touch knees?'

'I'm in a mood for high life. Enough rolling in the gutter. Let's do the Plaza.'

No use trying to put the quietus on this lunacy; once Trish put desire into word there was no turning back. 'Swell,' I said. 'Not in the Fancy Dan rooms, though. So much starch in those shirts, makes me itch.'

'All right, we'll lurk on the shadier side. 59th Street's more your speed anyway.'

'Damn straight. Trader Vic's?' I suggested, getting a big-league jones for a pupu platter – that *had* to be an aftereffect.

'So tiki tacky,' she said. 'Why don't we take in the Free Movement of Musical Air?'

'For real?' I asked. 'All right. Sold American.'

'You better be ready to tell me the once-upon-a-time.'

'Nine sharp,' I said, staring at that bagged bud lying on the counter. 'Don't go in the drunk tank before I make the scene. I'm bringing a surprise that won't mix with gin.'

'Everything mixes with gin,' she said. 'Toodles, noodles.'

In the Northeast, the Plaza's Theremin Room was the last of the Mohicans. There were still joints like it in LA and Frisco, and the one in Seattle in the Olympic was still there as far as I knew. They were the bee's knees back in the twenties and early thirties; then they found out the gizmos were bad, bad news anywhere within a two-mile radius of

Teslas. Thirty-block blackouts if the frequencies harmonized right and never mind the gas ruptures. Back in the big sky country they'd always favoured hydroelectric, so it wasn't as much of a problem; out west they claimed never using Teslas helped keep people out of tumour town but that was probably nothing more than xylocaine, something to ease the pain but not quite succeeding.

That night I headed uptown and once the witching hour struck I made my walk-on. Spotted Fabs at the bar, savouring a bilious toddy, a grasshopper by all indications. As I strutted over to her I glommed the stage. In the pit a rhythmiconist plinked out a series of overtones and five thereminists stood in front of diamond-shaped speakers, fluttering their fingers over their boxes' tone bars to evoke the countermelody. Two hepkittens in black leotards pranced atop the metal soundstage, shimmying away at some mean rain dance. Every move they took made additional notes warble by way of the oscillators picking up on the air currents, and the more they wiggled the more elaborate came the arpeggios and glissandos.

'Good to see you in one piece,' Trish said, and we enjoyed a mutual standing massage. 'Thought those rangerettes'd grind you up and spit you out.'

'I'm too chewy,' I said, and signalled the barman to dredge up a high head. 'What are –'

'Look who I bumped into on the way over,' she said. I looked; wasn't much taken with the sight. Trish had thousands of best friends, housed in every penthouse and gutter in New York, native-born and Euro, but not many hit the spot with me. Sometime earlier I'd met this one – Biff? Boff? whatever mater pegged him back in Beantown – and already knew he didn't come close to the mark. A Bennett without portfolio, somewhat more chiselled, with that lean Aryan look. Had that Art Moderne bone structure that makes the owners imagine the God of this world always has them in mind for bigger, better things. Didn't mean I owed them my lunch money, though that always seemed to be what these pussywillows assumed.

I offered my paw and he gripped it as if trying to break it off. I wondered what was giving him such a near-fatal case of the smirks. 'Walter. One of the Smith boys.'

'Burt,' he said. 'You're Trish's ex, aren't you?' Wasting no time in laying on the mustard plasters.

'That's neither here nor there,' Trish said. 'Burt was starting to tell me –'

'Best not to poke boils,' I said as the orchestra started in on a Beatles medley. 'Never know what'll pop out.'

'Quit it,' Trish said, laughing but failing to lull my suspicions. Luckily, she interposed herself in time. 'All right, Walter, so who were they? What's the story?'

'I was saying –' Boob started to say.

'Jersey girls,' I informed my henchwoman. 'Looking for a hot time in the big city. Did you have to call when you did?'

'Excusez moi. I hate to admit I was a nervous nellie,' she said, 'but you know what happened last night? At Max's?'

'Something happened?' I asked, hefting the glass the barman put before me and inoculating the mad dog.

'Somebody stabbed a guy in Max's after you left last night,' she said, stirring her green delight. 'Put icepicks through both hands. No suspects. Naturally I went off on a tangent and my stomach started doing backflips. Worried you'd wind up being done in by those Jill the Rippers.'

Figured it best not to mention Chlojo's tiny titty bumbershoots. 'I was safe as milk,' I said. 'It was copacetic. Don't let your hair turn white.'

'I don't understand,' Booboo interrupted, speaking twice as loud as either of us and not because he needed to shout over the theremin. His wardrobe was of the irksome prepster sort. He wore khakis and penny loafers and a cashmere sweater that would have paid my rent for three months. Orange, but that was probably what Perry Como was wearing and therefore acceptable. 'Anyway, before you got here I was telling Trish about something important, a great experience –'

'Muchas regretas,' I said.

Trish bounded into the conversation, filling up silence as quickly as she could. 'Last night Walter tried on his Casanova suit with these two sweet potatoes down at Max's,' she said. 'Muffies, I figured but figured wrong. When I called over there last night he was busy playing host with the most –'

'Fine, fine,' he said. 'But I was telling you about the experience. There's something this group can offer anyone –'

'Burt, I told you I'll check it out, but right now I just want to enjoy a cheerful beverage. Put a sock on the Dynamos and swill away.'

Something in Bub's eyes made me think his story had a few more twists and turns than I'd thought at first. I wouldn't say they were as empty as my ghost's, but there was a quality to them reminiscent of aggies and shooters that made me suspect he wasn't sticking as close to the high road to glory as he tried to make it seem. 'My apologies,' he said, giving me a highly suspicious onceover but baring his teeth nonetheless, as if thinking it a smile. 'My inner got the better of my outer.'

'Happens to me all the time,' I said. 'What group are you talking about?'

'The Personality Dynamos. My company sent several of us on their weekend programme. Fascinating. Confidence building. You learn yourself inside and out. I was telling Trish about it.'

Trish smiled, and put away the rest of her green goodness. 'Sounds too booga-booga to me.'

'What's your company?'

'Goldman Sachs. I'm a junior manager. Only a matter of time, though.'

'Till what?'

'Senior,' he said. 'Think, and it happens. What do you do?'

'I'm in government work.' Trish shot the daggers at me like we were the main attraction under the big top but I managed to dodge the sharpest ones. The thereminists moved on to the Rodgers and Hart songbook. Bobo looked absolutely dumbfounded.

'Seriously?' he asked. I nodded. 'Doing what?'

'Odd jobs,' I said. 'In the national interest.'

Had Booby said anything else of interest, I would pass it along, but he didn't. All he did was take up valuable space until both Trish and I were ready to go home. I don't drink more than one or two at a sitting; better to save the liver for more essential effort in my own professional field. 'You going east?' she asked, recapturing her coat from the check girl.

I nodded. 'Catching the El.'

'I'll walk with you far as Lexington.'

Trish lived uptown, on East 77th near York. Farther east than Newfoundland and almost as frosty and windswept come winter, but when anybody asked where she cooped her chickens she could put on the big light and say, *Upper East Side*. Among some in her sewing circles, that was de rigueured.

'Sure you didn't want to make the scene with Bart?'

'Burt. Please.'

'You know him from where?'

She stared out at the statue in front of the Plaza for a second or two, pulling her coat tight around her. 'I can't remember. Poor pup. Sounds like he's found a good home with those Dynamos, though.'

'He said it was a weekend thing.'

'Every weekend. He's into it. Next thing you know he'll be selling flowers at the airport, probably. Preps are such pigeons.'

It was after midnight, and a weekday besides, so only a few taxis cruised along with the cops, and we were the only ones taking a stroll. All the used book stores along 59th had rolled their tables inside and pulled down the grates. Neither of us said much as we perambulated on our merry way; when you're close as we were there's not always a need to chitchat. Besides, it was so tedious being constantly interrupted by Boohoo that we were both happiest to be hearing nothing, just then. The flakes eased off before we reached Madison. By the time we crossed Park the wind had started blowing the clouds away. A full moon, silver-dollar size, hung over the Waldorf like an Evacuation Day ornament.

'You know the Indians had a different name for the moon every month?' she asked. 'I forget what it's called this month. I remember September through December, that's all. Hunter's moon, Harvest moon, Beaver moon, Cold moon. Wish I could remember the rest.'

'You're doing all right to remember Indians,' I said.

'They're really going to land on it next year?' she asked. 'It's go with mission control?' I gave her a nod. 'When are they leaving?'

'Next summer sometime. June, July. Depends on the weather.'

'You're so scientific, knowing these things. And once they land on it, what do they do?'

'Anything,' I said. 'Anything at all. Main thing's landing there. That's as ultima groovitudina as it gets.' She hooked her hands tighter around my arm. 'You know I'd love to go there someday.'

'I thought you'd already been,' she said, smiling.

'You know what I mean,' I said. 'Wouldn't you want to go there, somebody gave you half a chance?'

'I'd just figure I'd do no better there than here,' she said. 'You're such a junior birdman, Walter.'

'Always had a soft spot in my heart for science fiction.'

55

'Heart, or head?' she asked. 'Think I'll start calling you Buck.'

I shook my head. 'Flash.'

Listening – don't know for what – I heard nothing but the sound of tyres shusshing over wet pavement and the tap tap tap of our heels. 'Aren't half the ones working on Apollo ex-Nazis?' Trish asked. '*They* probably have some ideas what to do, once they get there.'

Sad but true – it was another one of those things that leave you feeling drawn and quartered if you think about them too long. *Thanks to Nazi science, man would walk on the moon. We had to destroy the village in order to save it* – that kind of logic wears away the stone real fast. While under the influence of something, a little while back, I'd been reading the *Saturday Review* when I read what they called that numbness that sinks into your head like a bad cold when you start trying to keep two realities in the same place, and pharmaceuticals aren't involved. *Cognitive dissonance*; catchy. Seemed like something I suffered from more often than not.

The entrance to the East Side IRT yawned before us. 'Don't let the bedbugs bite, snookums,' she said, planting a wet one on me. 'Or Jersey girls.'

'You know me.'

'Too well,' she said, and skipped down the stairs.

A freelance existence has its advantages but stability isn't one of them. February is always the quietest month, but this year it was going way past dead and deep into embalmed. When I'd heard no word from my usual employers by the first week of March, I realized that somebody up there was trying to starve me into submission. Served me right: I'd ignored the key rule for junkies and freelancers alike, don't keep your eggs in the foxes' basket. Martin and I may have had a big something in common, but that didn't mean he'd always do *everything* I wanted him to do. At least he still took my calls.

'Walter,' he said, when he finally picked up the phone, 'if I had a job for you, you'd know it. I swear, believe me.'

'Wish I could.'

'Walter –'

'You know in the paper this morning I counted references to twenty-seven ongoing student actions, all Vietnam-related,' I said. 'Pretty amazing that none of 'em call for my kind of expertise.'

'Not exactly. Not until –'

'I agree to start singing "Danny Boy".'

Almost felt his breath coming out the phone when he sighed. 'Walter, what are you trying to prove?'

'Trying to prove nothing,' I said. 'It's just something I don't want to get into. Not with those Kennedys. They're crazy as loons, you know that.'

'I can assure you, there'll be no danger. It's not even a possibility. You're just cutting off your nose to spite your face. Would you listen to reason –'

'Could say the same about you when it comes to not using me.'

'It's out of my hands, Walter.'

That was a new one on me. 'Whose hands is it in?'

'They won't change their mind unless you change yours,' he said. 'Do us both a favour. Please.'

'I'll think about it.'

We both hung up on cue. This pissed me royally. Martin never was one for giving me public support but he'd always paved over the rocks in the passway in the past. Supposed it'd gone beyond that now. Didn't matter, I tried to tell myself. No matter how hard they pulled on this slave's neck chain they weren't going to drop me off in the briny deep. Worse came to worse, I could always get a *real* job.

For real? Of course not. Once you've gotten away living the boho life as many years as I had it's not easy to sneak back into straight society even if that's where you want to go. Like all blessed with a knack for the grift I had a salesman's skills but lacked the temperament; and no experience with doing the hard sell, considering how long I'd been working in a field where *convincing* the buyer he needed the product was never a consideration. Plus, I had the same problem Agency alumni face when they get thrown back into civilian life: the biggest part of your curriculum vitae is sealed under wraps, for the foreseeable future.

I'd paid March's rent already; that was good. Had two hundred dollars left in my account but no way to pay April's unless opportunity knocked; that was bad. Then my old gal Trish came through, once again.

We slid our treats out of their slots at the Times Square Automat and snared a table upstairs underneath the stained glass. 'Way you were talking I thought you'd reached the hot water and catsup stage,' she said, giving the onceover to my high-stacked tray. I didn't care; it was the first time I'd eaten out in weeks. When food cash ran short my strategy was to live on peanut butter sandwiches, gumming away at their sticky goodness while looking at the pictures in cookbooks and reading about twelve-course banquets. Imagination triumphant over nature once again.

'Better to exaggerate now than tell the truth later,' I said. 'So what's the deal? You say your friend Boff is involved?'

'Burt,' she said. 'All right, here's what he told me. You remember the time you met him he was going on and on about that group he was hanging out with?'

'Vaguely.'

'Well, here's their deal straight from the uncorrupted,' she said. 'These nutty squirrels are on the Upper West Side mostly, at least here in New York. Started out ten years ago as psychoanalysts and their patients. Adlerians, I think, maybe Maslovians. One of them got a big head, started telling the others what to do. Rather than saying go screw yourself royally they listened to him. Then his patients told their friends and the group grew, after a while things hit critical mass. They all went completely woowoo.'

'Krishna Krishna woo woo or Ronettes woo woo?'

'Closer to the latter, I suspect,' Trish said. 'Anyway, once the light hit them they confabulated an entirely new purpose in life. Everybody wants some of that of course so now they're all over the place, but mostly here and LA and London. Now along with these weekend programmes they have weekly meetings. Burt let on that after you're really into the group that's when they let you in on the next level.'

'Which is?'

'They sit around all weekend expanding the mind.'

That piqued my interest. 'Literally or metaphorically?'

'Along your lines,' she said, grinning. 'Got tired of shrinking it, I guess. Burt tells me they need a new supplier. The guy who had the original arrangement made deliveries once a month, found out another client of his was setting him up so he skipped. Burt came to me hoping that you might possibly be of help. I told him you possibly might be.'

'Possibly.'

She extended her arms as if she'd just jumped off a high wire in the centre ring. 'Tah-dah.'

'What do they need?' I asked.

'Mescaline,' she said. 'Chocolate, strawberry, any tangy flavour of your preference. Nothing stronger, certainly none of the things you put away for breakfast. Sounds like they have an intensive session first and unwind after. And it sounds like they've got thousands of members. That's a lot of action.'

'What's their guiding light?'

Trish shrugged. 'Sounds like the usual bushwah hey nonny no to me. He laid a brochure on me. It's no page-turner.'

I looked over the propaganda. Doctor Oscar – no last name – was the founder and Honcho Grande of the group Personality Dynamos Incorporated, whose members, having undergone

Mental Plastic Surgery, perfected the techniques of Opportunity Seizure. One session cost fifty bucks but special corporate rates were available. Looking at the back of the brochure I saw that, supposedly, executives of General Motors, Singer, Metropolitan Life and, yes, Goldman Sachs, had all undergone the Shake-Out; as had doctors, lawyers, dentists, famous movie stars and people Just Like You. Seemed reasonable enough, as these things go, but then I glommed the pitch:

TAKE YOUR MIND OFF ITS HINGES

Few people can deal with hard reality
— can you?

- Do you run from it?
- Fear it?
- Deny it?

Adults deal. *Children fear.*

WE OFFER THE TOOLS YOU NEED TO
DESTROY THE CHILD WITHIN YOU.

MAX YOUR PO through
PERSONALITY DYNAMISM

'Po?'

'Tential.'

I nodded. 'So I just deliver the goods and they make the payment? Right then and there?'

'You got it,' she said. 'Could anything be simpler?'

'Will they be having a séance while I'm around? Do I have to go?'

She shook her head. 'You've already maxed your po, if you ask me,' she said, 'but I'm sure they're always on the prowl for victims. They've probably got some fast talkers, too.'

'I'll carry rocks in both hands.'

'Good, Walter,' she said. 'I'd so much rather you did this than whatever you do for the feds. It's always better to be in business for yourself.'

Wasn't hard to lay paws on mesc; along with other useful material I kept enough of the stuff to turn on Hoboken in a safe-deposit box at my local Greenwich Savings. The next night, nuts in hand, I rode the West Side Local, going to meet the squirrels. When I got out at 79th I bounced upstairs and fell right into the middle of a gaggle of cops. Bad as St Patrick's Day, except none of them was drunk enough to shoot themselves or each other. Considering that I was holding so many psychedillies I could take down a regiment, I started to get a little weak-kneed. No need to fret, though, I was home free; the boys of Killarney had their hands full rounding up a different set of suspects. A kibitzer gave me the lowdown, said an Albanian dry cleaner had been gunned down in his shop and the bluecoats were rounding up the block's shiftier-looking Montenegrins. 'Kids,' we agreed and I edged past the holding area on my way uptown.

Two hundred feet further and I'd walked past a Hungarian restaurant, Serbian bookstore, Turkish candy shop, newsstand run by two Croatian women, Serbian shoe repair place, and at the corner of 80th and Broadway a grocery owned by a French

Commie. I'd met him at a party Trish threw – she knew him of course. He'd been on the losing side of a party dispute involving ersatz Roquefort and had to skedaddle, but he hadn't lost his principles in the free world; even named his place after the store he managed in Paris, Cheese Store Number Three, and made sure to be out of whatever cheese his customers wanted. New York tries on a new mask every ten years, but no neighbourhood in town had been put through its changes like the Upper West Side. It'd been going on twenty years, ever since the Soviets dropped the bomb in 1949 and evaporated Berlin, ending the war. Half the population that was left took the leap and landed in New York; nobody in America minded European immigrants, no matter what they'd been up to in the past. Even after everything went full-tilt Commie from London to Constantinople, people who wanted out bad enough managed to get to New York.

Since then the refugees had become one with the landscape. Packed into the West 70s and 80s like gunpowder in a pipe were Serbians, Albanians, Wallachians, Turks and Montenegrins; and scattered throughout, German and Hungarian Jews who'd gotten out of Europe in the thirties but hadn't yet made it to Long Island. After ten years of having their flats divided and subdivided into one-roomers and flops, all the big old apartment buildings on the avenues looked like wedding cakes left too long in a damp basement. The houses on the side streets were even more jam-packed, sometimes holding fifteen or twenty in a two-room apartment.

The Dynamos' HQ was on 81st between Columbus and Amsterdam, midblock, at the top of the hill. Most of the places nearby were slumlord specials but these boys had scratch, clearly, and owned their joint. I hopped up the stoop and ding-donged. It was one of those old Victorian whitestone jobs, with mahogany doors and gargoyles carved over the windows, heavy white curtains and thick iron grilles. They hadn't brought in the afternoon paper yet; the front page of the *Sun* read ONE MILLION IN VIETNAM TOO MANY, SAYS KENNEDY. Bobby, evidently; only bearable one in the bunch, but not by too much.

I heard a click, then a creak; then a cadaver in a black suit unlocked the door. Sounded like the start of *Inner Sanctum* when he dragged it open. 'Mister Jones?' he asked. I followed him into the entrance hall, padding over one of those forty-dollar a foot rugs. 'Please wait here. Be seated.'

I took him up on his offer and unloaded on a handy pew next to the parlour's open double doors. Skinny lanked up the stairs like he was being tugged by strings. A session was going on inside, and I felt free to look – nobody told me not to. Twenty-odd boys and girls sat in a circle on metal chairs. Most looked like insurance salesmen or executive secretaries, in their thirties and forties; they wouldn't have stood out of the crowd if they'd been alone in the room. In the middle of the circle was a tall balding fellow with grey hair. Doctor Oscar, perhaps? Not likely from my experience. Once the head men really get the racket rolling all they have to do is sit back and let the minions take care of the marks, doesn't matter if it's the carnival or the Department of Defence. This one was experienced, I could tell; he might have seemed like he was rambling but he was working his audience like he was the main act at the Copacabana.

'Now imagine this entire room is filled to the ceiling with shit.' That caught my ear. 'Imagine you know a priceless jewel was somewhere deep in that shit.' While he blew hot and cold he started turning, slowly, as if he stood on a lazy susan. 'Imagine that the only way to find that jewel was to burrow down through the shit until you found it. Would you?'

Judging from the glares a few of the participants shot him I gathered I wasn't the only one wondering what kind of produce he was on. Newcomers, obviously, and not used to the lingo.

'Aren't there adults present?' he asked. 'Only children? Every one?'

Two men and one woman lifted their hands gingerly, as if

they weren't sure. None of them looked altogether keen on being teacher's pet.

'*Zingo!!*' shouted the ringleader.

Skinny trotted back down the stairs. He handed me a brown paper envelope; I took a quick peek inside and, satisfied, passed him the goods. If I was cautious, three hundred would do me three weeks, maybe more, and I supposed these characters could become steady customers without much effort on my part. 'You're interested in the Shake-Out?' he whispered.

'That's this?'

He nodded. 'A five week programme ending in Ascendancy. The first week is the introductory period. This is second week, when the programme gathers momentum, and you roll with it down the hill of understanding. Sit here with open ears, if you choose. You choose?'

His lips pulled back over his teeth like his skin was starting to shrink. 'I choose,' I said, lowering my voice and speaking in a stage whisper, imagining that that was the way they preferred it be said. Give it that *I Love Adventure* twist.

'After visualizing your possibilities you may decide that you are ready to outside your inside,' he said. 'Let me know.'

'Definitely.'

He slid off down the hall as if he'd greased his shoes. When I turned my attention back to the parlour I heard the ringleader still going on and on about shit and the need to burrow through it. As you might have guessed I'm not much of a fudge queen so while he elaborated on his fantasia I ran my peepers over the rest of the parlour. There were some props on the far side of the room, and they didn't ease my restless mind. Lying on the far side of the circle, I saw several long wooden paddles, too small to be oars but too long to be fraternity memorabilia. In the corner of the room was a steel cage big enough for a Great Dane currently available to let. Two looped ropes hung down from the ceiling; they'd been attached with big u-bolts and looked like they'd support considerable weight. To my mind, none of this really *bode* well. On the mantlepiece, placed between two silver candelabra, was a twice-life size bust of someone I assumed to be Doctor Oscar; at least the bust vaguely resembled the photograph I'd seen on the brochure. Couldn't tell what the bust was made of from where I sat, but it looked like it'd been moulded by second shift cooks out of grainy chopped liver.

'What does an adult use?' the ringleader started shouting.

'Two feet only!' the group shouted back.

'What do children say?'

'Diaper me!'

'What do you tell them?'

'Take pain and like it!'

The top of the ringleader's head shone like a wet rock as he started heating up. Figured he'd work himself into some kind of preacher riff at any moment now, and I was starting to think he might be good at it. Good enough to empty the wallets of the congregation, at least.

'If you have to turn on the freeze to make your child undependent on you, how low do you go?'

'Subzero!'

The ringleader stopped rotating. Paused as if to catch his breath but it was easy to see he had plenty to spare. His audience seemed to be getting with it, somehow – it was all I could do to keep from laughing.

'If it's necessary to hug someone to evoke their child, what do you do?'

This may have been the second week but nobody acted as if they knew the drill. The sitters looked more than a little bumfuzzled. The ringleader made sure he had no expression on his kisser while they tried figuring it out. 'Hug?' one of the men finally asked.

'Zingo!'

The ringleader lifted him out of his chair and gave him a real rib-cracker, slapping his back as if whacking on a tom-tom. He started grinning like the acid was kicking in, and I wondered if the ringleaders were the ones who most often used nature's helping hands in their acts on cue.

'If it's necessary to kiss someone to make them outside their inside, what do you do?'

'Kiss them,' another man, more at ease, piped up.

'Zingo!'

The ringleader chose not to kiss that particular good student. He scooted off in the opposite direction and planted a big juicy one on the loveliest lovely in the circle, a tall blonde in a red shift. He rubbed his hand over his mouth and went wild with the dramatic pauses.

'If you have to beat the living shit out of a no-nothing,' he said, 'to drag their child to sunlight, what do you?'

That seemed to bring everybody up short. The ringleader pulled a stopwatch out of his pocket, clicked it and eyed the dial. 'Five,' he said. 'Four. Three. Two. One.'

Silence, no more than ten seconds' worth.

'*You stupid fucking assholes!!*' the ringleader began screaming. 'Assholes!! Every goddamned one of you!' His face turned beet-purple. 'Fucking stupid assholes!!'

It was like watching some poor soul getting set to take a sidewalk dive and listening to everybody in the audience shouting jump, jump, jump. The ringleader cursed like a sailor for two full minutes, spitting in the face of guys twice his size as he sputtered away, shouting at the women until every one of them, and three of the men, were crying. Finally, he ran out of breath, and stood in the centre of the circle, huffing and puffing, looking like he could really use a cigarette.

'Child response, no,' he said. 'Adult response, yes. One more time. If you have to beat the living shit out of a no-nothing to drag their child to sunlight, what do you do?'

Again, silence. 'Five. Four. Three –'

'Hit them?' one of the older men asked; a fellow in his early fifties or so.

'*Zingo!!*'

The ringleader wasn't that big but he had a punch like a welterweight. The good student almost fell over in his chair after he was hit, blood gushing from his nose. He'd never get the stains out of his suit. I'd have thought at that point there'd have been a mass sick-out, but no. Everyone looked terrified, except for the ringleader.

'Assistance forbidden!' the ringleader said. 'Assistance forbidden!' He walked up to the victim and pressed his hand down on the man's bleeding nose. Considering that it looked like he'd broken it I couldn't imagine it felt especially good. 'Response?' The man started to rain and his face swelled up like it was going to pop but he still didn't do what he was supposed to have done, clearly. 'Response?'

Again, nothing. 'Example!' The ringleader turned to his left and slapped a younger guy, sending his glasses flying across the room. 'Response?'

'Thank you,' said the younger man, getting out of his chair and kneeling in front of the ringleader. The older one didn't look like he could do much more than bleed. That was enough for me, and I started to make for the door.

'As an outgrouper and not an ingrouper, you may not view the programme in the right context,' Skinny said, emerging from the shadows under the stairs, grabbing my arm, hanging onto me like a leech.

'Maybe not,' I said, backing up, keeping my eye on him. I almost fell down the stoop on the way out, but didn't; got halfway to Broadway before I felt safe enough to catch my breath. Considering how they acted, straight, I shuddered to think what this bunch was like once they started flying.

My brief taste of potentially steady employment convinced me of the error of my ways. Next day, Martin called. He asked me to reconsider. I did.

FOUR

Next day at lunchtime I skidded over to the Old Town bar on 18th Street, two blocks from my crib; Martin said he was coming to town and that put me in the catbird seat when it came time to mark the turf. I put a reverse banana on my leather jacket, trying to keep those March winds from whistling inside. The Old Town's a 19th-century joint – ceiling so high and dark bats ought to be hanging from it, feeding pews too small for 20th-century keisters, a scarred mahogany bar with a dented brass rail, a mirror that makes you look drunk even if you've taken the Keeley. No one went inside in daylight but white-haired liver-wranglers, you see 'em lining up every morning before the doors open like they were waiting for Series tickets. Martin and his gang had expropriated a square table in the back. Hamilton and Frye were with him, and I'd expected they would be. The fourth member of the team wasn't Bennett.

'Walter, this is Hermann Sartorius,' Martin said. 'He's with the Justice Department. One of Hamilton's associates.'

'Welcome to New York,' I said. When I offered my mitt he gave me an icy road.

'I been before,' he said. Glass eyes, spun gold on the summit and accent thick enough to cut with a Luftwaffe

68

dagger. Even if Commies hadn't been unwise enough to present themselves as Commies, the boys in the marble halls would have still given the edge to Nazis; krauts were so talented, and so adaptable. But *Justice* Department! No question Martin felt the same way I did, sharing good air with one of these trolls, but if it gave him the queasies he managed not to need a flight bag.

'Good to see you, Walter,' Hamilton said. 'We're glad you've reconsidered. We gather things might have gotten a little dicey for you since we last met.'

'A little.' I signalled the waiter to haul over a beaker.

'Idle hands, the devil's workshop,' he said. 'Did you see today's papers, by chance? You do read the papers, don't you?'

I shook my head. 'No cats, no parakeets.'

Hambone puckered up like he'd been sucking lemons. 'Your hyperbole refreshes, Walter. In any event, you remember our previous meeting, I'd imagine. Do you remember my speaking of upcoming situations?'

'They came up?'

'When the moment came to raise or fold, all it took our leader was one word to decide,' he said, unfolding a copy of the *Trib*. Martin gave a wistful glance at the bar and I know he wished he still drank. Frye had a certain damp limpness to him, as if he hadn't been plugged in. Adolf sat there taking in the ozone, staring down from Berchtesgarten, looking like he'd forgotten to take the coat hanger out of his jacket before putting it on. 'One word.'

'Plastics?'

'Tet,' Hamilton said, kissing the word as he lifted up the front page.

PRESIDENT LODGE DECLARES HE WILL
NOT RUN FOR RE-ELECTION
States Vietnam setbacks played no part in decision.

'Some less agog than others,' Hamilton said. 'I'd think an intelligent man such as yourself will clearly grasp what this implies.'

'Incumbent's not going to win?'

Frye went off on cue. *Hmnf hmnf hmnf.* The Old Pretender fingered the rim of his glass as if trying to make it warble.

'I'm sure his unforeseen loss in the New Hampshire primary wasn't reassuring,' Hamilton said, shooting his cuffs to show off the links; small gold theatre masks, sweet and sour. 'The Democrats are greatly pleased by last night's surprise. Probably Mansfield went ahead and ordered his new desk for the Oval Office. There was, however, a new development this morning.'

'He's got competition passing the collection plate?'

Hmnf hmnf hmnf.

Frye wasn't the only one making with the chucks. Even Hambone gave a quick smirk before shooting me a death ray. Perching there he looked like he was some vicious old grandfather the littlest ones were always ratting on. 'You're a live one, Walter. A clam in the chowder.'

'What is funny?' Sartorius asked, cocking his head to one side like a parrot, maybe trying to shake water out of his brain. Clearly the more jive I slung around one-ball the more he'd be left in the dark.

'A private joke, Hermann,' said Hamilton, patting his arm. 'Nothing more. Passing the plate indeed. As you might suspect, the man in the aisle is Senator Robert F. Kennedy of the great commonwealth of Massachusetts.'

'And you wouldn't call that the bee's knees?'

'I'm a man of affable nature,' he said. 'Speaking for myself, there's no reason for these matters to concern me. Republican, Democrat. Both are equally adaptable in the right time and place. However, there are associates of mine who prefer that the Senator not run. Who, in fact, want to make sure he doesn't. I've assured them I'll do everything I can within realistic limits, but even so I can't do everything. Special abilities such as yours are needed to satisfactorily prepare the ground. Your sociability, your intelligence. The harmless impression you feign so well. Your willingness to –' He paused. 'Your adaptability.'

'I get the picture,' I said. 'Keep in mind I'm strictly make love not war.'

'What do you think I'm asking of you, Walter? We have a lead, we need a featured player. There's no need to be suspicious.'

'Told Oswald same thing, didn't you?'

No humfy humfs from Frye on that one. Sartorius blinked a couple of times but otherwise might as well have been a wax figure. Martin looked like he might have had a stroke if I'd kept pressing the point, but malicious I'm not. Hammy leaned across the table so I could hear his whisper. 'Walter, what do you take us for? This isn't New Orleans.'

I was still reading the papers in 1963 and remembered it all quite well. The '64 election, coming up fast. Nixon's thirty points up in the polls but every night he walks the halls in the White House, shaking his fists at his predecessors, wondering what they had that he hasn't got. No question he'll get the majority but old Tricky has a jones on for those Euro elections, ninety-nine per cent for Fearless Leader and the loser hung in a gibbet on the road out of town. There he is, managed to whip the opposition into shape and then along come those goddamn Long boys, puffed up full of themselves like old uncle Huey (luckily not to such a degree), upending the Hadacol cart by slapping their Republicans into Democrat duds, converting the state, *ergo* the Southwest. After the fact Tricky's henchmen swore it was his idea to strongarm Pearly Earl in person, but nobody bought that but the Commission.

Grab the banjo and let's cakewalk down to Dixie: whoever said it, it got said. Pat and cocker spaniels in tow, Nixon goes to New Orleans. Sunny September afternoon, he barks at his mugs to lose the bubbletop, he's keen to do his semaphore act all the way down Canal Street. Vietnam escalation sure to turn the tide. Off goes the Pierce-Arrow's roof; up go the arms; *Ka-chow!* sneezes the roscoe. Before the Trickster feels that warm Gulf breeze where the top of his head used to be he finds himself heading *way* down south, getting the purple-ass treatment from Satan's snickering imps, and belly-aching about how much better Ike's probably got it. Topside, nobody's surprised, not really. Nobody except Oswald that is to say, once he finds out he's not going to be working on his tan in Fiji after his work is done, after all.

'All right, I'll go along,' I said. 'So fill me in. What is it you want me to do?'

Hamilton leaned forward – conspiratorily, you could say. 'It's really very simple,' he said. 'We'd like you to make friends with someone.'

'Who?'

'You'll be ingratiating yourself with one of Bobby's brothers.'

Thought I'd dreamed what he said at first, and so ignored them. 'What's the punchline?' Their icicles suddenly felt mighty sharp when they started to land. 'Are you trying to tell me one of them's going to let me get in earshot?'

'Of course.' Hamilton was so calm he almost looked beatific. Thinking quickly I ran through the possible players. It wouldn't be Joe Jr., loser of the '60 election and Paramount Pictures head honcho; not John, Washington *Star* kingpin and Commie scourge; not Father Ted, up there on the Cardinal's throne in Beanville. Obviously not Bobby. That left –

'Bah, bah, black sheep,' said Hamilton.

Hmf hmf hmf.

'James,' said Martin. 'James Kennedy.'

I didn't remember ever seeing a picture of him when he wasn't in diapers. 'What's his game?'

'He has none,' Martin said. 'Not long before he died, the old man disowned him. Then a year and a half ago mom forgave and forgot.'

'Forgave and forgot what?'

Martin shook his head. 'There was an incident of some sort.' He looked over at his accomplices; Hamilton didn't shake his head, but he might as well have. 'It's not important. Not anymore.'

'Even so, the Cardinal preferred that his brother left Massachusetts,' Hamilton said. 'Joe Jr. didn't want him in California. Jack didn't want him in Washington. At Bobby's urging, they sent him to New York, where any leopard can change his spots.' *Hmf hmf hmf.* 'A year and a half ago they bought him a store, here in Manhattan.'

'Record store,' said Martin. 'Old records.'

'Specializing in 78s. Martin tells me you're an aficionado of music of the old days, Walter. That's what led us to believe you'd be perfect, that you'd have something in common. You and I may even share some favourite songs. Russ Columbo?' I winced at the thought of listening to any of those proto-crooners. 'It's a gritty little warren on West 82nd, near Columbus, next to a chinee laundromat. Any chance you know the place?'

Knew it well; best shop in town, even before he took over. Always struck me there was something familiar about the new guy but managed never to place it. *That's* James Kennedy?' Hamilton nodded. 'Pretty tightlipped cat but when it comes to wax he can talk your ears off.'

'Then talk to him about records. Talk to him about anything. Get to know him better. Do you know him already?' I shook my head. 'Let him get to know you. That's all we want.'

I wasn't enough of a sob sister to fall for that line, but

they were at least using the right kind of lure. 'Make with the gladhand and the bakery is back in business?'

In Bennett's absence Hamilton allowed Frye to light his cigar. 'Exactly. You'll receive a stipend of five hundred dollars a week, plus expenses –'

'*Bitte*, but what are these records?' Sartorius asked, his iron needle carving a ravine across Hammy's bouncy tune. 'Classical music?'

'Degenerate music,' I said.

'Pardon me?'

'Blues. Jazz. Spirituals. Music of African origins.' Sartorius frowned, but under the circumstances he didn't start slinging the braunsweiger. 'So all I do is be Jimbo's friend? Where does the flash, bang come in?'

Hamilton shook his head, but Martin wouldn't look me directly in the eye. 'There won't be any of that, Walter.'

'Still like to know how the play ends before I get too far into the first act.'

'Walter, we'll be operating under standard procedure,' Martin said. 'You'll receive no more information than necessary at any given point. You know that's the only way we can work –'

'What will you get out of this?' I asked Hamilton.

'The satisfaction of extending favours to friends,' he said.

'Which friends?' I asked. 'I call. Show your hand.'

Frye extracted a folder from his leather lunchbox. With pudgy digits he worked a few black and white glossies loose and flipped them my way. Giving them the eye, I saw myself; also saw Chlojo dragging me down the street, Eulie taking the lead. Didn't please me to know I was being followed but I can't say I was surprised.

'I sized you up as quite the Lothario, Walter,' Hamilton said, putting through a lecher to lecher call. 'Very striking, these women.'

'Picked 'em up at Max's,' I said, thinking it best to be as

nonchalant as possible. 'Jersey girls come into town to see the big city. Didn't get to first base, though. Pity.'

'Modern woman,' Hammy sighed. 'Even flappers never wore such dresses.' He studied the glossies as if reading the bill. 'The big one *is* female? Our observer wasn't absolutely sure.'

'I have a question, however,' Sartorius said, pushing one of the photos in front of me and stabbing at the girls' heads with his finger. 'Shape of the skulls, you see. And earlobes. Possible mongrelization, it seems to me. What was specified on their identifications?'

'Sorry, but I don't check teeth.'

He blinked a bit faster than was necessary, but otherwise didn't give the game away. 'This was of no concern to you?'

'Frankly, mein bruder, this isn't DC. When it comes to wretched refuse we wrote the book here in New York. Everybody you didn't catch before they got out of Europe. Shame all of you had to wind up here.' I fixed him in my sights; no way, no reason I should put up with Nazis. They were bad as Georgians. 'We even let Jews in.'

'These women appear to be more negroid than Jewish,' he said. 'Did you ask about their parents?'

'What do you do on a date, Herr Jones? Take blood tests?' No reaction: the Big Nazi Book of Laughs was a slim volume with wide margins. 'Strikes me I haven't seen *your* identification.'

Martin's eyes widened and I felt his shoe kicking mine, under the table. Hamilton's smile curled into more of a leer, as if he was really enjoying the way I didn't make friends.

Sartorius took out his wallet, flipping it open so I could see his driver's licence and be impressed by his American Express card. Then he put it away, and returned his attentions to the photos of me and my visitors.

'These women were strangers to you?'

'Pickups, like I said.'

'Even so, according to your Justice Department's edicts, those of questionable background are to be at least investigated –'

'Take Walter's word for it,' Martin said, interrupting at a timely moment. Hamilton shot my man a glare that could set fires. Frye slid the glossies back into his folder. I imagined they'd go back into the big drawer with the other pieces of string.

'Yes, Hermann, rest assured. We know everything about Walter that we need to know.'

The look the old codger gave me wasn't a pleasant one, no matter how big the grin underneath. There was no way they'd have anything on me; Dad wasn't even one thirty-second, and he'd burned the family records before he set foot in Washington state. As far as the official world could find out I was caucasian, that is to say the official world outside of Martin; he knew about me only because I knew about him. Even so, my nerves were starting to feel more than a little on the supercharged side.

'Better get to it,' I said, standing. 'Could use some subway fare, I think.'

Martin passed me two Jacksons and a sawbuck. I added them to the single in my wallet.

'Subway fare is twenty-five cents,' Sartorius pointed out.

'True,' I said. 'Better give me one more for the road.' Martin handed over a fifty.

'The coin in the coffer rings,' Frye said, wiping the corners of his mouth as if he'd just finished running his choppers over an ear of corn, or his wife's honeybin – the last seemed awfully unlikely. 'The soul into purgatory springs.' *Hmmf hmmf.*

Coasting away slow I eased past the sots lined up along the bar, deciding not to check my hair in the mirror. Bad, bad, bad; the Boche might make themselves useful at NASA or in the Agriculture Department, but let them stick a monocle in anywhere else and the next thing you knew they were using their break time to draw up furnace blueprints, just in case a less lax administration gets into office. Last thing I needed was some blonde beast nitwit rummaging through my ancestral laundry. I was sure Bennett somehow had a hand in this, somewhere; he always gave me the impression he suspected, he just never came out with it. I would have given it all deeper thought, but a voice I heard as I exited caught my attention.

'Walter.'

There they were, both my mutts bounding toward me. Seeing them, seeing how especially good Eulie looked, I instinctively switched into beach-strut mode, drawing in the gut so that no part of it would be visible. Then I thought of the genealogical voyeurs still hanging out in the bar, and decided we'd better make tracks. 'Hi hi. Around the corner, ladies,' I told them, leaning forward to cut wind resistance as I ankled past them double-time. 'Come on, follow me.' I steered my dusky delights down 18th and then up Park. They dressed down in daylight. Eulie wore an orange mini and knee-high boots – no jacket, coat or stockings. Even on the run I could see her pipestems pimpling up like plucked drumsticks. Big Mama wore leather, nothing but the old shiny shiny from bootsoles to collar. Looked like she came straight out of one of those magazines for special audiences. Inverted cross earrings dangled off her lobes, and I wondered if she was Cainite. As we kept up the pace I saw the stares were starting to load up, and figured we'd better slow down before we reached critical mass. Once on 21st east of Park I stopped at midblock and signalled they should join me. 'OK, this is good.'

'What disconcerts, Walter?' Eulie asked, laying one of her little paws on my arm. Let me tell you, that charged my battery right up. 'You're uncoloured.'

I nodded. 'Damn right. So are you if they ask.' Looking behind us, I checked to be sure we hadn't been tailed. Gave the surroundings a quick check, now that I knew

Hammy's boys could be playing Weegee on me whenever I wasn't looking. Lovely Eulie batted those lashes and my knees started clicking like castanets. Chlojo, idling, gave a hot dog cart a come-hither look. She licked her lips like she was deciding whether she should eat hot dogs or hot dog man first. 'Those were your supervisories?' Eulie asked.

'You went in the bar?'

'We sighted from without.'

'The guy who was sitting on my right, he's my boss. The other three, they're bad news. Blondie's all ubermensch and a mile wide, he's onto you two –'

Eulie didn't appear to hear a word I said. 'Walter, privacy essentials. Can we shack with you?'

My jaw dropped like I'd been poleaxed. 'How's that?'

'Go to your pad,' she said. When I gave her peepers a closer gander I gathered she'd almost hit the bull's eye when she first tried her line but it hadn't quite come out as she planned. 'Is it safe?'

'Come on.'

I ran them down 21st to Third, where we stood and waited for the light to change blue. The uptown clattered along the tracks overhead; it was a sunny day, and venetian-blind shadows ran the length of the avenue. Chlojo nearly bumped into a bum lowering his string down a sewer grate, fishing for change. A firetruck rolled by, and from the looks the gals were getting I suspected they'd try to roll by again.

'Where've you two been?' I asked. 'You said you'd be dropping back by. I could have died of old age at this rate –'

'Are you still sighting?' Eulie asked. Other people in passing cars gave Chlojo stares like she was the Loch Ness monster. One poor dope nearly slammed into an El stanchion before swerving back into his lane, nearly clipping a Seven Santini Brothers van.

'The ghosts?'

She nodded, and as we crossed the street I filled her in.

'I bring in spookarama in stereo every night.' I guided them down Third, past the pawn shops and thrift stores and bars. 'Mornings, too. Sometimes they try to talk to me. I don't know if talk's the right word. They know my name. He does at least.' Sweet petite looked like I'd told her the sun was made out of cream cheese. 'But he's all transmit and no receive.'

'They speak directly to you?'

'How'd they find out my name?'

'Unknown,' she said. I never saw anyone look so worried as she always did.

'No matter,' I said. 'Now when we get to 18th we're going to go through the building next door, go up to the roof and cross over that way, just to be on the safe side.'

'Walter, there's something you need knowing.'

'What's that –?' I started to say, but was interrupted.

'*Hey!!* Mama!' some too-manly voice shouted out. 'Where'd *you* two come from?'

Demolition men were taking down some old hovel at the corner of 19th, and we were lucky enough to be passing by just as their shift was ending. More than a dozen of them were swinging down from their scaffolds like rabid monkeys. 'Give us your number, baby. Who's that, your big sister?'

'Shake it, baby –'

'Pass 'em by,' I told my gals, quickening the pace, trying to reach the corner before they could cut us off. No go, though; Moe, Larry and Shemp walled off the sidewalk and their trucks blocked the curb.

'Hey, gals,' said the one in the centre, a red-faced lout with ropy arms and ham-sized hands. 'We lost our phone numbers. Can we get yours?' The one on his right, a wiry Italian, slid behind me as if I wasn't even there.

'We'll take it from here, buddy,' the one on his left said. This wasn't good, but if worse came to worse and these meatheads lost control of themselves, I'd go to the fallback position. I always keep five STP-12 patches hidden in my wallet in case of emergencies. I slid it out of my pants and got one ready; all I needed to do was slap one wherever they were bare and the lugs would be flat out on a ten count. The big one, I gathered he was the foreman, planted himself in front of Chlojo's face and switched the charm on high beam. 'Some tits, sweetheart,' he said. 'Got anybody takin' care of 'em?'

'You a go-go dancer, honey?' the Italian asked Eulie.

'You disinterest us,' she said. 'We'll proceed.'

'Baby, you going to give me your number?' the foreman asked Chlojo, giving her the eye-to-eye. 'Don't run into many my size.' He took hold of her hand, but then jerked it away as if he'd been burned. 'Christ Jesus,' he shouted. 'Your hands're rougher than mine. It's some faggot, get off –'

Her flight suit seemed to lack the special brassiere her earlier ensemble sported. What happened next happened very fast, and I can't truthfully say that I *saw* it. Chlojo seized his hand and pulled him towards her; her right arm moved, and the foreman fell on the sidewalk, wailing like a banshee. Chlo was still holding his hand, not that it was going to be of much use to him any longer. One time I gashed my thumb, playing Jack the Ripper on a bagel with a dull knife, and there was so much blood I feared I'd be leeched dry before I could curb the flow. That was just a paper cut compared; the foreman's wrist squirted like a hose.

'*Shit*, man –' his companions said, doing a quick reverse. Chlojo pitched the hand into a trash can and started to walk south again. Hard to say now, much less at the time, what was most upsetting – what Chlojo'd done, or the way Eulie took it in stride.

'Lay still,' I said, kneeling and pulling my belt loose from my pants. I wrapped it around his arm above the elbow and yanked tight, buckling it off. Two workmen ran out with a towel and stick, ready to tie on a tourniquet, and I gladly let them buy out my medical practice. We had already attracted a crowd, and under the sound of the el overhead I heard sirens coming up fast. Just when I'd have wanted everyone to pretend they were asleep and not hear anything, half the neighbourhood seemed to be running over to see. One woman looked at the wrist stump-on and let out a blast like a tugboat.

Eulie grabbed Chlo and pulled her back to the scene of the crime.

'Walter, are you coming?'

I really turned on the air raid siren. 'You can't do things like this,' I said, screaming at tall and frosty. 'Don't you know you could have killed him?' She nodded.

'Cops'll be here any second,' I said to Eulie, imagining what could happen if Big Bertha really went to town. 'Beat it. They'd haul you in in a second.'

'Walter, please –'

'Out! Go!' They heeled it down the street; one of the construction crew tried, briefly, to keep Chlo from getting past but she picked him up and slung him on top of the roof of a yellow cab and after that, no one else seemed willing to intervene. Seconds after they disappeared a paddywagon and five cans of Spam careened up, and out barrelled the boys of Killarney, waving their guns and clubs like it was Armistice Day.

'What's going on here?' one of the older cops asked me. He had a face like a pile of rocks.

'Psychos,' I said, estimating a freeform narrative would work best. 'Acidheads, probably. Goofballs. Jumped that poor guy, cut his hand off.'

'Cut it *off*? Christ –'

'They went that-a-way,' I said, pointing, figuring they were long gone.

'*That's* the fuck,' the Italian said, coming up and shoving me against the el stanchion. I really wished he hadn't been such a responsible citizen. 'He was with 'em all the time.'

*　　*　　*

Now in the Big Onion, only difference between being a material witness and being a suspect is that if you're chalked on the first cue, nobody beats you up until you get to the precinct house. Every twenty years the feds launch a new investigation into New York police brutality and, my luck, this was year nineteen. Back when the bosses built my precinct's pigsty this was the noted Gas House District, which took in the terrain from Third to the river south of 23rd; home turf to the Gashouse Gang, the East River Pirates, Sweeney's Gadabouts and the Kerosene Boys; by the time I came to town the gangs were long canned. The place was built when Bryan was president and should have been condemned before he left office. No matter how often they renovated, the screams still stuck to the walls and, my brothers, I wasn't keen on slapping on a layer of mine. My prints were filed, and as they bore the federal stamp they would have guaranteed my quick release, but no one seemed willing to look for them. The desk jockey tossed me in a one-bum drunk tank so I could consider the errors of my ways. A doped-up Chinaman two cells down caterwauled Beatles tunes.

Hour or so passed, then a cop led me down a hall lined with wooden file cabinets and pieces of broken chairs. He dragged open the vault in the back wall and bade me enter. The interrogation room had a damp concrete floor, tile walls and a row of lockers – only one with a door – and a big fan. Inside, two of New York's finest cooled their heels. Both wore Korvettes suits, tight on their arms as sausage skin. The taller one had slapped on so much Vitalis that his head looked flammable, and to enhance his tango-gaucho silhouette, let a tamed caterpillar snooze on his lip. The wider cop had toothbrush hair and a nose that couldn't have been broken less than eight times, no good for anything except supporting shades. I'd never met the day shift at my local establishment. They had me try out a wooden chair that wasn't broken yet. A sunlamp hung overhead, set on low instead of deep-fry.

'My name's Arnold,' said Nosey. 'Detective Arnold. This is Detective Benz.'

'Officers.'

'Construction worker's gonna live, but he'll need a hook,' said Benz. 'You get used to it, I hear.'

'Think his wife will?' said Arnold. 'Kids?'

'What'd your friends have against him? Just busting chops?'

'They weren't my friends,' I said. 'I'd just met them at the corner. Told me they were tourists. Kinda told me. No speaka the lingua real good.'

'Tourists.'

'Said they were looking for the Statue of Liberty.'

'They find it?' Arnold opened his jacket, so my view of his sap and his brass knuckledusters in the inside pockets wouldn't be blocked. 'Tourists. Where from?'

'Didn't ask.'

'Too busy looking to ask.'

'Witnesses said they were lookers,' said Arnold. 'You must have been looking.'

'Never saw anyone like them. Officers, speaking as a witness I –'

Benz shook his head like he was waking up. Not a hair came loose. 'A hook. How's he gonna pitch a few to the boy?'

'Lopped off like he stuck it in a meat slicer.'

'Like ham. Thin sliced ham. What'd she use? Machete?'

'I didn't know what happened till it happened,' I said, figuring it would do no harm to tell the truth. 'Guys were bugging 'em, I told them to ignore the assholes and keep walking.'

'Thought they didn't speaka the English.'

'Not well,' I said. 'Officers –'

'Boy probably won't make the team,' said Benz. 'Not without practice.'

83

Arnold walked over to the sole working locker, which he unlocked. He banged around inside for thirty seconds or so before he took out a radio aerial snapped off a car – sharpened, I thought, although that seemed unnecessary – a length of black rubber hose that dribbled its sand filling, and a Louisville Slugger with five long rusty spikes driven through the thick end. 'Then they just took off after that?'

'Yes,' I said. 'Seriously, officers, you ought to look me up in the files.'

'We gonna find something?' asked Benz.

'All in good time,' Arnold casually cuffed my right wrist to the chair's arm.

'Why am I being handcuffed?' I asked, starting to feel unnerved. 'I'm a witness, aren't I?'

'Tell us what you really saw, what you really know, you're a witness,' Arnold said.

'I'm telling you what I saw. What I know.'

'Let's take a look at what we got so far.' Benz extracting a small black notebook from a side pocket and flipping it open. 'Resisting arrest,' he said. 'Still resisting arrest. Two charges.'

'Possession of marijuana,' said Arnold, pulling on rubber gloves. I gave silent thanks to Sophia on high that I'd only been carrying brand X, and left my P-bomb muggles safe and sound back at the old homestead. 'Three.'

'Loitering with intent. Vagrancy. Four, five.'

'Accessory after the fact.'

'Add everything up,' said Benz, 'seventy years.'

'For *what?*' I asked.

Arnold looked over his collection before finally settling on the hose. As he picked it up he was careful not to let any of the sand slip out. Whipping it over his head, he brought it down on my legs just above the knees. Felt like a piano fell into my lap. 'That's for the boy.'

'What else you remember about those women?'

'Call Captain Thomason,' I said, not as loudly as I might have. 'He's night shift. He'll tell you.' Benz shrugged. Arnold tapped the non-pointy part of the spiked bat against the sole of his shoe.

'Tell you what?' Benz said. 'We haven't even charged you yet.'

'We'd like to avoid doing that,' Arnold said, winding up as if ready to send me out high over left field. 'If possible.' Before he could play the Babe, thankfully, the room's door opened. The desk jockey stuck in his head and gave us all the evil eye. 'Dammit, Dennis, put that goddamn thing down,' he shouted. 'Let him go. He's connected.'

'How?' Arnold whined, not letting go of the bat. 'Tammany?'

'Department of the Interior. Better luck next time, boys.'

The way Arnold slunk back to the locker made it clear his whole day was ruined. 'Thanks for coming in,' Benz said, unclasping my bracelet. 'You gonna be able to walk?'

'No thanks to you,' I said, making it to my feet. Glad they hadn't broken anything but it wasn't for lack of trying. Arnold glared at me as I walked out, but I was having none of it. When I reached the reception room I saw Martin sitting on one of the benches, looking more than a little peeved.

'Didn't need bail at least,' I offered, but he kept mum. 'Muchas thankas.'

'How long have you worked for me? How long? Shouldn't you know how to avoid these kind of situations?'

Martin was still Agency when he visited the University of Washington campus the one year I was there, looking for likely recruits. Soon as I looked him over I was able to peg his grandparents' line; his eye was just as trained and he did the same for me. In our unavoidable circumstances you always do what you can to help out your fellow passers, and he made me an offer. I hadn't found higher levels of academia any improvement over the lower, but I wasn't willing to commit, not yet. Called him not long after hitting New York, some time after I'd discovered my true metier. He was working the Department of Interior, which had its own operations going. Next thing I knew I was on the Sea Beach Express, barrelling toward Luna Park and Dreamland, casually spritzing testers to gauge how effectively an aerosol mood-alterant diffused within a closed subway environment.

'Martin, look,' I said as we reached Second Avenue. 'Wrong place, wrong time. Nothing to add.'

'Shouldn't I know who these women are? They were the same ones you were with last month, weren't they?'

'Did you see us?'

'I was on my way out. Think I wanted to hang around with that crowd any longer than I had to?' He sneered; I could only imagine the kind of small talk Hammy and his little Germ made when I wasn't around. 'They cut off a construction worker's *hand*?' I nodded. 'Walter, who are they working for?'

'They fed me some line about the Society for Psychical Research.'

'Don't feed me shit and say it's candy.'

'I'm not,' I said, but he clammed. We kept walking west; it was hard to say who followed and who led. When we reached Fifth Avenue we turned south. Shackmans toy store was at the corner of 16th; it was older than Hamilton, it had been there since Hector was a pup. Glancing behind us first, Martin peeled off to the left and went inside. I trailed, shoving through the revolving door and feeling worn wooden planks creak beneath my feet. There wasn't a toy in there made later than 1946. Reminded me of the old five and ten cent stores back in Seattle downtown, the bins on the oak tables full of tiny lead cars and soldiers, sets of jacks and hopfrogs, aggies and shooters and cats-eyes, airplane glue and balsa strips.

'Psychical research,' he said. 'You're fucking with me, Walter.'

'No I'm not. Why would I? Look, I don't know who they

are any more than you do. But they're definitely not ours or anybody else's, near as I can tell. They're –'

'What?'

'Hard to say. Look, I know they're not Agency. At first I thought Bennett might be in on it –'

'Not a chance,' he said, whispering. 'They'd have cut off his head first time he tried pinching their ass.' We flipped through a rack of paper dolls, marvelling at how many outfits you could get for Shirley Temple. On the wall to our right was a shelf lined with a row of mechanical banks, reproductions of early twentieth-century toys. Cast-iron Teddy Roosevelts fired pennies into trees, making cast-iron bears pop out the top; Uncle Sam dropped coins into his satchel and waggled his chin whiskers. There were others – 'Always Did 'spise A Mule,' where the latter threw a hapless pickaninny and the penny he held onto the ground; 'Darktown Battery,' where a pitcher was ready to lob a cent at a gangly, thick-lipped batter. These weren't entirely accurate reproductions; the once-black figures were all painted white. In the centre of the shelf was a bank I remembered seeing in stores when I was young; a bust of a man with one arm and a giant grinning head. The cast iron hair was curled tight, the nose broad and flat, the lips full, the ears protuberant. You put the coin in the hand and pressed the button; the arm raised to the mouth and the coin fell inside. The ears wiggled. On this model, the hair was blonde, the eyes blue, the face pale as Bennett's; but along the bottom of the bust the legend still read JOLLY NIGGER. It was the cheapest of the lot, at fourteen ninety-five.

'What's the kraut add to this gumbo, anyway?'

'I'm not absolutely sure,' Martin said. 'He's an associate of Hamilton's. Since he's at Justice I have no say-so in the matter.'

'And if he starts asking the wrong kind of questions about the wrong people?'

Martin gritted his teeth, and ran his hand over his bald head.

He shaved it every morning, so not a trace of a kink might show. Told everyone he'd lost his hair when he had typhoid, as a child. 'No. That won't happen.'

'You're sure?'

The clerk gave us a truant-officer stare, probably beginning to suspect we were waiting to lure away toddlers with candy. 'Sirs,' she said, 'we'll be closing momentarily.'

I nudged Martin and we headed out. 'It's not going to help matters if you keep being seen with those girls,' he said. 'The big one *is* a girl, isn't she?'

'And a mile wide,' I said. 'They haven't asked me if they can come around. It's hard to fight 'em off.'

'That's clear,' he said. 'What did she cut his hand off for? What did she cut it off *with*?' He shoved his mitts in his pockets after buttoning his coat. DC boys always cracked under the strain of New York weather. 'Look, I've got to get to the station.'

'Stag or drag?'

'They left on the four-thirty. Good thing for you I had to get a second fitting for a suit up at Brooks Brothers. When the police finally did look at your file they called my number, and luckily my assistant knew where I'd be.'

'Give her a raise,' I said.

'I can make the seven-twenty. When are you going record shopping?'

'Tomorrow,' I said. 'What should I know about this that they're not telling?'

'I'm not telling,' Martin said. We grinned, feeling fairly jolly ourselves for the moment.

The West Side Record Store was next to the Wong Kee laundromat on the 82nd Street side of the Endicott Hotel. Homicide Arms we called it, six people killed there every year on average: autoerotic fatalities, homosexual love stabbings, old drunks poking out each others' eyes with pocket knives, horse deals gone ruinously bad. Places like this attract good record stores; something in the air, I suppose. The jingle bells rang when I popped open the door. 'Hey there,' the owner called out, seeing me. 'Where you been, stranger?' Now that I knew who he actually was, it was impossible to miss. Tucked below that lush alky hair, beneath those chipmunk cheeks and the bags under his eyes, those Kennedy genes were there in plentitude.

'I've lacked liquidity, my brother. Led a pauper's existence. But down's up again and I've come to celebrate.'

'Here?' he asked, laughing. I was the only customer in the store; there were two lights in the ceiling and forty-seven thousand 78s in bins, files and cases. Hard to have gotten higher, no matter what I dropped.

'You got a couple of beauties I've been wanting to pick up for a long time,' I told him. 'Let me get their phone numbers.'

'Which ones?' he asked, not yet standing. While he wasn't morbidly obese, he was huskier – let's be honest, and say a real porker – than his brothers, all of whom were thin as motel blankets. Those mesomorphs couldn't be happier being seen pounding tennis balls, rigging sails, lifting cars, diving into volcanoes. Even Father Ted showed good form hoisting that loving cup every Sunday. Jim Kennedy must have always been the standout in the bunch.

'Skip James, "Devil Got My Woman Blues", Blind Tommy Walker, "Mean Old Blue", and Robert Johnson, "Malted Milk Blues".'

Oh, happy day when you make a store owner as happy as you when you buy something. 'You sure you want them?' he asked, smiling. I fluffed the green with a satisfying ruffle. He squeezed between the bins to reach the locked case, opened it and pulled out the prizes, laying them on a shammy he'd draped over his desk. 'Labels unfaded. Near mint, each one. They'll transfer to tape beautifully.'

'Numbers match up with Godrich?'

'Every one. And you know you don't usually find these in packages like this.' While Johnson was in a modern sleeve, and

Skip's original was still plain kraft, the one for Blind Tommy was a full-tilt Paramount Sambo special, bearing the logo THE POPULAR RACE RECORD, and a black-on-brown drawing of a big-lipped house slave whanging on his diddlybo. 'Walter, right?' he asked.

'Right, Jim.' Those Kennedy teeth gleamed like the moon. 'Wrap 'em up.'

As he padded my buys with cotton batting and newspaper I snaked over to take a look at what else was in the case. Several Enrico Carusos; but on a Brazilian label, not Italian or standard Red Victor. A couple of cylinders labelled, by hand, *T. Roosevelt Dec 1907*; the Emancipation speech maybe. 'Old Jimmie Sutton', by Grayson and Whitter, a sad sight; far as I had known until that moment, mine was the only existing copy. *Bud Averill Plays Songs by Stephen Foster*, a theremin recording on the Tech-Art label. A flat disc marked *Last Surviving 1812 War Veteran*; then several that I already owned, Geeshie prominent among them. And –

'Jim,' I said, 'how much for this one?'

'Twenty,' he said. 'I'll make it seventy-five total if you want that one, too.'

'Sold.'

'Dallas String Band. "Dallas Rag",' he said, reading the label. '14292 D. Coley Jones, right?'

'He's on there,' I said. 'Guy I knew had a tape. Magnificent stuff.'

'Let me tape it before you walk off with it. That all right?' I nodded. Jim stuck a new reel on his player, fed in the leader and tested the wires. 'Got it hooked into the speakers I use for the Victrola,' he explained. 'Picks it up directly.' He dusted the grooves, fixed the baby blanket on the spinner and then eased the disc down. He used a bamboo needle instead of a steel so even before the first note plucked I knew the condition was near perfect. You've probably never heard it, but if you have, 'Dallas Rag,' a two-mandolin beauty that drives like a Tennessee moonshiner is about as perfect as there is. Impossible to find, but I always had a working theory that most of the stock was in Warehouse 6, and went up during the 1930 Columbia fire.

'That's something,' Jim muttered, his eyes closed as he listened. Nobody listens to old records these days unless they've got the heart to hear them.

'Where'd you turn it up?' I asked.

'New England,' he said. 'Boston. Elderly abolitionist owned this and about two hundred others. Don't think he listened to a one of them but bought them to show solidarity. Boston used to be a good place to look for race records, but it's all cleaned up now.' I nodded; I knew. 'I'm hoping next year to take a trip down South.'

'Why?'

'Think of all the records that must still be down there,' he said, 'in drawers and closets. Basements. Barrels out back. You don't think so?'

'Broom swept clean, down in those parts,' I said. 'The records were dumped along with everything else. Never known a racer to show up south of the Ohio River.'

He nodded. 'Closing time,' he said. 'Glad you came in. This pays half the rent.'

'Jim,' I said, 'you ever want to go out for drink? Something?'

His face brightened, then dimmed slightly. Even so it was plain as the nose on his face that he'd have jumped over five fences to go out with anybody. 'I don't drink,' he said. 'Not anymore.'

'Never touch the stuff myself,' I said. 'Soda pop, then. And talking records. Let's say Saturday?'

'Sounds good.' But somehow he looked as if it sounded bad.

Maybe it was just events catching up with me, but I went all Blakey on the way back home. Sometimes when it's late enough, and I'm bored enough, or stoned enough, I hit the bricks and turn on my own personal Wayback Machine. Try it sometime: make sure it's after two in the morning, go to the right neighbourhood and then let your eyes unfocus – you'll see what I mean. It's one of the best things about New York, being able to live in past and present at the same time. Walk anywhere in the Thirties west of Eighth, and it's still 1941. Head down Ludlow or Orchard if you want 1894. Stroll along Fifth, in the Fifties, and you'll be right back in 1936. Keep your eyes above the cars, of course.

That evening I had a different kind of vision. It wasn't late, and I wasn't on anything; one second I was bouncing down Broadway with my new old discs, and then the next everyone and everything looked different. The usual Balkan gang assimilated; their clothes and hairdos got fancier, their faces took on the look of strangers. Pint-size cars and gigantic pickup trucks with cabins on the back rolled bumper to bumper down both sides of the boulevard. The bars were gone, the cafeterias, the dress stores, the Commie French cheese shop; I couldn't even guess what half the stores I saw sold . . . I nearly spun out, my brothers; but when I closed my eyes and then reopened, all was again as it should have been.

What was strangest was that I knew the scene I'd lightfooted into so casually wasn't in the gone world, or in the world of tomorrow, but in the *now* world; and whoever's *now* it was, it wasn't mine, at least not yet. Maybe my ghosts, or my gals, were having some kind of lasting effect on me; having had enough of Fortean phenomena for one evening, I snagged a cab and headed back to my castle doubletime.

FIVE

Man's walk tells you if he's buck, bull, or baby. Mine's a limber stride, when I set out I imagine that my legs roll in my hipjoints like they were fit with ball bearings. A walk like that lets the nosy parkers know no matter what shit comes down, it's not going to bug *you*. Jim Kennedy's walk told me that he was pretty much prepared for and expecting anything. His tightrope stroll along the sidewalk made me think of Frankenstein, or the Greek statues the Greeks sculpted before they learned how to sculpt. He kept his knees locked like they had pins inside, kept his arms glued to his sides, his fists clenched as if trying to figure out who to hit next. Jim moved like he knew in a place deeper than his bones that if he didn't always hew to the straight and narrow he wouldn't last longer than the time it took him to fall.

A bar called Shaugnessy's became our regular hangout. Place was your standard Irish dive, stuck between a cafeteria and a dry cleaners on Broadway, just north of 83rd before you got to Loew's. We'd keelhaul a booth, I'd order bourbon, he'd signal for the first of an endless series of seltzers. (His bicarb tab must have been frightening; he drank so much fizzeroo that I'm surprised he never blew up.) 'Down the hatch,' I'd crow and we'd down our respective poisons. The old traditional lost weekend isn't my favoured format but I'd learned how to drink when I needed to. Back in '63, during the Panama crisis, I earned my bones not only with Martin but with his bossmen, ingratiating myself as directed with a gang of commies in the Village. Half were Russian-born, and half of *those* were on the wagon, so I had to learn how to tie on the bag around sots and de-sotted alike if I was going to keep the wheels nice and greasy. During the first round of chuckle juice I'd act like I was guzzling a king-size snort, but I'd really only sip, and splash out the extra from the shotglass when I slammed it down; or, if it was a highball, artfully rearrange the ice, shaking the glass like a maraca. Made it look like I was just like one of the boozehounds, long as you seemed drunk as they were they were happy; and (most usefully when it came to Jim) by acting in such fashion the boys riding the wagon would think you'd never remember anything you heard once you sobered up. I had the poor bastards coming and going. On the last night I enjoyed their company (*enjoyed*, well; if you've ever been cornered by a Trot symp at cocktail hour you know there are more exact words) we went to the White Horse and I carried over the first round. First, though, I sprinkled their vodka with a little C9-Algernon4 (which, among much else, gives you Korsakov's Syndrome for the duration of the seventeen-hour trip). After I was done with 'em not a one was capable of any action, overt, covert or subvert, on Amity Street for the duration of the emergency.

The first week or so Jim and I got together it was hard for us to talk about anything other than records – put two obsessive shellackers in a room and they won't stop yakking till they pass out from lack of oxygen – and it was clear to me Jim was no dilettante. We spent one entire evening going over nothing but the Broadway 5000 series and whether or not the Reverend J.M. Gates and Congregation had recorded a version of 'Death Will Be Your Santa Claus' for the label (I thought he had, but Jim demonstrated to me he hadn't;

the number I thought matched the non-existent master was actually 5025; B 6927-1 and 6929-1, 'I Know I Got Religion' backed with 'The Funeral Train A-Coming.' Excuse my tangent; *you* may not dig the essentiality of knowing this for sure, but believe me, both of us did). Even so, the time finally came to talk about something other than discs, and so one evening as he ordered his third seltzer I bit the bullet.

'When did you buy the store, anyway?' I asked. 'I hadn't been in there for a dog's age till a few months ago.'

'A year,' Jim said. 'Took ages to get George to sell.'

Former owner Crazy George, that is, one of New York's more accomplished psychopaths. Always looked like he slept in the Indian cave in Central Park, hadn't had a bath since 1931, would as soon spit at you as look at you, but the man did know his platters. Knew 'em too well to ever find bargains in the bins, but I could have lived with that. Real problem was he was the kind of storeowner wouldn't sell you anything if he didn't think you were worthy. You may have *been* worthy, once, but things always change. Don't have to tell you that eventually no one was worthy – but then it probably saved him time, counting out at night, if he didn't make any sales during the day.

'He needed the money?' A chunky-shoulldered shrug. 'How'd you get him to sell, then?'

'The family handled it.'

Surprising to hear him say the word *family* himself; several times before that I'd use it in passing or we'd overhear it on the radio, or coming out of one of the barflies as the woozer beefed about the home life, and Jim'd go all pasty and woolly-eyed as if the very notion of what plays together stays together made his stomach try to hop out of his mouth. 'Never figured George'd give it up. Must have been pretty persuasive.'

'They can be,' he said. 'Mom took care of the money. Two of my brothers handled the actual deal.'

Hm, yes, that made me suspect George was probably spending his golden years in an oil drum at the bottom of the East River. 'Your dad help out too?'

'He's dead.' Jim smiled; not a chance he meant to, but he did. He shot me one of those grins where you know the grinner knows he shouldn't be happy but can't help himself. It gave me the willies now whenever I saw him flash the choppers, knowing his bloodline; every time this brother's teeth hit the high beams it was impossible not to see his four siblings.

'I'm sorry.'

'Heart attack,' he said, adjusting his stonepuss. 'Quick, at least.'

True enough, hearts tend to seize up fast when bullets plough through them. That was the last time Old Black Joe made the newsreels, back in 1954. He was just about bald by then but the hair he had left he treated first-class. Whenever he'd come to New York he'd see the same barber, regular as clockwork. The shop was a Fancy Dan off the lobby of the Ritz Carlton, over on Madison in the forties. He'd doff the chesterfield and the homburg, tuck the bifocals into his shirt pocket and lie back to be fitted for the shroud. Hitman that day was kind enough to wait till the barber clipped the last few strays around the neck before moving in for the kill. Splash of witch hazel, a quick whisk with the broom; *kerbang*! sneezed the roscoe. Barber conveniently had his back turned in that instant, dipping combs into the blue stuff – that was his story, anyway. Hooligan made tracks, ditching the gun behind him. No fingerprints, trail cold as Siberia. Word was Hoover was behind it, he was in a stew about how Joe'd sold McCarthy out once that gig was blown. Long before I knew I'd be palling around with any Kennedy, I asked Martin if he had any inside dirt. Looked at me like I'd asked him which route his mom preferred, French or Greek, and I didn't ask again.

'What'd you do before this?' I asked.

He shook his head, and brushed his hair back, trying to cover the shiny skin at the peak. Probably he'd started shedding soon as he stopped boozing; Sophia knew brothers in gin always kept thick rugs above the snowline. 'Wall Street. Day trader.'

'Seriously?'

'Had the knack for it when I was younger. Pressure got me after a while. That and the sauce. Couldn't take it any more.' He shook his head, and guzzled down the rest of his fizz. 'Went all blooey.'

'Blooey?'

'You know.' I nodded. 'Just had to take off. Told everyone that I was going to become the sheriff of Waco, Texas.' He pronounced it *whacko*, which wasn't the exact pronunciation, but from what I'd heard, it fit.

'Inventive.'

'Wasn't any of their business,' he said, and I heard a knife in his voice. 'Went back to my place. Got a suitcase and emptied it out. Went down to the liquor store and filled it with scotch. Checked into the Seymour over on 44th, stayed there five days. Mostly stayed there. Then they found me.'

'Who?'

He shook his head, and his eyes wavered. I was starting to think I should abandon this conversational tangent for the nonce. 'My brothers,' he said. 'Their mugs, anyway.'

I took a very, very small sip of my drink.

Needless to say while going through the initial motions with Jim I was still contending with my ghosts and losing three falls out of three. Though neither of my transparent moochers did anything especially annoying other than being there, the guy started trying to talk to me more often; seemed to try, at any rate. Never elaborated on his riff: *Walter*, he'd blow; *Walter*. Repeat for sixty-four bars, second verse same as the first. But however many times he spun the tune, no matter how I was sometimes disappointed if I didn't see them first thing when I walked in, I never stopped feeling those campfire shudders. It was anybody's guess when they would drop in. Usually after the initial start I'd be okay, but then sometimes I'd be sitting on the throne reading the paper, not hurting a fly, and suddenly Marley'd pour through the door laying on with that heavy moan. Make me want to pull the chain and flush myself down to live among the alligators.

My happy couple'd be there every morning come roostertime. When I'd get up I'd hope Eulie'd be there too, lurking in the kitchen or parking that cute keister of hers on my sofa, but every morning I was hit with a no-show. Wasn't hard to see she was the kind of cookie you couldn't keep your mitts on for long, but after two weeks dripped by I started to think they figured they'd put me through enough grief, and went off to haunt somebody else. The more I missed her, the heavier the black dog sat on my shoulders. I'm not one for the mushbowl – flowers and candy do nothing for me; as Trish knew well I can gape at a full moon and the only thing that makes me howl is how utterly groovitudinous it'd be to perambulate over its chickenpox scars. But when I thought of Eulie I knew considerably more than just the old kielbasa was involved; it worried me, the way I was thinking about her – I was never that serious about *anything*.

One cold crispy evening Jim was under the weather and since I had no desire to coop with the spirit world I paraded over to Max's. Got there too early for real action, showing up sometime around ten. That fabulous Trish was five deep in dopesters and jugheads at the far end of the bar, hard at work playing queen of the night. She heaved a bottle sky-high in salute and shouted at me. 'Get over here, Walter. Got somebody you should meet. Come on.'

No use fighting it. Hacking my way through the under-brush of coolies I waded across the room. Trish sloughed off her more useless admirers as I hit my mark. She struck attitudes with a lush little chickadee holding up the bar. Her pal was a five-footer tagged out in a shiny gold print mini; she'd swept up her blonde curlies in a bubblehead do. Standing next to Trish made her look like she was standing in a hole.

'Every time I'm raring to carouse I catch a glimpse of your pickle puss,' Trish said, slapping me in the chest. 'Stop sucking on those lemons. Here. Walter, Vivian. Vivian, Walter.' She prodded her silent sidekick with an elbow. 'He's prime suspect number one in my book.'

'Charmed,' I said, broadcasting over the din. 'One of the Vivian girls?'

She cocked a hand to her ear and aimed her noggin sideways at me, crooking her neck and looking like a parrot zeroing in on a cracker. She wore the kind of perfume that smelled like she bought it at Woolworth's even though you knew she hadn't.

'What?' she squeaked. Didn't sound like her voice had changed yet.

'*Enchanté*,' I said. 'Ma cherie.'

She threw me a flutter or two of the black rakes above her peepers. 'Oh, wow,' she said. 'You're French?'

Gritting my teeth I hauled myself towards the summit, looking forward to sliding down on the far side. 'Washington state,' I said. 'Where'd you get your diapers changed?'

Poor missy looked like she'd been hit over the head with a duck. 'Excuse me?'

'Excused,' I said. 'Where were you before you hit New York?'

The lightbulb went on, though I could tell it was flickering. 'Cleveland.'

Trish hopped in before I could make disparaging remarks about Euclid Avenue and her grand plan completely collapsed. 'Vivian works at Bonwit. She's in fragrances.'

As guessed. 'So I'll get a discount?' I asked. Got a blank

stare from Viv and an especially evil glare from my dishy delight. 'How long you been in New York, cookie?'

She seemed like she'd need an earhorn in a library. 'What?'

'Here. New York. How long been you?'

'Year,' she yelped. All tweeter and no woofer; painful to hear at top volume.

'Yeah,' I said. 'I'm an old hand in the batter, myself.'

'What?'

Our tête-á-tête continued in this merry manner until finally she smiled, I smiled, we signalled mutual toodle-loos and she let the crowd swallow her up. Best to put these kinds of moments out of their misery as soon as possible. Once she disappeared from view Trish punched me on the shoulder like a schoolyard bully.

'What'd I do?'

'You're so malevolent,' Trish said. 'Rolling over her like Ike over the Japs. Deliberate miscommuniqués. You know you can send any smoke signal you want if you want to.'

'I was coming in on the beam,' I said, perusing the room, hoping to spot Big Bertha and my little sweetie as they looked to sweep me off on some madcap, potentially life-threatening adventure. 'Now I know you didn't think we were perfect match. She still in junior high, by the way?' Trish frowned. 'Can take the girl out of the hay, can't take the hay out of the girl, notwithstanding her trendomatic threads. I'm sure she meant well, but –'

'Maybe she can't tell Blind Lemon from Blind Asparagus. I could?' She fired up one of her long and leans. 'Be nice if you could flap your tongue about something besides slipping discs.'

'I do, I do,' I pleaded. 'But what was the point here? None. So why waste –'

'Where's your mystery date been, anyway? Talk about dying calf eyes. I'm going to bring over the bucket and start calling you Bossy.'

'She said she'd be back. She's just –'

'Flaky,' she said. 'And you're not going to convince me she's not a Holiday Girl. Maybe she acey-deucy's if Wonder Woman's not looking but all the same –'

'You're just jealous,' I said, but I knew better than that. There wasn't a jealous bone in Trish's carcass; whole time we were together, until she decided it was time to snap the twig, she'd kept an open mind. Then suddenly the madness took hold, she started talking about putting up a wigwam and making a basket for the papoose, I started feeling the need to set back out for the high country and the next thing we knew we were both back on our own again. But jealousy had had nothing to do with it. Only money, and how much of it I had, or didn't have, and where I got it.

'Bordo, get over here,' she shouted across the room. Our mutual pal was already winging his way in our direction, tippytoeing over like he was sneaking up to the cookie jar. 'What's shaking?'

'Overseas assignment,' he said, 'Feeling 1A?'

'I'll enlist,' she said, hooking my arm and hauling. 'You too, Walt. This'll be just the ticket to bring you out of this.'

'Maybe better call it a day tonight.'

'You'll be sorry if you don't stop making with the sourpuss,' she said. I'll admit it, my brothers; I'm not much of one for physical threat. 'Join the glee club and let's go. You can't wait forever for Rapunzel to let down that hair.'

Knowing it was useless to fight I cried uncle, and fell in with the parade. We took the air and started off down the street. It figured the one time I'd finally meet somebody of interest she'd be harder to catch than I was. No matter how often I tried prying Eulie out of my head she was a hard tenant to evict.

'Walter,' Trish said, shaking my arm as we crossed Seventeenth, heading down Park. 'What's got you hypnotized?'

'Just distracted,' I said, watching steam rise out of the street

101

over by Union Square. The usual gaggles of junkies and hooligans were scuttling through the underbrush, waiting to snare stray passersby. Far too many lackies on white crosses and mean reds for me to deal with; I hadn't been in that park for maybe eight years. Rather deal with a D train full of Fordham Baldies. Steam oozed upward from the Belgian block, circled slowly and curled around, tried to gel and blew apart. For a second I'd thought my ghosts were on the prowl. 'Nothing more.'

'So where's the circus?' Trish asked Borden.

'Go east, young girl.'

'Not without a chauffeur,' Trish said, lifting her hand and giving the high sign. A yellow Checker shot across three lanes of honkers and screeched up to the curb. We hopped in, Trish and I taking the chaise lounge and Borden commandeering one of the jump seats, shouting directions at the hack all the while.

'Wake up, Snoozy,' Trish said, poking my side as we hit Fourteenth and cruised past Luchow's as we sped under the el. 'What kind of trip are you on tonight?'

'Nothing natural,' I said. 'Out of body experience, I guess. Don't clip the cord.'

Turned out the bash was down in the East Village on 12th between B and C. The sensible man steered clear of the neighbourhood even at high noon these days, but when in the company of the adventurous one tends to stop fighting the current and swim faster towards the waterfall. Two blocks from where we were heading was New York HQ for Hell's Angels; uptown Tong wars broke out weekly on 10th and 11th; the Third Balkan War was in its fifty-second year at the corner of A and 13th. Nothing that untoward, considering, but then the hippies showed up. Starting the summer before all the nitwits who couldn't figure out that San Francisco was at the far end of the country started pouring into town, flower girls and gurus and Sergeant Peppers, every one a fat little pigeon waiting to be plucked. Now ten months later the wreckage was all over town, plucking lutes in Herald Square, wandering back and forth in front of Saks hustling spare change, drawing the cops no matter how low they tried to lie. Bad scenes all the way around; last October, in the block we were shooting towards a Greenwich deb who'd dropped out of NYU got her 36–24–36 run through a meat grinder and fed to her boyfriend's Alsatian after she complained he spent more time over the meth boiler than with her. He called himself Otter; she called herself Trout's Dream. Let me tell you, my brothers, the world of altered consciousness used to attract a much more sophisticated element than had lately been moving in on the territory.

The party that night was in what New Yorkers call a back house. For you non-Gothamites let me elaborate. Back in Dead Rabbit days, long before the tenement laws, a landlord could build his sheds any way he wanted – walls a brick thick, two room apartments with no windows and one door, no plumbing or wiring or roof. But sometimes unexpected pangs of guilt caused them to provide light and air; when that happened they'd throw up the usual seven-storey walk-up at the front of the lot, but one shorter than usual; leaving a small paved courtyard and a small wooden two or three-storey house, behind. That was the back house. Even in the old days it took a special kind of individual to live in a back house. Trish and Borden and I fell out of the cab when we got there, found the street entrance to the alley – an archway cut through the building façade, next to a junk shop renting the storefront – crept through the dark until we reached the court and then made our way up the wooden stairs that led to the second floor door. Things were swinging by the time we got there, and pushing into the room was almost as challenging a job as squeezing into Max's.

No sooner did I begin to scope the action than my usual suspects started to find me. 'Walter,' somebody shouted.

When I gave the looksee I spotted Marv Ballard, Ogilvy scribbler by day, gutter lounger by night. 'How you doing?' he said; I heeded the gleam in his eye and counted five. 'You holding?' Goes without saying I was; that killer bud Chlojo left me rested in my inner jacket pocket. Weeks in the open air and the potency hadn't lessened a bit. Hard to say how much moolah the frugal man can share, keeping a permanent stash. When it came to sharing the wealth I've always been a Huey Long, mind you, but Marv couldn't stop asking for seconds until he reached nineteen.

'Fieldstripped, my man,' I lied. 'Lighter than air.'

'Bummer.'

His eyes lit on new arrivals, and he vamoosed. 'Bumbadiered,' I called out after but he was already hard at work. Before I could slip a hand into my pocket and hold that bud beneath my nose long enough to slip into overdrive I spotted Gaspard, inconveniently close. Turning quickly I managed to miss his eye. Even if he hadn't been such a blowhard we'd likely as not have called him Gassy, it just fit. He was the kind of art boy who never found the right gallery, and definitely not the kind of individual best fitted for the field of mind expansion. Couldn't drain a half cup of mocha java without spinning into a tizzy. Best tale I heard, he'd gone upstate to see a friend, ran into a powdered donut man coming back from Buffalo. Next thing you knew old Cokey Joe'd done half an ounce of snow and called the local constabulary, shouting *I know you're looking for me, coppers.* Coppers tried to tell him they weren't but he was so insistent they finally went to his hotel. Lucky for him, by the time they got there he'd done up the rest of the bag. No evidence of anything save for aggravated stupidity. They kept him around till his head reattached itself and then stuck him in the first Northern Line heading back to New York.

Borden wandered over, a panatella-sized spliff in his claw.

Smiled like the cat who'd swallowed a dozen canaries. 'Savouring the moment?' I asked.

He drew in enough to fell a mule; tried to speak, couldn't, and tottered away. Trish broke out of her huddle and slithered over in my direction.

'Having fun?' Across the room Auden sat in a chair, pulling that poet routine so as to better lure the chickadecs. Horror of horrors, I eyed some Fenster Moop in the corner whipping out his guitar and starting to plink out his version of 'Tom Doola'. Wasn't Grayson and Whitter's, I can tell you that much. Made me want to go over with scissors and cut the strings but he didn't take too deep a stab at it, some kind stranger was good enough to put on a mambo album. 'Glad now you took my advice and came out, aren't you?'

Before I could say anything I realized that some unexpected crashers had made it through the door. My evanescent wallflowers lurked near the kitchen, giving me the fisheye. Only other time I'd caught them outside my crib was that time I saw them in DC, in the Willard. I tapped Trish on the arm.

'Look in the corner. Over there. What do you see?'

She chinked her eyes as she focused on the mob. 'Long Island girls out of their league. Borden holding up a wall. Two bowls of potato chips –'

'That's it?'

'About covers the terrain,' she said. 'What's up? You look like you've seen –'

'All good fun must come to an end,' I said, suddenly wanting out. 'Must run.'

'Stick tight, it's early.'

'Maybe I'm coming down with something,' I said. Nerves, to be sure, but I didn't say it. 'I'll call you. Got to talk.'

'Heart to heart?'

I nodded.

'Fabulous. Whenever, wherever.'

She made with the double air peck and I started to push. After a few minutes of rush hour IRT I got through the door. Stepping into fresh courtyard air, I felt like I was popping out of a submarine into the ocean, except in this case the water was inside. Felt thirty degrees cooler once in the ozone so I zipped up my jacket. My shoes clicked on the bricks underfoot as I headed for the passageway to the street. Over the entrance was an idea-sized light bulb; at the far end of the tunnel, a streetlight. Then I thought I saw something move at the end of the tunnel as well; whatever it was slipped into the ink. I hung back, my brothers, listening for the sounds of lurkers in the dark; mugs and thugs loitering by the exit, picking off party guests one by one as they stumbled home. I gave the passageway another onceover. One second the streetlight was still there; then the eclipse started.

'Here chick-chick-chick.'

Young snarl, Polish or Irish or Italian, full of Catholic blood. I'm no gunslinger, brain takes brawn down two falls out of three and when it doesn't, that's where feet come in handy. Problem was, in this courtyard there was no place for feet to go. The guy started to come out of the passageway, pasty white, a head taller than me and a foot wider, Puerto Rican fence climbers on his feet and something long and metal in his right hand. Didn't think he was looking for the eighteenth hole.

'Hand it over, faggot,' he said. 'Whatever you got –'

If you'd been watching this on film you'd have figured some big wind came along, just then; his feet lifted a good six inches off the pavement and he disappeared head first into the passageway. I gave a look down the passageway, but saw no light; something big still blocked it. Noise I heard sounded like a dog cracking chicken bones.

'Chlojo?'

No answer, but I had a hunch. Those dames were first class when it came to going incognito. The streetlight appeared at the far end of the passageway and I started in. Listened to broken glass crunching underfoot but thank Valentine didn't step into anything slippery. I gave the sidewalk a one-two when I made it outside.

'Chlo? Eulie?'

A street or two away I heard a garbage truck crushing up the day's leavings. A beaten up Rambler rumbled down the street, some old codger behind the wheel. Under the streetlamp shine I saw a pair of mens' shoes in the gutter. The toes were as pointy as fence climbers get. Mysterious debris indeed so I sidled across the sidewalk to get a better view. The shoes seemed to be propped up over a sewer opening in the curb. When I stepped into the street, though, I saw that the shoes still had feet in them. The feet were still hooked onto the legs, but those disappeared some short distance into the opening. Couldn't say how much more of my unlucky assailant was still attached but I decided I could live without knowing.

So I walked briskly toward nominally safer Avenue A, at which point I headed north to Fourteenth. Didn't see my lady pals anywhere; although this kind of suggested to me that even though they weren't there, they were keeping an eye out. Can't say that made me feel more comfortable, though I wished it had. When I reached Fourteenth I went over to Second, and then up and finally back home. My ghosts must have caught a cab; they were waiting for me when I got there.

Time came soon after that when I realized I had to let Jim know I was already in on his game. Clearly this wasn't a subject he liked to brag about. Now as I said, in my field of interest there are a lot of handy techniques that work when it comes to scoring info. Ingratiation is the easiest, long as you've got any personality at all. A little cadging here, a little cajoling there, and soon enough they're eating out of the palm of your hand. (Something all ladies know from birth, but it amazes me how hard it is for gents to comprehend). Problem was, though, that ingratiation is a two-way street. During the weeks I'd spent hanging out with him I'd gotten to really like old Jim – for one thing, he was the only obsessive I ever met who knew more about those golden discs than I did. Martin was lying low, and that was just as well; but whatever it was I was doing, for whatever reason I was doing it, started to gnaw at me. So I figured it wouldn't hurt to be upfront with him, at least about my being more than a little aware of who those relatives of his actually were.

Next time I went to the record store, however – couple of days after that party – I didn't get a chance, at least right off. 'Look at this, Walter,' he said when I strolled in late one afternoon. He picked up a platter and a shammy to swaddle it in and cradled it in his hands like it was his firstborn. 'Ever seen one?'

Poor cynic me; before I scoped I figured it was something I had – I didn't make much of my holdings that often, bragmasters wear on everybody's nerves – but I was wrong. I nearly dropped on the spot. It was like seeing ghosts. A plain kraft paper sleeve insulated an Okeh labelled platter, serial number 847773. *Said Goodbye to My Baby* backed with *Black Harvest Blues*. 1944. Performer, T. E. Barnstable, lay preacher in the Reformed Christian Church of Jesus, onetime performer in crow's nests up and down the Pacific coast, onetime escort on the Underground Freeway; and most notable to the majority, perpetrator of the Crime of the Century. Everybody knew his name, nobody said it. When it came to his kind of action, Nat Turner and Caesar Blanchard were pikers, compared. I stared at the label as if I was staring into the sky and saw the Sons of Light descending, ready to rumble with the archons one last time. Now hear me, my brothers; you know well as I do that no group can be completely wiped out, no people absolutely erased. There's always traces left on the paper, a scent left in the air, the memory of a memory of a memory. Never mind the records; if that was the case, I wouldn't be here not letting loose on your ear. But when it comes to individuals, though, that's something else entirely. Judging from what was left of Theodore E. Barnstable, you'd have thought he lived a thousand years ago.

'Is it legal to own one?' I asked, unnaturally fretful.

'Maybe, maybe not,' he said. 'Can't say I'm overly concerned.'

'You've listened to it?'

'Not yet. Going to when I get home. Want to join me?'

It was closing time, and he slid the disc in a Halliburton case, the kind with the hard vanadium shell and padded inside; the kind of accoutrement only Kennedys can afford. After locking up we flagged down a cab at the corner of Columbus. As we hopped in it struck me that I had no idea where Jim lived.

'Dakota,' he told the hack. Only about eleven blocks from store to home – well, Jim was big, but he wasn't big on exercise.

'So where'd you get it?' I asked.

He smiled. 'Guy came in this morning, used book dealer I know. Usually picks for Pageant and Abbey down on Fourth Ave. Knows as much about records as we know about rocket science. He'd gone through the collection of a dead rabbi out in Flushing. Nothing but religious books and male pornography. The sacred and the profane.'

'Horse and carriage,' I offered.

'He lugged in a boxful. Didn't know how to pack 'em, so some of the ones on the bottom were broken. You know to expect that. Started going through the batch. Some nice cantorial stuff, a few Hungarian cymbalon pieces. Then some of the old Negro preachers. The usuals, McGee, Rice, Reverend Gates of course.'

'The guy was a rabbi and he had these?'

'Maybe trying to hedge his bets,' Jim said. 'Then I spotted this. Thought I'd have a stroke but I kept a straight face. Offered him a dollar per record. He said great, I gave him the money and he went out the door a happy man.'

'You're keeping it?' I asked, hoping he wouldn't but knowing he would. He was considerate enough not to rub it in by answering me.

'Wasn't even officially issued, you know. Month it was pressed he —'

'Yeah.'

'Somebody always walks away with a few under their coat, though.'

We pulled up on 72nd in front of Jim's building. I'd passed by this joint a million times, but like most New Yorkers had never gone inside. Upper West Side's full of those old Victorian monsters with dragons on the fence and demons over the door and old possessed women staring out the windows, cackling, but the Dakota was the biggest monster of all. 'Keep the change,' Jim said, handing the hack a bet to place, and we clambered out. The little brass house nodded as we walked into the dark courtyard. Jim lived in a corner apartment on the fifth floor. From the windows you could watch people getting mugged in the park. It was nominally three-bedroom, but all three were full of records and Jim slept – apparently – in a murphy he'd installed off the living room. As I looked around I started wondering how he could even have noticed his family, growing up. He had maybe twice as many records as I did, and he wasn't really much older than me. Most of his furniture looked like he'd bought it in a job lot at W.J. Sloan. Jim's professional unit was deeply impressive, though: a 1928 Victrola with a solid golden oak cabinet, lovingly polished, and a sterling silver crank. The interior of the box was plush red velvet. The doors of the bottom storage compartment were open, and I saw he'd installed a *very* good German tape-recorder. Probably a gift from Adolf to Old Joe.

'Want a drink?' he asked. 'Fruit juice? Soda?'

'Want to hear the song.' He smiled. He laid protection down on the turntable, and installed a new needle in the arm. 'You don't actually have to crank it, do you?'

He shook his head. 'It's electric. Great looking, though, isn't it? Which side you want?'

'Black Harvest Blues.'

'Me too.' Jim slotted the needle in the groove and adjusted the switch until the table started to spin. Barnstable's voice was strong, though he didn't always stay in tune, and the way he fingered his guitar made me think it was a cold day in the studio, and he had to wear gloves. Even so, he managed to get his message across. It was like hearing somebody singing on the moon.

> *Late one evening, baby come crying to me,*
> *Oh, late one evening, baby come crying to me.*
> *Time they say to take 'bo away*
> *Black harvest here at last Lord Lord*
> *Black harvest here at last.*

My brothers, I'd never before heard a song that didn't exist even as I listened to it. Barnstable was a *prophesier*, that's what my father called him; it was only a shame that he did what he did, the way he did it – one way or the other the writing was on the wall, but thanks to him the period was put on the end of the sentence sooner than it would have been. While I listened I almost got all weepy, once or twice; hard to admit but I'm not going to deny it. Didn't want to give my *own* game away, going overboard, but I had a hunch Jim wouldn't have cared, if he knew; and maybe he did know after all. He didn't look too happy himself, listening; and for a second I thought that maybe at least after the fact this was a way caucasoids could really dig precisely what it was they'd done – even though the way I saw it, they never would; what was in it for them? Neither of us said anything until the last chord decayed.

'Terrible sound, considering it's Okeh,' he said, lifting the arm and flipping over the disc. He switched off the tape recorder, removed the reel and marked the plastic with a series of laundry-marker hen scratches. 'Must have been a rush job. Ten to one this was the only take, though we'll never know for sure.'

'Probably hard song to sing more than once,' I said, standing up. He didn't get it; no surprise, really, but it couldn't help but work at me. Old Jimbo would check this off on his 1944 Godrich, slide it into the B shelf between Blue Lu Barker and Barrel House Annie and play it no more than once a year or so; probably less, considering that I seemed to be the only fellow obsessive he hung out with. A collector's item, no more; as truly meaningful to him as a Yoruba mask is to the Natural History Museum.

'Imagine so,' Jim said, but he couldn't imagine. Not that I could, to be fair. 'You doing OK with that drink?'

'Yeah.' Across the room, where the hall began, there were a number of framed black-and-whites on the wall. I strolled over and peeked: they were all there, every one. Mother Rose, Old Black Joe and the boys, boys together; boys separate. Joe and Jack in fine wool Brooks Brothers suits, Bobby in mountaineering togs high on Mount Roosevelt, young Father Ted looking like he hadn't realized how tight those clerical collars would be. And Jim himself, in skinnier days, all Kennedy teeth and Kennedy hair; and a look in his eye like he was sorry to have been blessed with either. He caught my eye when I turned back around.

'See 'em often?' I asked.

'We keep our distance,' he said. 'Kind of close in here,

don't you think? Let's go back out, if that's okay by you.'

'Fine,' I said, and we put on our coats.

'You ever get along with 'em?' I asked, once we were back up at Shaughnessy's, and ensconced in our usual booth.

He shook his head, and drank his third club soda. Going by his face, and the grey there, I suspected this was one of those evenings where, if alone, he started instinctively slowing down, passing every liquor store. 'Bobby calls me once in a while. We always got along. Not sure why, he's the toughest one in the bunch. He was the one convinced the others to give me another chance down here.'

I wondered what he possibly could have done that was so bad, within the context of his family. 'Good of him.'

'He's staying out of touch this year, though,' he said, smiling. 'Long as the race is on.'

'Probably what his henchmen tell him to do.'

'They don't tell him anything he hasn't told them first.'

Sometimes you look at somebody and you can almost see the clouds take shape overhead. Jim looked at that instant like the only one to have gotten out of the family alive, and at the same time looked like he wished he hadn't. 'What happened, anyway? What'd you do to them to give 'em such fits?'

Looking at the ceiling, he stuck out his hands palms up, as if expecting rain, or pleading his case. 'The curse of the Irish.'

I nodded. Say what you would about them but that was one grave the Kennedys always kept clean. 'How long you been off the sauce, anyway?'

'Two years. After the first anniversary they got me the store. Bobby said it was only right. I could live like I wanted down here, long as I was down here. That was the deal.'

'Good deal?'

'No room for argument.'

'So how do you manage?' I asked. 'You go to AA?'

He shook his head. 'Long as you know you have to stick with something, you do. Long as you got will power.' With a quick jerk he downed his fizzy like it was a triple highball. Good as any reason to explain the cat's stare he'd sometimes get, looking into the corner of an empty room as if spotting his own ghosts. Alkys who get with the programme say if you break the habit on your own you're not really sober, only dry, and they know their stuff. Soon as the shades come down, next thing you know you're looking at the bottom of a bottle of Old All Bets Are Off. 'Knowing about the family,' he said. 'That make any difference to you?'

'How so?' I asked.

'People have strong opinions about 'em,' he said. 'I always worry it carries over. I'm not like them, you know. I never fit in.' I nodded. 'Never liked football. Flunked out of Harvard, it wasn't what I wanted to do. Didn't make any difference downtown, of course.'

'What'd you want to do?'

'What I'm doing,' he said. 'What I'm doing now, anyway.'

However often I left my conscience somewhere behind me it always came crawling back, begging to be let in; and I'd always weaken, and throw open the door. No way I could see that Jim could be of any assistance to those DC clowns, no way I'd agree with at any rate. Started thinking I'd let things taper off; tell Martin that the truck wouldn't start. I was tired of playing their reindeer games, anyway.

'Lady, stop!' I heard somebody shout. Jim and I turned around to see what was up. The bartender, a white-haired potatohead from the old sod, looked as if he'd just been told his mother was a child molester. Some of the barflies appeared as bumfuzzled but I couldn't see what had them in such a tizzy. 'What the hell, lady, you can't come in here. Women aren't –'

'What's meant?' *Eulie.* She stepped between a couple of hulking louts as she sidled into the bar, brushing past elephants terrified by a mouse. Chlojo didn't appear to have made the scene, else I suspected the patrons wouldn't have been quite as vocal.

'Jim,' I said, standing up, 'you'll have to excuse me.'

'She belong to you?' he asked, smiling as he took in the melodrama.

'Vice versa. I –'

'Lady, what is it with you? Please, get out of here. Fucking Jaysus –'

'See you later, Walter.'

I shot over to where Eulie stood, slouching as if waiting for the crosstown bus. She had on a bus driver's jumpsuit, black instead of grey. It looked three sizes too small. Some of the sots were so dumbfounded that they were slumping against the bar, nearly in tears, but a few of the younger – as beefy in head as they were in body – clearly wanted to mix it up.

'Get your hoor outta here, you fuckin' idjit,' shouted a balding lout with broken teeth as he shoved me into the bar. The man in the apron leaned over and fixed a lobster claw on the back of my neck, squeezing hard as if he wanted to break it.

'Get her out of here,' he said. 'Bring her in again, you're eighty-sixed permanent.'

Eulie grabbed my arm and we stumbled to the door, trying to avoid the imbeciles who kept sticking out their feet to trip us. When we finally got outside we walked as fast as we could, south down Broadway until we were sure nobody was coming after us.

'Okay, we're safe now,' I said. 'Where've you been? I –'

'What problematicked back there, Walter?' she asked.

'Irish aren't big on women in bars. You didn't see the sign?'

'Sign?'

I sighed. 'Where's She-Beast?'

'Chlo, meant?' she said. 'Around, but not present. For security's sake.'

115

'Considering the last time –'

'Walter, updates essential. Tell.'

'With my ghosts, you mean?' Seizing her elbow, I made a quick turn east onto Seventy-eighth. 'Let's take the scenic route.'

'Contact continues?' she asked.

'We're not having heart to hearts. It's like I said, he knows my name. He says it, sometimes. I don't pay that much attention anymore. Where have you been, anyway?'

'Are they gaining mass?'

Once she got her teeth in she clamped down like a bulldog. 'What are you talking about?'

'Do they look any more solid?'

'Clear as a clean windshield,' I said. 'When'd you get back into town? If you'd called, I could have –'

'Today,' she said, looking at a Greek grocery at the corner of Amsterdam. Lambs and squirrels dangled pink and bloody in the window, a fan stirring them into life. 'Only today.'

'You sure about that?' Much as Muscles would have come in handy with the sons of Erin back at the bar, I still felt leery that she'd pop out of a manhole at any second and kill everybody in sight. 'I was at a party downtown the other night. Almost got mugged, but seemed like I had a guardian angel.'

'I've only been back today,' she said. 'Chlo stayed at my direction. To see that you were all right.'

'I can take care of myself,' I said, but didn't make much of an argument.

'When you see them, are they moving?' We continued along the street. Two long ammo belts of trash cans lined each curb. 'Have they appeared outside your apartment?'

'They were at that party,' I said. As soon as I spoke, Eulie went all pale – that's to say she turned light olive as opposed to her usual café au lait – and looked like she'd swallowed a bad oyster. 'What's the matter?' She shook her head.

116

'We anticipated other, even though our AV confirmations predicted.'

'AV?'

'Audio video,' she said. 'Radio. Television.'

'What's television?'

She didn't fill me in. In the streetlight shine Eulie looked fourteen, very young and very scared. Can't deny I've broken the Mann Act now and then in my life, but this was another kettle of fish indeed. Never been a candyman and didn't want to be mistaken for one. At least she didn't act like any teenager I'd ever come across. 'You were going to tell me something the last time you saw me,' I said. 'What?'

'It's difficult to detail,' she said. 'A tree, multibranched.'

'All right. Why don't you start by telling me who these ghosts used to be.'

'She was a Russian scientist. He was Dryco's security chief. Identifier, Jake.'

'What's Dryco?'

'My owner.'

'Nobody owns anybody,' I said, speaking – it seemed to me, when I listened – with my father's voice. Frightening; I'd never expected to hear him again. 'You don't mean literally.'

A pause, way past pregnant into nine-hour labour. She eyed me as if she couldn't fathom what I meant. 'It's a subunit of Dryco. I officiate.'

'Not the Society for Psychical Research?'

She shook her head. 'The Lucidity Institute.'

'Whatever,' I said. 'Look, is this ghost business some kind of a psyop? Am I the guinea pig?'

'Psycop?'

'*Op, op*. Psyop. I'm no chicken in the basket. I have ears. Stories fly in.'

'Walter, you're baffling,' she said. 'Clarify.'

'Baby, I may not look the part but I'm pretty tight with my

ninth circle connections. They don't know you from Lilith. Who are you with?'

'As stated,' she said. 'Dryco. I can't detail further, not presently.'

'Why not?' No response. 'Why is this Jake character hanging out? Why can't he go on to where he's supposed to go?'

'He wouldn't know how. He's been in his state for thirty years.'

'Why's he showing up now, then? In my apartment?'

'We have theories,' she said. 'But actualities, unknown.'

Seemed to me I may as well have been speaking in Choctaw for all the info I was getting out of her, and finally I gave up. Figured when she really had something to tell me, she'd tell me; and all I could think of now was how much I wanted to see what was under her jumpsuit. We reached Columbus Avenue and crossed against the orange. Within the park, beyond the trees, rose a dark black hulk. 'What's that?' she asked.

'Natural History Museum. Awful place.' A new idea popped into my head, and I figured it wouldn't hurt to try it on for size. 'Are you and Chlo poltergeist girls?'

She stopped dead in her tracks. 'Iterate?'

'All right, so maybe you're the guidance counsellor, but you can't tell me Chlojo's not experimental.'

'Chlo's perfected,' Eulie said. 'Poltergeist girls? Detail, please.'

'I've read some of the studies. Little missies who divert raging hormones into useful trades. Lock 'em in a room and they go to town. Think about people who did them dirty. How much they hate their mothers. Whatever, doesn't matter long if they get upset. Once they build up a good head of steam, they let 'er rip. Break all the glasses in restaurants. Tracks in a freight yard bend out of shape. Cows spontaneously combust.'

'Cows?'

'My main man told me they did a trial run at Khe Sahn last year. Every man on the battlefield cooked from the inside out. Experiment succeeded, soldiers failed. I have to keep up on these things if I'm going to do my job right. What's up with you two? Bringing the war home in a *different* way?'

We strolled into the park. Didn't think it'd be too hazardous this time of night, Central Park West was the place in this part of town that suffered the heavy action. 'What is your job, Walter, and how do you do it right?'

We stopped under a light while I tried to put it into words. 'Government work. I freelance. Go where the market takes me. Satisfy the needs of –'

'Yes?'

Came to me that I didn't think I was satisfying the right needs, just then. She looked at me, and I couldn't say another word. I've always heard that the first tongue you touch other than your own is the one you never forget. Back in Seattle, Karen and I were both fifteen, and it was outside the school before the ninth grade dance. I remember my surprise at how wet her mouth was, how sharp her teeth were. Didn't work out in the short or long run; wasn't but a week later or so she fell in love with a quadriplegic, ten years older. (He'd taken shrapnel in the spine while he was in the Jackson Brigade, fighting Nazis in France.) I got over it, but never forgot that kiss. But when I kissed Eulie I knew I'd remember that kiss even longer. She didn't try pulling away; she held me just as close as I held her, she up on her toes, me craning my head down. Each of us took a step back when we came up for air.

'Ah, gee,' I said. 'Eulie –'

She didn't look scared, not at all; but suddenly she turned and hopped over the broken benches to our left as if she was wearing springs on her feet. I saw her running deeper into the park, into the darkness where the streetlights didn't shine.

119

No telling what kind of characters were laying in wait down there. 'Hey,' I shouted, 'wait a sec. Eulie! *Eule!!*' I clambered over the bench, managing not to fall over it. I heard her feet crunching over the dead leaves somewhere between me and the museum. Just when I thought I was closing in somebody let off a flashbulb, or at least that's what I thought it was; but who was there taking pictures? One of Frye's photogs, no doubt. 'Gimme that film, you son of a –'

But nobody was there, after all; not a wandering shutterbug, not Chlojo, not Eulie. A cold wind blew through the park, rustling the trees; for a few minutes it sounded as if it were starting to rain, and then I felt small plops on my shoulders and head. I started walking back toward the light, wondering how she'd pulled a Judge Crater so completely, wondering who'd taken a photo, wishing I had an umbrella. It still seemed to be raining when I reached a streetlight. The sidewalk wasn't wet, but it was covered with what had been falling. Little green frogs, no bigger than a dime, hopped across the concrete, looking just like the ones that always fall in July thunderstorms. But it wasn't July.

SIX

'You're working up a sweat, Walter,' Bennett said. 'Taking too much of something?'

'Yeah. You.'

We hooked up in a gloomy knock'emback called the Expressway Bar, down at 40th and Eighth, just below the last Manhattan exit ramp before the Robert Moses Bridge. At my demand Martin arranged a meet and greet when he hit town the next Monday. As punishment, though, he showed up with his dopey sidekick; and while he'd left Hambone and Chuckles back in the swamp, Sartorius hitched a ride as well. I hadn't wanted to let those louts in on anything I had to say but there was no getting out of it, and it wasn't long before I understood why.

'What is it, Walter?' Martin asked. From the moment he parked himself he sounded peevier than usual; he hadn't given himself the usual close shave that morning, and a faint five'o'clock darkened his dome. Whole time he sat there he tapped out a semblance of a beat with his fingers against the top of the table – he'd lived too long in DC to have any sense of rhythm left.

'Before I go any further with this you've got to fill me in on what the long-term goal is.'

'With what?'

'With Jim Kennedy. What's the master plan?'

Sartorius sipped his coke and tried on a variant sneer. His expression made me wonder if he'd slipped a blood sample of mine under the microscope and didn't like what he saw crawling. Bennett looked unnervingly calm, as if he were already in on the joke. Martin was sweating, though it wasn't hot. 'Family reunion,' said the weasel. 'Leave it at that, Walter.'

'Why is this bothering you now?' Martin asked, his voice raw. Sounded like he'd been up three nights in a row preaching.

'Always bothered me,' I said. 'I'm just being more upfront about it.'

'Treat it like all your assignments,' he said. 'Drive in the nails and don't worry about what you're building.'

'My brothers, mayhap you don't get me. What I'm saying is, if you don't tell me what I'm doing, I'm not going to do it.'

Sartorius held his fork tightly, as if ready to spear out my eyes, but he didn't budge an inch. Bennett cracked his knuckles. 'What's the matter, Walter? Turn over a rock and find your conscience?'

'You can't quit, halfway through the assignment,' said Martin.

'Look, I was squeezed into this assignment, it didn't fit me –'

'You let yourself be squeezed.' He had nothing to add; I didn't like the way he wasn't looking at me when he spoke to me. That's never a good sign. I couldn't get why he acted like he was almost taking his cues from Benny. 'Walter, you didn't answer my question. Why is this starting to bother you now, when it's never bothered you in the past?'

'You know as well as I do this isn't the usual gig,' I said. 'Generally, I don't have to see who the joke gets played on.

Jim's family may be straight out of Charles Addams but he himself isn't hurting anybody –'

'Not presently,' Bennett said. 'Walter, time's come to move on to step two. This is where your previous experience'll come in handy. What you'll be doing –'

'You heard a word I said?'

'Every word. Doesn't matter. Walter, you'll –'

'No offence, Bennett, but how is it you're slinging the do this do that around? Far as I know you're just a tall root on the government tree.'

'Acorns, oaks.'

B-boy could toss off a real death's head when the joke was on somebody else. I looked over to Martin, and the second I did I could tell that at some point, for some reason, somebody heavier'd sat down on the teeter-totter since the last time we hooked up. 'Walter,' he said. 'At Hamilton's request, Bennett is now playing an active role in this operation.'

'An active role, or the active role?'

'You *can't* quit, Walter,' Bennett said. The Germ fell into line as he suddenly drew himself into the vertical. 'There's no need to add anything. Martin, your boy seems to find it hard to handle change. So you tell him about step two. See if he listens.'

'I haven't left the room, you know,' I pointed out. Bennett didn't say a word; the edges of his mouth – couldn't really call them lips – pulled up over his teeth, as if the skin on his face was starting to shrink. 'We'll be outside. I can't sit in this dive any longer.'

Sartorius gave us both the old so-there stare and trundled off after his American cohort. 'Only animals could,' he muttered, sending his remark in Bennett's direction but making sure it richocheted off our heads first. The two of them strolled casually out the heavy wood door, almost arm-in-arm. Through the filthy window I saw that they stationed themselves on the 40th Street curb outside, looking up at the expressway as it began its leap across the Hudson as if seeing someone getting ready to jump

'Fill me in fast,' I said to Martin, not raising my voice, but not whispering either. Before I could say anything else he put a finger to his lips and reached under the table; peeled away what looked at first like an extra-lumpy piece of chewing gum. Before I could wonder what he wanted with such a disgusting souvenir he pointed to the two small silver wires sticking out of the purple clot. Placing the bottom of his glass on top of it, he pressed down until it chirped a cockroach crunch.

'This is your own damn fault,' he said, sounding about as angry as I figured I sounded. 'Your ultimatum was all the excuse Hamilton needed.'

I snuck a peek out the window. Sartorius tapped his ear with his hand like he wanted to get the water out of his brain. 'Who are you working for now, Martin? Who've *I* been working for? Interior Department or Hamilton? Or the kraut, for that matter –?'

'Be quiet,' he said, looking like he'd stayed so long at the blood bank that now he was running on empty. 'Walter, nothing about this operation is clear-cut. It's not officially a government action –'

'Nothing I ever do is,'

'But with Hamilton involved, it has an ex-officio primatur,' Martin said, and rubbed a hand along his head. Frick and Frack, outside, probably were starting to wonder why they weren't tuning in to the afternoon broadcast, but didn't give any indication they were going to head back inside. Sartorius was pointing up at the expressway and frowning, as if he'd spotted patches of Jewish concrete. 'I don't always see what's being built myself, Walter. Like you, I just drive in the nails I'm given –'

'I'm thinking this time we're driving them into our coffins,' I said. 'How'd that little punk Benbo get promoted so fast?'

'Within the bureaucratic structure he's still my associate,'

Martin said. 'But he's been all peaches and cream with Hamilton ever since they met.'

'What a sob sister.'

'And what happened, he was in my office when you called. Overheard my first reaction.' Which had been explosive, granted. 'He ran off and got ahold of Hamilton while we were still on the line. Half hour after you hung up Hamilton called. Gave me a real line. Said that considering the fruitful working relationship you and I had had for so many years that as the operation moved into step two it'd be preferable to have a more disinterested hand on the wheel, as he put it.'

'Bennett'll steer me off the first bridge we come to.'

'I know, you know, for all I know Hamilton knows. Doesn't matter.' He leaned closer towards me, and in his deep brown eyes I saw all the way down to the pit of his heart. 'Walter, I'm begging you. Don't run out now. I think Bennett's got ahold of something.'

'There's nothing on me,' I said. 'I've seen to that.'

He shook his head. 'My grandmother was octoroon.' I nodded; mine was quad, but they'd been mixing it up in my line all the way back to Charleston, which had blessed me with my pale, pale face. 'She was born in Jamaica. The British were bad as the Germans, they kept everything. Her records are still down there, Walter,' he said. 'Or were, until Che and his boys rolled into Montego Bay.' Martin moaned; he sounded like a ghost, although not the ones I knew. 'You know Commies, they'd've sold Lenin to the Nazis if there'd been a way to make a profit by it. Ten to one the Germans have already dug in to see what they could turn up, just to have on hand when times get tough.'

That was the problem with the silent treatment; it only worked if everybody kept silent. The biggest, darkest Masai warrior could have been under-Secretary of State as long as he didn't make noise about it and as long as his usefulness was such that the ones he worked with, and for, refrained

125

from pointing it out. But let the first shoe drop, the first hint turn up somewhere down the line, and as soon as some kind of proof on paper could be run down, that'd be that. If you were passing and got caught, you were dead gone, even if the offending ancestor had been a seventh cousin twice removed. If you were over thirty, and got officially nabbed (which was the only way to be found out, Sophia help you if some local nitwit got it into his head to set the dogs loose), you'd be sent off to sunny Guatemala, or Costa Rica, or one of those welcoming Central American countries; but during the past couple of years, if you were under thirty and the cat got out of the bag, well, you'd be sent South, all right – down on the delta, that is to say the Mekong delta.

That year, I was twenty-nine. Not a good age, considering.

'Why hasn't he sent word to Hoover yet, then?'

'Hamilton wants the job to be done,' Martin said. 'Chances are good Hoover wants the job to be done. If it is done, then chances are good Bennett'll get bumped upstairs and you and I, and everybody *we* know, will go on their merry way. Otherwise –'

'So what's planned for Jim? You know, don't you?'

He looked out the window. The louts still cooled their heels. Sartorius was sucking on a candy bar. 'There is a pharmaceutical aspect to this, Walter.'

'Figured as much,' I said. 'What? They want me to dose the family, drop a little something off Hyannis?'

'You know much about hypnosis?'

'Doesn't work on me. That's about it.'

'Years ago, they found out that if it did work on you, and if you were hypnotized, you could be told to do something, no matter how ridiculous or dangerous, and ninety-nine times out of a hundred you'd do it. But if on the hundredth time you were told to do something you wouldn't ordinarily do – hit somebody, steal something – you wouldn't do it, not under any circumstances.'

126

'Kill somebody,' I said. I was always good at math.

'There's been further development lately completed on a readaptive agent,' he said. 'You've never tested it. As near as can be told, from what I've heard, it works perfectly every time. Hypnosis in a bottle, essentially. And guaranteed to work on anyone.'

Martin chewed his nails like he needed the calcium. 'So I'm supposed to give some to Jim?'

He nodded. 'And give him directions. Help him along, I suspect, though I don't know for sure.'

'Help him do what?'

'You aren't supposed to know this yet,' he said, and this time he did start to whisper. He gave the glass-smashed bugged gum another crunch, for good measure. 'Remember your worrying you were going to be made the Oswald in this?' I nodded. 'You won't be.'

'Jim?' He nodded. 'They want him to kill who? Humphrey? Paxton? Mc –'

'Bobby.'

I looked out the window; Bennett was checking his watch, and I had a notion he'd be traipsing back in here shortly to drag Martin along. Sartorius had turned his back to the street, and was staring at the windows of the bar. 'Who's back of this?' I asked. 'Who the hell is Hamilton working for?'

Again, a whisper, this time directly into my ear. 'The Kennedys.'

That send more shivers down my spine than since I'd first laid eyes on my ghosts. Even for that bunch, this seemed pretty cold-blooded. This was something I didn't think was safe to even dream about, much less talk over, whether whispering or screaming. I was almost scared to move my head, and look anywhere else, thinking for at least a moment or two that surely, at the mention of their names in this unfavourable context, Joe Jr and Jack and Father Ted were all going to suddenly burst through the door, give us a sendoff with tommy guns until we were nothing but Swiss cheese, and then pile back into their black sedan and screech off back to the hideout at Hyannis, whooping. 'Which ones?'

'Well,' said Martin. 'Not Jim. Not Bobby –' He shrugged.

That night I didn't sleep more than a few hours. In between bouts of nightmares I'd sit on the edge of the bed, try not to pay any attention to my ghosts as they hung out in the front room, calling out my name every once in a while just to shake me up. Time to change partners, I knew, but how to do it? Until the year before it'd have been a simple enough matter to hop on the train to Montreal and scoot up to the border, get off at the last town on the New York side, pay off a fisherman to take you across the river and then lose yourself in the midst of our neighbour to the North. Unfortunately, so many had been taking that route since the war escalated that the borders were clamped down tight. Mexico? Back in the fifties, maybe, but they were too keen on making sure nobody used the drugs they produced in-country, and that would have made for rough going while I tried to get back on my feet. Back to Seattle? Nothing for me there, not any more. Mom and Dad both gone and the place had changed too much since they'd built the nuclear plant on Vachon. Europe? The Commie cheese shop was as close as I wanted to get to our Soviet neighbours, and where the Reds didn't control the turf the Nazis still did.

Africa? Took a different kind of passing, to get by there. But if I could get to Hawaii, there were boats that went around the Pacific; and outside of Vietnam, the state of flux the other former Japanese territories were in was somewhat more hospitable to strangers – the Phillipines, perhaps, or Fiji; or Nauru. Move somewhere and become the Guano King. The more I thought about it, the more possible it seemed –

But as ever the old problem of funding came immediately to mind. At the moment I had about a thousand bucks;

128

that'd buy the ticket, but I needed more. I got up around five; walked into the music room. Looked around at my shelves, at the collection. Jim'd buy it, that was for certain; but that'd also be a certain giveaway that I was planning to skip; and even if I left them for a while, I couldn't imagine losing them forever. There was only one of me, sure; but with half my records, there was only one of them, as well, and I was too used to serving as cultural custodian, keeping them all safe and sound until the day when they might be appreciated – more to the point, when the people who made them would be appreciated, finally, for what they did and for who they were.

Granted, in this country I figured that'd be a pretty long wait.

I sat in my chair until close to nine the next morning, my ghosts keeping me company in both of my front rooms, in form both evanescent, and flat, black, and shiny. A little after nine, Trish called.

We met at noon at the fountain in the middle of Roosevelt Centre at Broadway and 66th. 'Let's chat and sip,' I said, taking her arm and leading her toward the café in Alma Mahler Hall.

'You're such a charmer,' Trish said. 'You look awful. What were you up to last night? Your tag team show up and start tossing you around the ring?'

'Couldn't sleep,' I said. 'Money worries.'

She laughed. 'Let me take those off your mind.'

Once inside, in the café area, we ordered up the old mocha java. I needed a triple dose bad; as soon as the first cup was drained I signalled the waiter for seconds and thirds. At that time of day we were surrounded by music matrons decked out in heavy matinee frou-frou, tapping their biscuits with white gloves to shake the crumbs loose before downing them. Every so often I caught some of the grouchier ones eyeballing me like they suspected me of sneaking around, waiting for the right moment to make off with the Stradivari.

'I never thought you'd agree,' she said. 'When Burt called, I told him I'd give it a try but –'

'You say they'll slip me the cabbage on the premises?'

She nodded, brushing away her own crumbs. 'Ten thousand. You can get them that much?'

'What I have on hand's a little stronger than mescaline,' I said. 'But they'll be able to make it stretch. What is this thing tonight, anyway?'

'They have these public get-togethers once in a while. Invite people in to get a taste of the treatment. They won't be giving them any of what you'll be bringing along, of course.'

'Could be hazardous if they did,' I said, thinking of the one meeting of theirs I'd glimpsed. 'They'll need to dilute it. I can provide full details once I make the trade. Will I give it to him? He didn't look like he could keep two things on his mind at once without practice –'

'Don't be cruel,' she said. 'Poor Burt, he's deeply into this. I haven't seen him for a month. I think the only reason he called me was because he remembered you. After you met I filled him in on your hobbies, since I remembered how useful you'd been to the Dynamos in the past –'

'Muchas thankas,' I said. 'This is a real life preserver, it really is.'

'You that much behind?'

I shook my head. 'Trish, listen. I may be going away for a while. Things have come up.'

'What things?'

'Things that make me think I'd better go away for a while.'

'Business or pleasure?' she asked, smiling.

'Nothing fun about it,' I said. 'Not till I get there, at least. I'll let you know, roundabout, once I'm settled.'

'Settled? Are you moving? Walter, is something wrong?'

'No, no,' I said, knowing she knew I was lying; that made it easier. 'Don't worry about it.'

'Walter —'

'Valentine,' I said, caught by surprise. Jim had just walked through the door of the hall, and was shuffling slowly toward the ticket booth. He'd shaved, wore one of those blue blazers with the pocket crest, and had pressed and spitshined to within an inch of his life. If it hadn't been for the hair, and the walk, I didn't think I'd have ever recognized him. He picked up some tickets, it looked like; as he turned, I waved my arm, and caught his attention. He started toward us. Trish turned to look; didn't seem attracted or disgusted when she circled back my way.

'Who's that?'

'Friend of mine,' I said. 'Surprised that he's out in public. Usually, he stays in his store —'

'Store?' she repeated.

'He's a record guy.'

Her face fell like a rock. 'Really?' she asked. 'He's got the build. Looks like he bathes occasionally, at least.'

'He's very well groomed, considering.'

'He looks familiar, somehow,' she said. 'What's his name?'

'Jim —' I said, but stopped myself before I provided ID. As he made his way between the tables he stuck out his hand before he reached us. For a second I pictured him standing outside a factory gate in New Hampshire, trying to get any one to stop and take a button.

'What are you doing here?'

'My brother got me some tickets,' he said. 'Ring cycle starting in May. I was picking them up.'

'What's with the old school drag?' I asked. 'Don't you have any of those pants with the little whales on them? I thought those were required with these jackets.'

He made a face. 'Don't wear 'em. You dress right when you come to places like this.' Both he and Trish looked over my

131

standard wear, black pants, white shirt, black leather jacket. 'Well. Some of us do, anyway.'

'Jim, Trish.' I said, laughing. 'Trish –'

'A pleasure,' he said, grabbing her hand, shaking it up and down as if trying to pump the well dry. She made an expression that reminded me of a smile.

'Have a seat.'

'Thanks,' he said, and as he plumped himself down in an unoccupied chair he managed to bump against the table, which bumped against my knee, which caused me to spill half my third cup of percolations into my lap. Luckily, it had cooled off and I suffered no traumatic burns to delicate areas. 'Walter, I'm sorry –'

'No trouble,' I said, standing, shaking off excess drainage. The waiters looked at me but didn't seem anxious to assist. The biddies made with the glares and I sat down again. Walter seemed to be working himself up to saying something else, but before he had a chance he managed to shift his elbow onto his coffee spoon, flipping it into the air. It sounded like a whole drawer of cutlery hit the floor when it landed, the joint was so damn hush-hush. Good thing he didn't go out much; seemed like he could do more damage than a Gatling gun without even trying.

'Walter says you're deep into the record game,' Trish said. 'Bad as he is?'

'Worse, I think.'

Her eyes shone like an anaconda's, spotting a warthog. Something about him appealed to her baser instincts, I could tell – she'd never minded looks as long as the attitude was there, and Trish had the perceptions of a shrink when it came to sizing people up. Valentine knew what she was making of Jim, but she seemed to like it.

'Hey, Walter,' he said, grinning; at the sight of those teeth, little wheels seemed to click in Trish's head. 'You having a party or what?'

'What're you talking about?'

'Over there. Going to introduce me this time or just mix it up?'

Still damp in the lap, I turned around and I saw Eulie and Chlojo, strolling across the big room, looking like they were trying to figure out how to reach the loge. My sweet petite wore a sleeveless black dress that stopped at an agreeable distance above her knees, and shiny leather boots. Chlo, ever stylish, wore a black jumpsuit, baggy as a bus driver's; except bus drivers tend not to favour fabric that resembles rubber when you face left and snakeskin when you face right. Her own boots and gloves – also black – were comparatively understated, except they would have been big on Jersey Joe Walcott. The waiters didn't look like they wanted any part of these customers, and vanished behind the bar.

'Well, well,' said Trish. 'Gang's all here.'

When I stood and hugged Eulie she hugged me back, as usual seeming strangely inexperienced with where the various hands should go. Chlo flashed us her standard warm stare but, thankfully, kept her lip buttoned. 'Where've you been?' I asked as Eulie worked herself free of me. Didn't seem like the time to force an answer, so I fell back on sociability. 'These are friends of mine. Jim, Trish, meet Eulie.' They nodded, but neither one was looking at the smaller of the pair. 'Ah, yes, and this is her friend –'

'Chlojo,' she said, giving her high-pitched growl.

'A pleasure,' Trish said, examining their threads, sizing and resizing. 'I've heard tell.'

'About?' Eulie asked.

'You know.' My evil one grinned to beat the band, sloughing off the nasty looks I shot her way. 'Did you give Walter a two-for-one deal?'

The noise I heard myself making bore no relation to a laugh. 'We require him,' Eulie said. 'Agreeable?'

'Of course. I can't keep my paws off him, myself,' Trish

133

said, getting up, sliding the straps of her Hermes bag over her arm. 'Jim, tell you what. We don't want to be fourth wheels here. Walter can certainly handle himself, not that it'll be necessary. You got time to grab a bite?'

'Sure,' Jim said, eager as a puppy.

'I adore the Ring,' she said. 'Who's conducting?'

'If you insist,' I said. 'So Burp'll be expecting me?'

'Burt,' Trish said. 'Don't do anything I wouldn't do.'

'Likewise,' I said, shaking hands with Jim, giving Trish double pecks. Although I'd have liked them to take Chlo along, I didn't think Eulie would have been in favour of it. The second my pals were out of earshot I tried to take Eulie's hand, but she worked out of my clutch. No matter; I was used to her playing impossible-to-get.

'Where'd you run off to, last time?' I asked. 'Why didn't you come back before now?'

'Departure essentials, Walter,' Eulie said, taking my arm and starting to lead me out of the café. Chlo was giving the remaining matinee ladies a stare that I'd have found awfully disconcerting, but they were a hardy bunch and stared right back. 'Please.'

'Wait a second. Whose departure where?'

'Officeways,' she said. 'Our office. It essentials.'

'For how long?' Eulie smiled, but didn't tell. 'I've got something to do tonight. I can take off once I'm finished.'

'Finished when?'

'I got to go to the Astor Hotel. Meet up with some people and drop something off for 'em. Get there at seven, I'll wrap it up by eight. Boom, bang, cat, bag, bag, river. Then I'm free and clear.'

'AO,' she said. 'We'll accompany.'

Wherever the gals planned to take me, it wouldn't be as good as Hawaii; but I would get there sooner. All the same, I wasn't going to pass up ten thousand big ones; that'd be the best deal I ever swung. Briefly, I considered the millions of ways things could go wrong that evening, if I decided to swing this gig drag rather than stag. Considered that this meeting of the Personality Dynamos, unlike the one I'd glimpsed before, would be going on in a public venue and not back at their den of iniquity – what could possibly happen? Considered that if I let Eulie take off without me now I might never see her again; that made up my mind for me. 'All right, but it could be tricky. These people I'll see tonight are –' I stopped to consider the best way to phrase it. 'Funny.'

Chlo didn't smile. 'Comedy funny?'

'Psycho funny. You can come with me, but don't do anything that'll attract attention.' Chlo cracked her knuckles, and the sound was like a floor caving in. When shifted from boot to boot her suit changed from rubber to snakeskin to rubber again. 'You didn't happen to bring any evening wear, did you?'

'What evening?'

'Okay,' I said, 'follow me.'

We weren't the high point of the day for the ladies at the Big Gals Shop on West 72nd '"*No Miss too hard to fit*,"' I said, pointing out the slogan they had plastered all over the window. 'Where's truth in advertising?'

'Sir, I'm terribly sorry,' the assistant manager said, avoiding Chlo's glare. I got the idea she was having flashbacks of a real bulldozer of a gym teacher. 'I don't see how we can possibly –'

Then the owner came back from lunch. 'Can't possibly what?' she asked, stepping back onto the floor of the shop, wiping her lips with a napkin. She had on harlequin glasses and red ensemble coordinated down to her toenails. 'What's the problem?' Chlo stepped into her field of vision. 'What've we got here?'

The sales girl tried to explain, but didn't get far. 'They're looking for an outfit for the, uh –.' She gestured toward Chlo

135

but still didn't look at her. '– their friend. I've told them we simply can't help them, we don't have anything –'

'Nonsense,' said the owner, not missing a beat. 'You are a big one, sweetie. What size are you? That'll save us time.'

'One hundred thirty-seven,' said Chlo, after giving it some thought.

'Oh, we don't use European sizes in this country, dear.'

'She's from New Jersey,' I interrupted. 'Needs something for an evening event. Nothing fancy, just nice. Within reason. Better than nice. Know what I mean?'

Even if she didn't, she'd have never let on. 'Oh, sure,' she said, taking out a tape measure and wrapping around Chlo's various attributes. 'Usual trouble areas don't really present a problem,' she said. 'Problem's not height but your width, dear. Your shoulders and arms are somewhat oversized –' The sales girl made a barely noticeable expression, and sent up some kind of enigmatic retail smoke signal. 'May I speak frankly for a moment?'

'Shoot,' I said.

'The lady is a lady, isn't she?'

I wasn't sure what to tell her, and looked to my lovely little one. 'Chlo,' Eulie said. 'Denude.' With a long single zip, Chlo opened her jumpsuit and stepped out, sliding it over her gloves and boots. Since she wasn't wearing underpants, and favoured a close shave down in Happyland, it was obvious right away which side of the fence she'd landed on. Her basic structure was hourglass, kind of, though it turned out her spectacular fore and aft were to some degree artificially enhanced by her outerwear. No matter; what got me was that from the scars on her neck, between the metal bra holding her casabas, all the way down to the honey pot, there was what looked like a flesh-coloured plate. It would have looked like the bottom of a turtle shell if a turtle shell was made of telephone plastic. Her skin was puckered along its edges like it had been glued on. Sticking out of her bra were two metal nozzles right where the nipples were – I guessed – and then I remembered those little bumbershoots she'd used on Romeo, first night I saw her. Her legs and arms looked like they'd had some work done as well, but there they'd used chrome steel to fill her out. She wouldn't rust, at least.

'Judas Fucking Iscariot.' The owner probably meant to whisper, but didn't quite pull it off. 'What happened to you, honey?'

Our naked glamazon just blinked.

'Car wreck,' I said. 'Touch and go for awhile. Complete success, under the circumstances. Modern medicine's a miracle, isn't it?'

'Dear, let's get you covered,' said the owner, suddenly conscious of the scene any new customer would encounter, walking in; she helped Chlo pull her suit back up.

'So what's the verdict?' I asked.

'Frances,' she said to the sales girl, who was standing behind the counter. If there was a bat back there I'm sure she was ready and willing to grab it. 'That shipment from Hawaii. The island wear for summer. I think we can work something out.'

'This essentials?' Chlo peeped, growling at me.

'We're still observed,' Eulie said.

'Not as much,' I said. 'Trust me, it's better than it was.'

The owner had taken two muumuus, as she called them – one with pink and green flowers, the other with green and blue – and in no time at all her gals in the back managed to put the two together, kind of. Colours clashed a little but I've seen worse off the rack, especially on hayseeds. Her new frock hung down to her boots – you could still see their sharp metal pointy toes, but only if you looked for them – and they'd wrapped a long blue scarf around her neck. She insisted on wearing her jumpsuit underneath, but it only showed on the arms. We were still getting rubberneckers, true, but not as

137

many as before. I still wasn't sure how she'd go over that night, and figured when the time came with luck she'd be willing to dawdle in the lobby.

'Believe me, you're dressed to kill,' I said.

'Always,' Chlo said.

'Weren't we there?' Eulie asked, pointing across Columbus toward the Natural History Museum.

'Yeah, in the park,' I said, remembering that night, that kiss, those frogs. 'You never have said where you went. I looked all over –'

'That museum. I minored zoology,' she said. 'It's seeable?'

Not my favourite place in town; not by a long shot. 'You'd like to see it?' She smiled, and any resistance I might have offered melted away like dew. 'Just behave yourself.'

Zipping across Columbus we wandered over to the 77th Street entrance, underneath the big arch. The old ladies manning the counters looked about as upset as the matinee crowd back at Roosevelt Centre but they were probably more used to seeing visitors from faraway climes. I led the gals upstairs, through the long marble corridors, past the glass ferns and the stuffed parrots and the big painting of old Teddy. Didn't strike me as odd that a Jersey girl, even one with a fondness for animals, wouldn't have gotten to the museum before this. A tourist trap, on the one hand, and on the other something to keep eugenicists happy. Eulie looked pleased, though; and Chlo seemed to have calmed down enough that I wasn't as worried she'd suddenly start pulling those construction worker tricks.

When we reached Akeley Hall, where they keep the gorillas and the rhinos and the herd of elephants in the middle of the room, that was when I really started to wonder about them both. As soon as we went in they stopped dead in their tracks; they looked at the lit cases with three-year-old's eyes. Eulie looked especially upset, considering she'd wanted to go the zookeeper route. True enough, though, I never found Jersey

138

girls, even down in Devil territory, in the Pine Barrens, to be any more adept than New Yorkers at dealing with animals more exotic than Airedales. I stood there with them for maybe five or ten minutes before I realized that both Eulie and Chlo were letting loose with the waterworks. I'm no stone heart but like many gentlemen of my acquaintance, I never know what to do when a woman breaks down with a bad case of the boohoos. 'There's more to see,' I mumbled. 'Come on.'

'They're alive now?' Eulie said as we stumbled back into the brighter light in the hall, hooking her arm into mine. I tucked her in close to me as it sunk in to my thick head just how much the place seemed to be upsetting her.

'They had their day in court,' I said. 'Look real, though, don't they –?'

'*Nya*,' she said, dabbing her eyes with my sleeve. 'In habitat, meant.'

'Honey, I don't get you. What's wrong?' I glanced at Chlo, but she looked as sad; perhaps not as willing to seek comfort.

'Extinct,' she said. 'They're not extinct?'

'Course not, not on this floor,' I said. 'You want extinct, we got to go up to the fourth floor and see the bones.'

The two of them sat down on a marble bench, looking like they'd just come out of a four-hankie matinee. Eulie's makeup ran, turning her eyes all raccoony. Nothing I said seemed to bring them out of it. 'What's the matter with you two?'

'We've only seen visuals,' she said.

'I don't get you two,' I said. 'Half the time you act like you're in charge of the show, and half the time you act like you'd spend your life savings buying magic beans.'

They started drying up.

'Cognitive dissonance,' I said, remembering the phrase. 'Why don't we go?' I asked. 'I never thought this was a good place, myself. Come on, this way.'

We stood up, and I led them down the hall, thinking I knew

139

a quicker route to the exit from where we were. I waited to see if they were going to say anything, but they were trying to pull the old speak-no-evil again. It wasn't long before I realized that we'd wandered right into the Hall of Man. I hadn't been in the museum since I first hit town; once was enough. 'Not this way,' I said. 'Over here, I think –'

But Chlo had already spotted what I'd tried to avoid seeing, and strode across the floor, almost knocking over an elderly couple passing away their remaining time. 'Eulie,' she said, whispering – of course, she could have whispered in the basement and you'd hear her in the attic. Eulie sidled over to where her big pal stood, blocking the view. I heard her say one word.

'*Godness.*'

They gave the exhibit the old looksee over and over again, like they hoped to get some kind of reaction out of those black glass eyes. They looked at it probably the way I looked at it, the time I'd seen him before. I'd read about the exhibit back in Seattle, and found it as hard to believe as it was easy to believe – cognitive dissonance popped up all over the place, once you started thinking about it. They'd set him up just off Akeley Hall when he was first installed, I gathered; I suspected they wanted him there so the curious could conveniently size him up, *vis-à-vis* the gorillas. Then foreign tourists – the ones that mattered, Canadians and Argentinians and Australians – raised enough of a ruckus that they moved him here, where at least he nominally fit in within an anthropological framework.

'Sambo?' Eulie said, giving me bugeyes.

'Nickname,' I said, reading the label on the mahogany part of the case. 'First one of his kind ever brought over.' I reconsidered. 'Of his tribe.'

'Masai,' she said. I couldn't remember what his real name had been; remembered it sounded just as made up. He was as tall as Chlojo, but only half as wide – all muscle, posed on one foot, a long spear cradled in one arm. His skin was as dark as an oxblood loafer, I suspected they waxed him periodically, to keep him fresh. 'He's Masai.'

'May as well be Cherokee.'

'Brought here in 1917?'

'And sent to the Bronx Zoo,' I said. 'Didn't stay too long, though. Died in the pandemic.' I tried to remember the name of the disease no one caught anymore, the one that took all four of my grandparents. 'Brainbuster.' Eulie and Chlo looked at one another and nodded, and kept staring in the case, at the man who wasn't man, not officially, not here. You'd have thought their moms would have warned them about things like this, but maybe they never had the chance. Or maybe they were Canadians after all, and sheltered from the more mindboggling acts of their neighbours to the South.

'Zoo?' Chlo asked.

'Genetic upkeepery,' said Eulie. 'None protested?'

'Only ones'd protest would have too much reason to complain,' I said. 'Maybe it's not that bad a thing. Long time from now, I don't know where I'll be, but chances are good he'll still be around.'

I turned down the volume; we seemed to be alone in the room, but you can never be too careful when it comes to acoustic tricks in these old Victorian barns. 'Even so, speaking personally, I can't hang out in this joint without thinking I might wind up in one of these boxes myself.' I started to think that if I stuck around much longer, I'd start making with the boohoos myself. 'Come on, ladies. I need to pick up something at my place before we make the scene tonight.'

141

SEVEN

The *something* that needed picking up before we hit the Astor was a standard-issue test tube containing 30 parts distilled water to one part phenylethylamine isoergine-144, an especially delirious new compound tagged by the Interior Department's pocket protectors as Pi-R2. Now it strikes me as probable that some of you have passed what idle newspapermen call the acid test. Six months earlier, while the finishing touches were still being put on, I gave Pi a try. Let me tell you, my brothers, the difference between the trip LSD-25 gives you and the one you get from Pi is like the difference between your old granny pinching your cheek and the Homicide boys hauling you into the back room and making you believe you took a razor to Shirley Temple. And like that perm-a-muggles Chlojo gave me, you only had to let your finger do the walking through the stuff to get the right size hit, that is, one which dropkicked you right there into a twenty-eight-hour ride on the Cyclone, *nineteen* hours of which consisted of the old peakeroo.

The wise man knows that that way lies dementia praecox. Once I splashed down, and spent a week recovering, I presented my report, suggesting that it might not be a bad idea if they just stuck Pi in the storage room, back there with the smallpox and anthrax, but I don't have to tell you that in the land of the blind the one-eyed man is ignored.

Considering that to the best of my knowledge the Personality Dynamos weren't familiar with anything stronger than strawberry mesc, dosing the punchbowl with Pi would make sure that if the hapless Dynos had personalities of even an animal sort prior to sipping, they would be *tabula rasae* afterward. But a further mixing would bring the trip down to a bearable state; I simply wasn't sure how much mixing would be necessary.

We made the Astor at six forty-five. I'd changed into my dullest suit, a slate-blue single-b model that made me look like an accountant who could be persuaded to forget how to add. In her little black mini Eulie blended in beautifully. Chlojo, however, still presented problems no matter how good the camouflage. Her muumuu was colourful enough as street wear, but in close quarters it made her look like a one-woman parade float. Every time she took a step those silver-spiked boot toes of hers poked out from beneath the hem, and even though Eulie convinced her to finally ditch the gas station gloves it didn't really help, considering that she could have palmed a honeydew one-handed.

The pre-theatre crowds scattered before us like minnows before sharks. Sad to say I began to realize as we left the subway that if the salesladies had had problems believing Chlo to be of the weaker sex, the hotel dicks were sure to size her up as a drag queen the moment we hit the revolving door. Bust the three of us for loitering before we had a chance to corrupt the three-dollar bills that kept the Astor Bar in business. 'Follow me,' I said, guiding the gals down 44th to Schubert Alley. By taking the stage door route I could pass them off as theatre people if anybody asked.

Didn't bump into any watchmen so I steered my escorts into the rear lobby.

When Times Square became Times Square the poor old Astor was one of the first hotels built, and while it retained a certain raffish charm its glory days weren't even a memory. You couldn't have called the joint a flop but it didn't seem like it'd be that long before they strung up the hammocks. The ceiling was two storeys high, and a balcony ran entirely around the lobby at mezzanine level. There were crystal chandeliers big as a Volkswagen, looked like they hadn't been washed since the market crashed; the way they swung a little even when you couldn't feel a draft made you hesitate before doing the mistletoe bit underneath. On the floor were oriental carpets big as a school gym, with long rubber runners thrown over the places two million feet had worn through; near the floor, the walls were full of holes – not rat or mouse holes but where kids had stuck their fingers through the plaster when their keepers had their backs turned. In the past the bellhops would've had the dicks lay into the Dynamos with saps if they'd dared to even walk past the place; but you could tell it wouldn't be long before management finally wrapped its mouth around the gas pipe, and let in sci-fi conventions.

Doctor Oscar's flunkies had been hard on the case in preparation for the evening. Not only was his smiling puss hanging down from the balcony in black and white, but they'd stuck one of those chopped-liver busts parked on an oak table in the centre of the lobby. On either side of the grand staircase's chipped marble balustrades they'd stood up their sandwich boards, the usual eye-catchers.

'Spiritual group?' Eulie asked.

'Personal growth.'

She took another gander at the photos of Doctor Oscar. Chlo was tapping the bust with a finger, seeing what it was made of. 'Growing how?'

'This won't take half an hour,' I said, irrationally optimistic. Working my hand into my left trouser pocket – damn Continental cut of this suit – I felt the tube within its triple-thick sleeve. A couple of lounge lizards ankled past, heading upstairs to the meeting, giving her the fisheye all the while.

'What's done here?' Eulie asked.

'They're getting together, pressing the flesh. Cats looking out for fresh pigeons. Now let's go through the drill,' I said. 'Remember what I told you, don't pay attention to anything they say. I listened to 'em once and couldn't make heads or tails of it. Just turn on the charm and make with the chit-chat, and while you two circulate I'll handle the dirty work.' Chlo cracked her knuckles by making a fist. 'Chlo. You don't talk. OK?'

'AO.'

'Once I've done what I need to do, I'll give you the high sign. Like this.' I scratched my ear. 'Then it's scootsville to wherever it is you want to take me. Believe me, I'll be happy to go.' Chlo swayed slightly from left to right, rocking on her silver heels. 'And ixnay on the swillage. One toddy, no refills.'

Eulie looked like she'd bit down hard on a lemon. 'We're disalcoholic.'

'Wise decision on your part,' I said, and saw more characters heading up. 'Looks like the lambs are ready for the slaughter. Come, ladies, his master's voice is calling.'

We made our way to the mezzanine. When we got to the Oregon Room we found ourselves bringing up the rear. At the entrance to the hall two Dynamos were lurking. One was a lantern-jawed Aryan with a blonde crew that was so perfectly flat I figured his barber used a paper cutter. The other was good old Biff Baff Bop, still wearing his orange Perry Como underneath a bright burgundy jacket. If either had had whale appliques he'd have been the toast of Hyannis.

'The Shake-Out awaits,' Crewy Lou purred, giving us the old Brought to You By Ovaltine voice.

'Walter,' Burt said. 'Good to see you. And you've brought open minds.'

I looked behind me, supposing he met my companions. 'That's not all I brought,' I said, starting to go through the door. 'Where can we –'

'You choose?' asked Crewy Lou. His complexion was so rosy I'd have liked to compliment the embalmers on a job well done.

Burt nodded, suggesting to me that I should do as asked. 'I choose.' Odd to be my age and needing to say the secret sign to be let into the treehouse but I've done stranger. I gave the ladies a nod and they chimed in. The gatekeepers blinked, hearing Chlo's pipsqueak snarl, but if it troubled them they didn't make a production number out of it.

'Enter,' said the buzzcut one. 'Seize opportunity before it seizes you.'

The Dynamos didn't seem to be as dynamic as I'd thought they might be when it came to pulling in the marks. There weren't more than sixty people in the room. All the Dynamos, like Burt, wore burgundy jackets and looked, to a man, as if they were getting over concussions; they numbered about fifteen. The rest were comparative innocents, the same batch of semi-professionals, executive secretaries, dental hygienists and veterinarians I'd seen back at the HQ.

'Burt, listen,' I said, 'I'd like to go ahead and get this taken care of.'

'There's no rush,' he said. His grin had grown goofier since we'd first met, and I started to think that once you were finally accepted into the Dynamos, the next step was to have the frontal lobes removed. As I looked around the room I marvelled at the fact that this seemed to be a mixer where nobody mixed. If they'd been playing musical chairs earlier, they'd stopped; everybody'd already taken seats in four different rings spaced throughout the big room, which was one of those Louis the umpteenth places with the mirrors and red plush bagnio curtains and little gold cherubs in the corners leering at you. Three of the ring-leaders stood in the centre of their circles, looking like they couldn't wait to start laying down the old zingo. 'Friends,' Crewy Lou intoned, creeping up behind us, 'find seats. Take them.'

'Walter,' Burt said, stepping away; not a pleasant sight, under the circumstances. 'Take the opportunity to let your outside command your inside. We'll take care of matters following the shake out.'

147

'Really, I was hoping we'd be able to move along,' I said, the tips of my fingers beginning to twitch. Trying to calm myself I stuck my hands in my pockets and started fiddling with the tube. 'I had another appointment –'

'It can wait,' Crewy said, sliding around to interpose his body between myself and Trish's lobotomized pal. 'Find seats. Take them.'

'I don't think you get me –'

Crewy Lou leaned forward, his eyes as warm as a coyote's, and repeated his riff. 'Find seats. Take them.'

Just at that moment my nerves got the better of me, my brothers, and I pulled a trick that would have shamed a greenhorn. As I jiggled open the tube's sleeve my finger slid inside, and jarred loose the cap. That cool cool wetness, enough to assure that I'd be sailing like Icarus through the next day and a half. Removing my paw as if I'd set it on fire, I rubbed my hand along the hem of my jacket, but it was too late.

'If you say so.' The three thousand things running through my mind just then kept me from remembering how long it'd taken to blast off the time I'd tried this stuff before. No question I'd soaked up more this time around. 'Any recommendations?'

'Sit here,' he said, pointing to empty chairs in the nearest circle. 'In my nutshell.'

Sudden gushers spurted from beneath my arms as I sat but it was too early to know if it was simple nerves or the first symptoms. My chickadees perched on either side of my roost. While Crewy was shedding his red threads I wasted no time laying down the bad news.

'Emergency,' I whispered, nudging Eulie. My nose was already starting to get cold as the capillaries began to close off.

'Pardon?'

Glancing up I felt a shakiness coming over me, noting

that I could already perceive the pink border outlining each chandelier bulb's light. 'I dosed myself. Accidentally.'

'Dosed how?'

'Hallucinogen,' I said.

'Walter, what's meant?' Eulie asked, her lowered hiss loud enough to catch Chlo's attention as well.

I nodded. 'We can't stay in here long. Get me out if I start –'

'*Greetings!*' Crewy Lou interrupted. 'Attention. Focus and concentrate.' That grin was so fixed he was starting to look like he'd been carved for Halloween. 'Focus and concentrate,' the three other ringleaders said, some five seconds after he did. That wasn't going to help, having the sound noticeably out of sync even before the echo came in. Burt, that nincompoop, was parked in the circle farthest from ours; not a chance I'd be able to make the exchange and get out in time. 'Open yourself to the shake out, and see what'll fall out.' He started to turn slowly in place, giving each one of us the snake eyes, that grin never slipping an inch. 'As Doctor Oscar says.' Looking up at the chandelier I watched circular rainbows take shape around every single bulb. On the floor, the carpet's nub started to deepen. I started to think of Bryce Canyon. 'Accept the inmost deep within you.'

That old stiff strychnine feel swept in along the back of my neck. Soon as Crewy turned to face the far side I started rubbing, trying to loosen the muscles before they had a chance to knot up. Wanting to give Eulie a sign all was okay so far, I winked, twice.

'First,' Crewy said, 'imagine this entire room is filled to the ceiling with shit.'

What *was* it with these clowns? Rough toilet training was all I could figure. Realizing I'd have to hear this spiel in replay made me feel like I'd puke. Eulie's face seemed kind of antsy, like she was watching somebody set off fireworks in a dynamite factory. I took a breath, and thought a while

149

of what air felt like, inside my lungs.

'Dig through the shit, through the shit, the shit –'

The ringleaders sounded as if they were enhanced for stereo, badly, each one of them said almost the same thing almost simultaneously. Even as I grew to like the sound, I made a point to remember that the last thing I wanted to do during the shakeout was open my head up wide enough for something to fall in.

'No adult's adult while the child hides inside –'

Tried humming internally, calling up favourite songs to try drowning out the Dynamos, be they 'Little Maggie' or 'Canned Heat Blues' or the Ted Weems Orchestra playing 'Cheer Up', but not a one could get through a chorus without some nitwittery piercing the veil. 'The jewel is in the shit and the shit is in the jewel,' 'Master potential or it masters you,' 'Not a cough in a carload,' that kind of blather. Chlo leaned forward in her chair, her long blonde ropes dangling down, hiding her face. If I stared at her hair long enough I knew I'd see them move like snakes of their own accord. Eulie tapped my arm. I couldn't tell what she wanted, and she finally stopped. Shadows in the room were two o'clock sharp. Bad sign when I realized I couldn't remember if minutes earlier there'd even been shadows. Couldn't help but notice how odd my feet felt, within shoes, and was about to take them off –

'Zingo!!!'

Didn't like the sound of that; looked up and saw him slapping a red-headed secretary sitting across the way. The faucets let go and she acted like she was going to run off, but her seatmates held her down. Taking Eulie's little paw in mine I tightened my grip, thinking that might let her know I was having second thoughts. She didn't act as if she saw me, she was whispering something in Chlo's ear. It didn't seem to bother Chlo. Sharp white shafts started poking, longer and longer each time I blinked, out of the lights' surrounding spectra. Forgetting that I had my eyes open, when I devoted my attention to the circle once more I saw everybody start to look at me, one by one; everybody except Crewy Lou, and he was still ranting on, perfecting that grin. I knew by now my pupils were as big as quarters; and knew that if I closed my eyes, no one would see me.

'Zingo!'

Reopening I saw Chlo watching Crewy really put his shoulder into a punch as he let a middle-aged man, insurance agent probably, have a hard one in the kisser. When Crewy stepped away it looked like he'd tried to put red lipstick on the fellow, but hadn't quite mastered the fundamentals of cosmetology. Then he feinted to his left, and jumped, and I thought he was coming to try out a new line on me. Sense tried to crawl back into my head but now the opening was too small, and sense gave up. I couldn't understand why Eulie ignored the subtle facial gestures I was sure I was making. The corners of my mouth began to ache and I realized my grin might be noticeable. At least I'd fade in with the rest of the crowd.

'If you have to beat the shit out of a nonadult,' Crewy said, 'in order to drag their child into sunlight, what is needed? What?'

Jamming a hand into his pants pocket, he yanked out a stopwatch. There're trails and there're trails, but this was something else entirely. As Crewy Lou performed that action I saw its progression take place in about fifty individual static frames. Think of a strobe going off in a black-lit room, but without black light. 'Five,' Crewy counted off, though as I expected the sound no longer issued directly from his lips. 'Four.'

'Eulie,' I said, trying to squeak it out under my breath. When she turned to look at me I know I gaped when I saw her make hundreds of facial expressions, nearly all at once and every one sequential, as earlier described. I'd experienced

151

this effect many times, in milder form – under the influence of any of the LSDs, once after swallowing (to be on the safe side) a baggie full of dried *stropharia cubensis*, and again following the intake of a number of other derivatives of vegetable agents, notably toloache. But comparing those to this was like comparing automatic vaudeville to 3-D Cinemascope.

'*You stupid fucking assholes!!*'

Crewy was going into overdrive. While shifting my head to look at the dozens of him I felt the blood shoot down into my feet and then shoot back up twice as high. All the Crewies moved simultaneously, jabbing in all directions, lifting scores of legs. The words didn't come from them, or underneath them, or above them – they just landed on my ears and tumbled in. As I heard them I perceived the fugal music underpinning speech, neuronic Bach.

'Fed up. Fed up with you. Fucking. Fucking People. Fed. Up. With You People. With. You. You people.'

I thought I said *Eulie*, but I didn't hear myself say it, after the fact, and she gave no sign that anything had distracted either her or Chlojo, both of whom appeared to be watching these dynamic escapades wide-eyed. Their hundreds of faces flowed, slowly, toward Crewy. All ten thousand of him were shifting, floating like gulls, toward me. Then the echo severely kicked in.

'Iffff youuuu. Haave. Toooo beat theeee livinginging. Shititit out. Of Aaaaa nooooo-nothing –'

Blue and brown blended into dirty violet as he swerved away from me. Crewy now hovered directly in front of Chlo, who was now vibrating like a tuning-fork. Even so, since she wasn't moving, per se, I was able to focus in on her, imagining I could see her various aspects merging into one until they actually did so. Once I had her fixed, she and everything around her started to move as if floating through clear syrup. Her jaws moved, slightly, as if she were chewing something. Veins popped out on Crewy's temples and that

152

bloodless face of his took on the colour of an August tomato. I heard hummingbird wings abuzz somewhere in the back of my head.

'What. Do. You. Do. What. Do. You. Do? Do? What? Do?' Then Crewy started counting out again. 'Five.' An hour passed. 'Four.' Another. 'Three.'

Then I heard Crewy say the next word:

'Two.'

The notion passed through my head that old flattop was getting ready to do something he'd regret.

'One.'

I felt myself trying to get up, briefly; then sensibly stopped trying. Eulie's grip tightened on my arm. I started to think about how much I wanted to get down on something soft with her and making with the appassionatta till all the glasses in the cabinet broke.

'Response?'

Some want to know the experience without having the experience, but there'll never be a way. Most people shouldn't even think about the experience. But maybe I can give you a hint. Think of the clearest dream you ever had, the sharpness of the colours, the facial expressions of the people drifting through, the fast-shifting backgrounds, everything in reach yet not in reach, the profound silence that falls when nobody speaks. Think how the dream felt more real than life, and as greatly unreal. The non-hallucinatory part of the experience is twenty times as clear, but exactly the same.

'Zingo!!!'

Crewy's hundreds of arms swung consecutively forward until they suddenly stopped. Chlo caught hold of them somewhere between the wrist and elbow. His and her facial expressions riffled through my line of sight more slowly, a dealer's casual shuffle. *Chlo*, Eulie shouted, *Nyah*. Chlo put her hands around his neck and tightened till you couldn't tell he had a neck. I wondered what he was thinking.

Stop her. Oh my God.

Crewy's head lolled in her grip like it was made of rags. I heard a crack, thunder after lightning. A black blur passed through my eyes, clouds over the sun, and then saw light glossing over Eulie's crow-dark hair. When Chlo and Crewy emerged from eclipse she had one hand around his neck and the other clamped down on his shoulder. She roared like winter. *Stop* somebody said. Judging from her movements it seemed like Chlo was starting to push in two different directions. Her mouth opened, wide and then wider until I thought her head would split apart. Her back teeth were filed to, or capped with, points. Other people in the room seemed to be getting up to dance and I figured they'd be dancing to 'Venus In Furs' rather than 'Telstar', since I heard both playing. Two long red whipcords shot out of Crewy Lou's neck. Where did his head go? She took her hand from his shoulder, and there it was, in her hand. She threw it.

Trails.

Utmost fabulousity. I felt myself floating towards the floor. Eulie was tumbling with me. We hit the ground and I bounced up. I wondered if I could bounce higher when I landed the second time but Eulie held me down. She was saying something.

Walter

'Kiss the boot,' I said, 'of shiny shiny leather –'

What

'Waffles,' I said. 'Waffles, waffles, waffles –'

Looking upwards into a dome I saw ourselves apotheosized. Chairs flew across the dome like grey metal cherubs; and then I saw Chlo hovering like a gigantic hummingbird, holding a chair under either arm, her blonde ropes loose and swinging around her head. She'd shed her muumuu and was back in rubbery lizard black. There were dancers on the stage when she landed, running back and forth. The percussion drifted

154

in from somewhere in the wings, crazed polyphonists beating out Gold Coast rhythms as the mamas wailed.

'Whoa daddy,' I said. Eulie began fading in again, her signal stronger this time.

'Walter, connect! Walter –'

Chlo flung chairs like she was dealing cards. The dancers caught them and, once partnered, leapt with them to the floor. The chandeliers overhead swung back and forth, stirred by wind, their glass chiming. Chlo snapped her dozens of right hands and things slid into them, flexible black sticks; one stick. She lifted her arms and a ten-foot long silver cord shot out. Letting the end swing free, Chlo began pirouetting like a ballerina. Eulie pressed my face against the floor, the rug burned my cheek. Managing to stare up between her fingers I glimpsed the corps de ballet removing parts of themselves and tossing them, chair-like, towards heaven. Fireworks burst red.

'Stay down,' Eulie said, this time sounding strangely near. For a moment I imagined it was morning, and we'd just woken up.

'Chlo's a good dancer.'

'She's activated.'

'Pixilated?'

Eulie didn't answer. She faded. The next thing I knew she'd hauled me to my feet and I was standing; the sudden rush of blood to my head cut the buzz down to size. This clarity wouldn't last, no question about that, so I figured I might as well make the best of a difficult situation in the meantime. There was no one else left in the audience. Chlo whipped a large heap of clothing on the floor. I saw Burt's orange sweater, covered with tiny red whales. The rug squished beneath my feet, sounded like we were walking in a swamp, down deep in the reeds with the two-headed men. Eulie was speaking again.

'Disarm, Chlo. Disarm! *Disarm!!*'

She reached up behind Chlo's neck and massaged it. The big gal stopped at once, shook her arm and her stick slid back into her sleeve. She panted as if she'd just run here from Philadelphia. Drool hung from her lower lip, and her face was the colour of Harvard beets.

'Maxed po,' Chlo gasped.

Eulie shook her head. 'Overreactive, Nonthreats, all. Level, Chlo, level.'

'AO.' Chlo nodded, and tossed us a beatific smile; for an instant, she was her father's little girl again. 'Guide.'

'Interior transfer nonsustainable,' Eulie said. 'Outside us.'

I felt Eulie take my arm as my blood started to simmer again, and without feeling my feet in the swamp we started moving toward the ballroom's closed doors. The doors started to breathe in and out; then started to shout.

'Chlo,' I heard Eulie say, 'activate.'

She lifted one of her silver-toed boots, followed by the other. Looked as if she were levitating, five feet off the ground, it was the old rope trick. The doors splintered and opened as soon as her heels hit the knobs. It looked to me that she turned at least two somersaults before coming down boots-first on gents who had the look of house dicks about them. Others – bellboys, desk clerks, the concierge – ran towards us, pouring up the marble stairs. Chlo lifted her arms until they were perpendicular and jerked her body; something shot out of her from the front – couldn't tell what, but every single guy trying to make it up the stairs took a tumble before they were halfway. Once they were all down Chlo ran, kicking them out of our way as Eulie and I followed. At the foot of the stairs Chlo grabbed the bust of Doctor Oscar and we bore left. I wondered why she'd wanted it until she threw it at the man blocking the back exit. He caught the bust and leapt backwards through the door. Breaking glass chimed like chandeliers in the wind.

'Chlo, pause,' Eulie shouted as we stepped into Schubert

Alley. It was intermission, and dozens of playboys and girls were out there stretching their legs, getting quick smokes, making with the wry eye. On the wall directly in front of us were posters for *My Darlin' Aida* and Cole Porter's *Out of This World*. The colours were Kodak sharp. Eulie fumbled in her bag until she found something the size of a transistor radio. 'Tighten grouping. Hold Walter –'

'*Freeze!*'

A sudden rush of blood to my head, and reality lurched briefly into view. Running down the alley at us at top speed were two boys of Killarney. One had the old reliable Smith & Winchester .44, and the other held tight onto a twelve-gauge. Chlo stepped in front of us and started walking towards them. Sound of gunshots and of hail on a tin roof, *fortissimo* shouts and murmurs in the background *molto presto*, playboys skedaddling, Chlo not breaking step as the cop fired his gun. Then a cannon-blast as his partner unloaded both barrels. Chloe's right arm took leave of her body. The metal part, no doubt; erector set sticking out of her elbow. Didn't faze her. With her left arm she swung forward, hitting the cop's neck with the side of her hand while plunging the sharp stump of her right arm into the shotgun cop's breadbasket. He fired again, directly into her midsection. A butcher shop, the display counters full of schnitzel and weisswurst.

'*Chlo!*'

As the big one fell backwards Eulie gave her neck a fast one-hand clamp while with the mitt she ran her digits down the sides of her little black radio. There were more cops coming down the alley, a lot more cops. But I didn't hear them saying anything, which seemed surprising. Suddenly I saw the cops still running towards us, but now as if from far down a country road, seen through the shimmering orgone as it rises off asphalt in the heat. Chlo and Eulie stood in front of me, and the three of us looked solid, but they didn't move and I couldn't either. Schubert Alley was hit

157

by a blizzard; everything around us whited out; but there was no movement, no wind, and I thought I'd even stopped breathing. There was an absence of air movement. I hardly felt I could breathe, but I was. Then my ghost appeared, now solo, without his friend. Old see-through wasn't a ghost any more. His suit might have looked white once. He had brown hair and pale skin, and ran towards us, never seeming to get any closer, never falling any further back. Seemed like we could do this for hours, but then my internal organs felt as if they'd been filled with hydrogen and getting ready to take the zeppelin route. Closed my eyes as I doubled over, the blood leaving my head like the tide. Saw nothing but millions of multicolour flashes, Pi-addled phosgenes. Then I felt breeze on my face; heard background sounds – low humming, the rustle of traffic, distant *sotto voce* dialogues.

'Walter,' I heard Eulie say. 'Walter.'

Eased open my eyes, not sure what I was going to see. A world of colours once again, though I couldn't tell how real these were. I faced a big yellow circle. Two dots and a curve glowed red from within. Then I heard Eulie again. 'Home,' or 'Chlo.' I was projectile vomiting when she said whatever it was she said, and couldn't be sure.

'Walter?' Eulie asked as she gave me the maraca treatment. My brain wobbled like a plate of Jell-O; looking up I saw Eulie's face, and beyond them both two big green Coke bottles taller than the Empire State building. No doubt I looked like a turkey in a rainstorm. She wiped my mouth with something that felt like terrycloth and looked like bubble gum. 'Done?'

'I think I maybe –' I heard myself sputter and then gave up. Someone else was there, an older woman with brown hair. With dozens of hands she gave Eulie something.

'Walter,' she said. 'Hold.' A paper punch going in, right where my arm met the shoulder, as if she were giving me a vaccine. When I blinked again, I was no longer hallucinating; was in fact dead sober as a park ranger. 'Clarified?'

'What?' I asked, shaking my head, unable to imagine that I'd come off the trip so soon. 'What'd you give me? Antihistamines?' The woman and Eulie helped me get to my feet. Then, my brothers, I realized that even though I should have been staring deep into my own imaginings, I wasn't. We stood in the midst of a circular plaza, maybe a hundred feet across and surrounded by low metal carports, real Levittown specials; atop the ones that were facing me was that big yellow circle with the dots I saw when I first opened up. The Coke bottles were buildings, all right; there were twelve others just in my line of sight even taller, their tops swallowed in deep grey felt. The other buildings were in colours other than green – blue and purple and red and yellow. Some had tubes running along their sides, looking like the piping on Marines' pants. Running horizontally between most of the buildings were other tubes, in other hues and I wondered if those helped the things stand up. All the buildings looked as if they were made out of the same kind of plastic used in telephones. Hundreds of little bugs flitted around the tall boys. 'Where are we, Eulie?'

'New York,' she said.

'No. Where are we? Where are we now?'

'New York,' she said, looking down at the ground. Chlo lay there, not moving. She'd lost the muumuu I'd bought her, earlier that day, and wore only what remained of her jumpsuit. A sharp metal shard emerged red from her elbow, and the rest of the arm was missing; as was a good deal of her midsection. Her blonde ropes lay all around her head, and I thought of those clocks they used to make in the fifties, the ones that were supposed to resemble suns. Eulie knelt down, and stroked her face; with her thumb and forefinger, pulled her eyelids shut. 'My New York. Come on, Walter. Come with me.'

159

'Chlojo?'

'Retired,' Eulie said. 'Come on, Walter.'

Streets sloped downward all around the plaza, on hills steep as San Francisco's. In the sky, clouds of lighter colours kept showing pictures. 'She's dead?'

Eulie wiped her eyes with her hand. 'As risked. Come on, Walter.'

The woman with brown hair and a couple of large guys in black were wrapping Chlo's body in clear plastic; once she was enshrouded, it turned opaque. They lifted her up and carried her across the plaza, towards one of the carports. I started trying to walk, but while we were in transit I'd gone all gimpy; it felt like I was trying to stroll across gravy.

'Where're we going?'

'Required checkover and superior notification,' Eulie said. 'Necessaried to reduce potential harm.'

'To?'

'You.'

When we reached the edge of the plaza she lifted her arm and a lemon whizzed to a stop. The rind peeled away from the top, the sound of birds chirping floated out and Eulie helped me climb in. Between the front seat and the back seat was a heavy black barrier with a tiny slot. The windows were tinted a deep Rayban-green.

'Dryco,' Eulie said. One second we were parked, the next we were shooting off at a fast clip.

'We're making tracks where?' I started to ask. No sooner did I open my trap than somebody else started outyapping me; a recording, I gathered. Couldn't see the speakers, couldn't tell if the speaker was male or female, grownup or kid. When I tried to make out the lingo I felt like a missionary among the heathen chinee.

'Interavesting per sliptimper transgratisfy allayvoo –'

'Not the old klaatu barada again,' I said, turning up my speaker to be heard over the foofaraw. 'What happened to

160

Chlojo –?' But it got louder every time I did.

'Doublatar whilomit extronon whang –'

'Eulie –'

Thinthin delavooz maximate coladwalpter –'

'Eulie, what the hell –'

'URGALL VOX MAGNAWAIL BLAP –'

'EULIE –!!'

She fixed her mouth on my ear like she was going to slip me some tongue. 'Taxitalk impossibled, Walter,' she shouted. 'Adspace precedents. Mute til we decab.'

That made as much sense as whatever the taxi was saying, so I just lay back and gave a listen to some sexless goofball sputter out songs of the Pogo. I kept looking to my left, thinking Chlojo would still be there, but of course she wasn't. All at once the cab stopped without braking; we slid forward a little on the seat and then slid back. Eulie pushed a little white card into the slot in the black barrier and something clicked. 'Come, Walter.' I looked out over another plaza as she helped me out, this one wide as Washington Square. In the centre of this plaza, where broom-dry grass sprang up between the cracks in the terrazzo, was a statue of some husky boy in a plumbers' suit and a high collar. He held a pipe up to his face as if thinking he'd see what clogged the drain.

'Who he?' I asked.

Eulie glanced over, muttered 'E,' and kept walking. In front of us was what looked like an upside-down golf tee. Piss-yellow, round at the bottom like the top half of a globe, the shaft getting narrower as it rose. I couldn't see the top of the damned thing. Probably no one could. This plaza, unlike the other one, was populated; hundreds of people wandered about beneath the shadow of the plumber. Felt like August, but there's never this many people around at that time of year in the city. Everyone had the look of a typically cheerful New Yorker but there was one big difference, the difference that gave the game away. The faces were different colours –

au lait, milk chocolate, chopped liver, blutwurst, espresso. I'd never seen so many coloured folk in my life.

'Eule,' I said, as my sometimes-slow mind started to click in. 'We're in the future?'

'My present. Come.'

Eulie pressed her hand against the side of the building when we reached it, and where there'd been a blank wall, a large door opened up. Two teamster-size characters in dark suits stood just inside the entranceway.

'Tarcial,' Eulie told them. 'Gamamye.'

Something like that, anyway. Didn't look like their suits were tailored to conceal weapons. Before I knew what was up, Vinny from Local 136 had my shoes half a foot off the floor as he held me up by the jaw. Rocco had pulled a bright green popgun out from under his jacket and looked set to let it fire, right between my peepers.

'Aggro *nya!!*' Eulie said, intervening. 'Approval met.'

'Explitail!' he shouted back. English fell by the wayside and some odd combo of Hungarian and Urdu took over. This Buck Rogers business was the last thing I needed, just then. Couldn't help wishing I'd been more of a futurian, might have been ready for anything under those circumstances. I thought of what you were supposed to do if you found yourself in the future – look to see how the market was doing, check out property values, tell Nixon to make sure he went to New Orleans, try not to kill your own grandfather – no, that was what you did if you found yourself in the *past* – so hard to tell the difference, sometimes.

'Walter, come.'

Having appeased the teamsters, Eulie guided me into the building's lobby. I thought the walls were marble, at first; found out they weren't when I ran my finger along the wainscotting and carved a line through it with a dull fingernail. Hanging from the ceiling, six storeys overhead, was a long chrome steel bar – seventy feet long, maybe –

162

that slowly glided back and forth, barely missing the surface of another chrome steel bar that rose up out of the floor. Words were engraved into the sides of each bar. DO GOOD, read the bar that moved. FEEL REAL, read the one that was stationary. Looked around for anything that said OR ELSE, but no go. I supposed anyone they caught in this building without permission would wind up strapped onto the gliding surface of their choice of bars.

'What is Dryco, anyway?' I asked as Eulie pressed her hand against a wall on the far side.

'Dryco,' she said. I nodded, figuring there was no point in pressing the issue. An oval opening appeared in the wall. Eulie stepped forward and put her face against it. A quick blue flash on our left and an elevator door opened. Inside, it looked like an elevator.

'Eighty,' Eulie said, and the door disappeared. It seemed like we were going nowhere, until suddenly I felt my head attempting to slide down through my body, as if not feeling safe until it nestled at my feet. As I slumped against the wall of the elevator I looked at her; she was crying as she had back in the museum, just that afternoon, and I pulled myself forward until I could hold her. Then gravity got the better of me again, and I blacked out.

EIGHT

By the time Eulie picked me up off the floor the elevator had stopped. This high up it took half a minute for the door to open – took time to depressurize, I assumed. Blood poured out of my nose until she put some more of that bubblegum against my face and I was once more dry as a bone. 'Where now?'

'Essentialled protectives,' said Eulie.

'What kind?'

'Med. This way.'

In New York – my New York, that is – there's probably a hundred sawbones happy to deal with the scurviest clientele – old geezers who'll tear off scrip for reds or beauties or barbs if a three-year-old came in describing symptoms. Not many deal in my brand of esoterica though, so it was a rare thing for me to need their services. Croakers have their uses, but by and large I steer clear. This'd be the first physical I had since I was fourteen – wouldn't hurt, I figured, to have one. Eulie led me down a white-walled hall to a small grey room with two red couches, a metal door and a low table covered with magazines.

Eulie pointed to one of the couches, took something small and blue from her bag and tapped its surface. While she busied herself I picked up one of the magazines, thinking I might be able to figure out something more about where I was. Silly me. At first I thought somebody'd gone one better on *Life* and got rid of the articles, leaving only pictures; then I noticed that at some angles, if the light hit the pages right, words popped up out of the photos. Even so, the type was so small that you'd have needed a magnifying glass to read it. For the life of me, I couldn't figure out what kind of magazine it was; there were photos of what looked like the insides of transistor radios, followed by photos of naked women – too skinny for my taste, and one was missing a leg – followed by landscapes that would have looked like Arizona if the sky hadn't been pinkish-red. There were pictures of that plumber whose statue I'd seen outside, looking somewhat livelier (if fatter) and some other characters who didn't appear to be the sort you'd trust alone with either your brother or your sister. There were several pages where I couldn't tell what was even being photographed, that is to say if what I was looking at were photographs in the first place.

'All's prepped, Walter.'

'You'll read magazines?' I asked. 'Are these magazines?'

She shook her head. 'I require treatment as well. Same procedure, different space. I'll meet you here when I'm done.'

I walked through the door. There was nothing in the room but a chrome table shiny as the bumper on an old Pontiac. I was admiring my profile in the reflection when I heard the lock behind me click.

'Denude,' the ceiling said, speaking with the cab's voice.

'Come again?'

'Denude and prone.'

I was getting better at figuring out the lingo – I took off my clothes and got ready to lie down. *'Beelzebub!!'* I shouted, hopping on the slab and immediately flash-freezing my ass. Didn't get much chance to complain, though. Without

165

warning, the table had me in a full body-lock. Grey plastic bands came out of the table and wrapped around my wrists, something I couldn't see came up under my back and my feet sailed into the air; two big chrome clamps popped up and locked them in place, leaving my toes wiggling hello at the ceiling. That was pleasant, compared to what happened next. Two steel octopi with beady red eyes rolled up on either side of me. Their tentacles were tipped with needles and thermometers and sanders, and without a word of warning they started drilling in. Felt like I was sealed inside a wasp's nest, rolling downhill. 'Mute,' the voice said, but I didn't care to oblige. Goodbye a moment later to the metal monsters as the table rolled forward toward the wall. The wall opened up and I slid right into what looked like a white plastic sewer pipe not much wider than my shoulders. Thousands of bright green flashbulbs went off and something began to hum. Felt at first like I was lying out in the sun copping rays, but as you might have figured this bunch couldn't keep from going overboard, and I started to develop a crispy outside crust while staying moist and juicy on the inside. The hum turned into a hiss and something wet spritzed over me. Refreshing for a second or two, and then it started to sting, then burn. Just when I thought I was going to pass out yet again, I was shot out of the tube back into the room; the table tilted as the bands holding me disappeared, and I slid down onto the floor which – like the table – was freezing cold.

'Clarified,' the voice said. 'Regarb.'

'Refreshed?' Eulie asked when I finally managed to stumble back into the waiting room. She sat on the couch, staring up at a tiny movie screen built into the wall. I couldn't tell what it was; whatever was playing made as much sense as the magazines.

'What is that?' I asked, but she turned it off.

'Follow, Walter.'

We walked back into the hall and she did the face thing against the wall again. Nothing happened. She tried it again, and again nothing. I looked down at my arms; my skin was lingerie-pink, as if the top layer had been sanded away. 'We'll take the service lift.' She pressed her hand against the opposite wall and it slid open. I followed her in, but before I could jump back out the door had disappeared. In the service elevator the walls, the roof and the floor were transparent. It was like stepping off a cliff. 'One forty,' she said.

'Ascending,' said the elevator. We reached one forty, five minutes ahead of my stomach, but my nose didn't let me down this time. The door reappeared and we stepped into a hall that was much wider, with a shiny black floor and sky-blue walls that must have been twenty feet high.

'Identify.' The hall spoke with a different voice, some gravel-throated yegg who sounded like the actor Larry Tierney.

'Eulalia Bax with outland transient,' she said, not breaking stride, heading the end of the hall. Just when I thought she was going to lead us straight into the wall another door appeared, and we entered what I assumed was a reception area, uncluttered by receptionists. There were six king-size bruisers, orangutan-armed, all in black, tall as Chlojo and twice as wide. Only one had ears. They were all female.

'As appointed?' the biggest asked, speaking with the voice of a Barnard grad. I started to think that City Hall in this New York must be headquartered down in the Duchess Club on Sheridan Square.

'AO,' Eulie said. Big Bertha twisted her bracelet and yet another opening appeared in yet another wall. Doorknobs must have been as much use as buggywhips around here. Eulie led me through, and it didn't make me unhappy that none of those Junior League linebackers followed. Now we were walking through another hall, one that seemed normal

167

at first until it struck me that everything was just slightly larger than it really needed to be.

'Where we going?' I whispered. Somehow, as in a museum, or church, it seemed like the thing to do.

'Superior notification.'

'Who's superior? I thought you were the director.'

'Of the Lucidity Institute, yes,' she said. 'But this is Dryco.'

'And now we're in executive bathroom land, in other words.'

No answer, but I didn't expect one. At the end of this hall was a sight I could not have predicted – doors that looked like doors. Eulie stopped before going in, and knocked.

'Madam,' she called out, and the door creaked open. I couldn't help but think of *Inner Sanctum*, but there was no grisly-voiced host in sight; only a round space as wide as the plaza we'd first come out in. I wondered why we weren't given sunglasses before going in; the floor was shiny as a ballroom and the walls were toothpaste white. At first I couldn't tell where the light in the room was coming from, even though there were windows; the walls were nothing but windows, in fact, the closer I looked. Remembering that it had seemed like a cloudy day outside, near as I could tell, and recalling how high these buildings seemed to go, I could only imagine that we had to be somewhere up in the midst of the stratocumulus. Just as I was starting to get my bearing a thin white wall as wide as the room came up out of the floor. The wall glowed from within, and at any second I expected to hear the voice of W.C. Fields saying, I Am Oz the Great and Powerful but no such luck. The voice that came out of the wall was female, and old; grandmotherly, you might have said, but there was a quality in the tone of her voice that made me think grandma was packing heat.

'Eulalia Bax, Lucidity Institute. Madam?'

Grandma answered. 'Speak.'

The wall lit up like a movie screen, and then I saw the old

battleaxe. The picture was clearer than any movie I'd ever seen. I suddenly remembered an invention I'd read about in *Amazing Stories*, back when I was a kid, before they'd started running that Shaver nonsense and I realized there wasn't any future in science fiction – *visual radio*. Every home was supposed to have it by 1960, but as with so much else whenever the future came into it, somebody missed the boat. I tried to listen to Eulie and Ma Barker as they gabbed away, talking in Estonian or Hungarian or whatever they liked to use when they talked to each other over here, all the while staring up at the big screen. Granny's head was maybe fourteen feet high; the little hair she had left was chalk-white, and she'd lost her choppers. The veins on her temples looked like snakes beneath the skin. Her eyes were about sixty years younger than the rest of her, and from the looks she threw us I suspected she'd be just as happy to squash us like bugs if the mood struck her. But what I really couldn't get over was the fact that she was as dark as milk chocolate. I had a hunch she'd have slapped you down if you even brought up the question of passing.

'This is your man from over the mountain?' I heard her say, surprised to hear anything that was recognizable as English.

'Node and conduit.' Eulie said.

'Current status?' Granny's head started rolling upward, fluttering and I wondered why the projectionist wasn't paying attention. Then it was brought home hard to me that this was no movie. 'Walter,' she asked, 'How are you?' I was glancing out the window, thinking I saw something fly by. 'I'm speaking to you.'

Eulie nudged me in the ribs, and I gave the old gal my full attention. 'Feel like a top,' I said. 'Couldn't be better.'

'Fabricator,' she said. 'Bestill yourself.'

Those shifty eyes of hers returned to my tour guide. The two of them started jawing again, louder and faster this time. They sounded even more incomprehensible than the taxi had. Sometimes, as if accidentally, phrases in English burst through the static, but faded out just as fast. Finding my eyes drawn back towards the windows, I watched some kind of little blue helicoper whiz by. The thing didn't have any windows, and the only thing I could figure was that the pilot used a periscope to get by.

'Comprehended,' I heard Eulie say. The old woman nodded, and peered down at me, shaking her head. The screen went blank. Her expression hadn't really changed throughout the entire conversation, so I assumed that whatever Eulie had told her, it hadn't been anything different, or worse, than what she'd expected to hear.

'Let's go, Walter,' Eulie said. 'Superior notification continues.'

'Who was that?'

'Madam,' she said. 'Chairperson Emerita of Dryco.'

'She's not the head honcho?'

Eulie's face was blank as the clouds outside. 'Her granddaughter publics Dryco. We see her now.' Eulie tried out a smile but it looked more like a grimace. 'Follow, Walter . . .'

'Eule,' I said. 'Is everything all right?'

'With us, yes,' she said. 'With everything, no.'

'I'm sorry,' I said. 'I'm sorry about Chlo. I never thought –'

'Unavoidable event,' she said, pushing open the doors. 'Follow, Walter.'

Then it was back out in the reception room, a nod to the Holiday Girls, out and down another hall and then into another elevator, this one thank Sophia not as see-through as the last. I began to understand why so much time passed between Eulie and Chlo's trips over to my neck of the woods – clearly, once they were back home they had to spend whole days, maybe even weeks, just going from one office to the next. When we got out of the elevator I was glad to see we'd descended, and not risen higher – it was hard to tell while we were still inside. At least this was what I thought when we emerged; windows seemed to line the hall, and it was only after a minute or so that I realized the blue sky I thought I was seeing was actually a very good paint job. We weren't the only ones in the halls down here; there were dozens of wage slaves roaming about, and save for the fact that they came in all colours, most didn't look so different from the people I saw all the time back in my neighbourhood.

'The old lady start all this?'

Eulie frowned. 'Madam succeeded the successor.'

'That would have been Dryco?'

'The successor was Mister O'Malley,' she said. 'The founder, Dryden.'

She stopped long enough to touch the nearest wall, and another picture took shape – it wasn't on a screen; the wall became the picture, that's the only way I can put it. Three goonpusses huddled face-on, evidently in some steakhouse, judging from how dark it was. The central figure was a nasty-looking woman filling the seat of a wingchair, flanked fore and aft by a pair of stupes. The younger one was wearing what looked like a shirt and a leotard, and lay at her feet as if ready to give her a pedicure. Some rough old piece of work stood behind the chair, lean and hungry, using a baseball bat as a walking stick. Real dark alley characters, that was for sure.

'The Drydens. Still present, not voting.'

We walked a little farther down the hall, until we came to yet another spot where she could put her face up against the wall. Another magic door opened up with a clank.

'Here we are, Walter. Mute yourself.'

'Why?'

'Granddaughter is difficult,' Eulie said.

The room we entered looked almost like a receptionist's office as I might have known it. There was a desk, and chair; on top of the desk was a small pad with another little movie screen. Probably no need to add that there wasn't a receptionist in sight. There were, however, a couple of bruisers – males, this time, about the size of the teamsters downstairs. They wore black suits with a close-in neckline that fell somewhere between Beatle and Mao. Both of them resembled funeral home bouncers hauled into service whenever the box proved too heavy for the pallbearers. Eulie nodded at them and they nodded in return, and one of them opened the door to the next room – once again, at the top level, there were real doors with real knobs. As I followed Eulie inside, I immediately wondered what exactly she was leading me into.

'Lucidity girl,' said the granddaughter, spotting Eulie. 'I've problemed. Assist.'

In her haste to get us down here, my little co-conspirator had neglected to mention that the old bat's granddaughter couldn't have been any older than fifteen. Granted, the older I get the harder it is to tell, but in this case I'd have been willing to bet money. She sat yoga-style on top of her desk; it looked like she'd cleared a space by throwing everything onto the dark brown carpet – at least I thought it was a carpet. Not much of it showed through beneath the tossed-aside clothing, purses, shoes, empty boxes and all the standard teenage girl debris. This room wasn't as big as the old lady's, but it wasn't small, and had a fireplace, which blazed away even though the air conditioning was running full blast. On the wall behind her desk hung the original of that picture Eulie'd called into existence out in the hall. Judging from the holes in the canvas it looked like the little minx had been using it as a dartboard, with icepicks.

'What troubles?' Eulie asked, holding tight to my arm as we cleared a path through the undergrowth.

'This unworks. Alice unhelps,' she said, holding out a shiny green hockey puck. 'Command her.'

'Alice has silenced,' Eulie said. 'Show me.'

Although the little missy wasn't more than five feet away

172

I did everything possible to keep from looking at her. It's always been my experience that girls her age are shy even when they're running around beaches half naked, but this one didn't seem shy at all. She was dark as a Greek, and wore her hair pixied; probably couldn't get the kink out, and didn't want to flaunt it. That wasn't what distressed me so, however; granddaughter wore what looked like pink pipecleaners in her ears, dirty white ankle socks and a purple stripper's gaff, and nothing else. It didn't seem to matter to her who might have seen what.

'Dislodging,' said Eulie, taking the puck and tapping it. Trying not to even come close to catching granddaughter's eye, distracted by a buzz of voices, I craned my neck around and saw, behind us, a wall covered with about fifty of those little screens. Every single one was showing a different movie; on the second row from the bottom, on the far left, I even recognized Humphrey Bogart. It was impossible to hear what was really being said on any of the screens, though; music – I guess that was what it was supposed to be, although it didn't seem to be much more than a steady driving rhythm – filled the room. Wherever the speakers were, they must have been concert-size. Granddaughter had incense burning in several different censers, but the smell of the room, and of granddaughter, still came through painfully clear.

'Corrected,' said Eulie, handing her back the puck. Granddaughter lay her little mitts on it and then shoved it into her mouth as if intending to swallow it, but she didn't. All of the pictures on the screens as a single big movie filled the entire wall. It was doubly unsettling to suddenly see a much larger version of our hostess, wearing even less, stomping through what seemed at first to be a toy city, until I realized it was some actual anonymous burg – Omaha, or Cleveland, maybe. She knocked over buildings, crushed people underfoot, slung cars through the air like frisbees.

'We've paid respect,' Eulie whispered to me. 'Follow.'

173

Eulie bowed down before Topsy, and as I took her literally I did as well. No surprise to find out that I shouldn't have. Without taking her eyes off the wall she snatched up a rock-hard plastic mug and bounced it off my noggin. It didn't break the bone, or even the skin, but it wasn't a sensation I enjoyed. Soon as I recovered my footing I backed out of the room, fast. Neither of us said a word until we were back in the elevator, heading somewhere below.

'Apples don't fall far from the tree,' I mumbled. She shook her head.

'Adopted,' Eulie said. 'Childhood friend's daughter, heard. Friend died postbirthing. Cancered. Father in absentia, dead.' She shrugged. 'Environment, heredity. Onesame.'

Thought it best to keep the talk light while we were still in hearing range of Sassy Sue. 'She's older than she looks?'

'Thirteen,' Eulie said. 'Figureheads, sole, installed by Madame. Dryco runs itself, or did until recent disruptions.'

'What disruptions?'

'We'll homeways now, Walter. You need knowing.'

'Homeways where?'

'My home.'

'Where's that? Up here in the clouds, somewhere –?'

'Jersey.'

So I was right, after all. As we plummeted down I still tried to get it through my head that the Pi had somehow been removed from my system; that none of this was a hallucination. I'd be just as glad, I thought, to get out of New York; because how much weirder could their Jersey be? Her place, as well. Taking another gander at those sad, glistening eyes of Eulie's, I felt that old springboard go. Forgive me for being so blunt, my brothers, but it was the only thing on my mind at that moment; that after months stuck in drydock, I thought I was finally going to get my chance to open the savoury bivalve. But I should have known better than that.

*   *   *

174

Even though I'd figured we'd hop another cab, once we popped back out into the free and clear I saw we were in a parking garage, same as any you've ever seen except that this one was shiny bathroom white. When cars drifted past us, looking more like bugs than krautwagons ever looked, I couldn't help but marvel at how quietly they ran.

'Oh,' Eulie said when I noted this, 'they're electric.'

After walking down a series of spirals we reached her car, a pathetic little runabout that looked like something FAO Schwarz'd sell to the Kennedy boys to put in their nephews' stockings. A pink bunion with Radio Flyer wheels is the only fair way to describe it. She must have been hauling pig iron in the trunk; the thing didn't sit five inches off the ground.

'What kind is it?'

'Stimray,' she said, waving her hands over the car's side. Nothing happened. She started pounding the roof till the doors came open.

'Double as a lawn mower?' I asked, squeezing myself inside. I could have rested my chin on my knees if the seat hadn't strapped me down so tight the second I sat down in it. While not a half hour earlier that would have probably made me jump up and run off screaming. I couldn't help but be aware of how quickly I was getting used to the way things worked out in the territories. Eulie pressed a sky-blue button on the floor with her foot and we slid out, gliding through the aisles until we emerged at what looked like the Harlem River – it was too narrow to be either the Hudson or the East. She edged the car along a narrow ramp running across the river and then onto a much bigger expressway, one that vaguely resembled the Cross-Bronx except that it had eight lanes, not eighteen, and ran across what must have been Manhattan. Bright green signs proclaimed it to be the Morrie Feldman Transitory.

175

I asked, of course. 'Unknown. Major Deegan, JoeDiMaggio. Who knows.'

'Who?' I asked, but her mind was on what lay ahead. Transitory, so-called; seemed more like a parking lot than a highway. For over a half hour we rolled slowly along, surrounded by six or seven thousand other cars the same size. There were also what looked like trucks, but they were twice as big as the ones I was used to; nearly as big as locomotive engines. Everybody tried to steer clear of those beasts; it'd be like a rowboat getting in the way of the *Queen Alexandra* if you changed lanes at the wrong moment.

The real breath-stopper, though, were the buses. From where we were I could count fifteen to twenty at any given moment. They were half the size of the trucks, but the people hanging onto the sides, and lying on the roof, sort of fattened them up. As we crept past them I could see that there were hand-holds and foot-ledges stuck all over the sides of the buses. The commuters must have been used to travelling this way; a lot of them were looking at tiny little movie players they wore strapped to their chests. As we crept up the ramp leading to the GW bridge – the bridge looked the same here as it did in my New York, except that here it was painted Army green – I saw one of the passengers on a bus some fifty feet ahead of us lose his footing, and tumble down into the traffic.

'Eulie,' l said, trying to see if he'd landed on a hood or something, but spotting neither hair nor hide, 'didn't you see that? He fell off. Shouldn't we stop?'

'Why?' she asked, genuinely puzzled. Four lanes to our right, I saw another commuter slip down between the lanes. As we continued across the bridge – moving a little faster by that point, maybe ten miles an hour – others came loose, here and there, from other buses, and I realized that this must be one of this place's drawbacks of commuting. Never saw one of them get up, once they fell. After a half hour more we reached the Jersey side, and by the time we passed under the Fort Lee exit sign I'd stopped counting.

'These people work in the city?'

'Workers and drones unhiving,' she said.

'What do they do? Office work?'

'Whatever's essentialled.'

She turned onto a six-lane highway that wasn't as crowded as the bridge had been; then, pulling onto another ramp, steered us onto the New Jersey Turnpike. This almost looked like home – fourteen big lanes, plenty of space, and everyone speeding along – except our turnpike wasn't walled off on either side by tall green and grey glass buildings. None of these buildings had any signs; none of them had any windows – the walls were glass, but you couldn't see in, and I felt safe in assuming that no one could see out.

'Where do you live?' I asked.

'Maplewood,'

'Wouldn't the tunnel have been closer?'

A blink, a stare: recognition. 'Tunnel's flooded.'

I looked over to my left. There weren't quite as many buildings along the road in this stretch, and I could catch glimpses of New York's taller buildings – the Empire State, notably, and several other taller, boxier towers. 'How's that possible?'

'Rising water table necessitated the shift north. Before my birthing.'

'Manhattan's flooded?'

'Here.'

'Eulie,' I said. 'It was my fault Chlojo was killed. If I hadn't –'

'If she didn't guard me,' she said. 'Six, half dozen, twelve either way.'

That was the last she said of her big friend; I supposed that it wasn't so much different from falling off a bus in the long run. The farther we got from New York the more there was to see, to a point, even though the sun – that is, the light that shone through the clouds – was going down. Most of it, however, looked about the same here as it did there – power lines, buildings, bits and pieces of what was left of the Meadowlands. If I didn't look too closely it almost seemed as if I was back where I came from, heading out to visit Newark or Jersey City. By now I'd been up close to thirty-odd hours, and I felt Morpheus starting to get the upper hand. Somewhere around the time Eulie made a right onto a new highway, I let him put me in a full nelson, and snoozed.

It had seemed like only a couple of minutes passed before I felt the car bumping up and down; it felt as if Eulie, for some reason, had decided to use the Erie-Lackawanna tracks the rest of the way home. When I opened my eyes it was twilight, and we were on local streets. Headlights were blue, streetlights were yellow, and, surprisingly, stoplights were red and green.

'Where *are* we?' I asked, looking out the window, instinctively reaching for the lock, though there didn't seem to be one.

'Maplewood,' Eulie said. Her face was pinkish in the dash's purple light.

'What happened to it?'

Eulie shook her head, and we stopped at a light as it turned red. A bug, or bird, hit the windshield; there was a bright colourless flash and a sizzling sound, and whatever it was, was gone. We were driving through a neighbourhood that must have been built in the teens or twenties – or would have been built then, on my turf – the kind with enormous old houses, and elm and chestnut trees on both sides of the street, and green lawns; cars in the driveways, and kids on the sidewalk. Eulie's Maplewood didn't look quite that respectable. Almost all the houses we passed – the ones still standing – were boarded up, or burned out. Some had

178

collapsed in on themselves, but in a few there were lights on in the parts that were still standing. Most of the trees along the streets we bumped along were stumps, or stubby, or even broken off halfway up. The yards were worn into dust, or blanketed with little cars. Everything in the neighbourhood looked like the white trash had been sharecropping too long without a foreman.

'This is a substandard area,' Eulie said, pulling out as the light changed to green; she must have seen the look on my face. 'I'm gated.'

I didn't have the faintest idea what she meant, and was just as glad. There wasn't anyone else on the street, whether walking or driving. If it weren't for the lights I saw in the houses I'd have assumed the entire state had been emptied out. In another five minutes or so we drove up to a high concrete wall that blocked the entire street. Although I thought she'd have to get out and walk over and touch it, she didn't; all she did was punch in some keys on the dashboard and a heavy metal gate in the middle of the wall rose, and we rolled through. Eulie's neighbourhood seemed never to have been as well-to-do, but it was in somewhat better shape – every house, and every yard, was surrounded by a high fence of some kind – wood, iron, chicken wire – and every wall was topped with rolls of sharpened wire. There were no cars parked on the street; the owners kept their vehicles in the driveway, within each fenced-off perimeter.

'Here we are,' she said, easing the car to the right. A beige metal gate opened as we rolled through it. She pressed a button and the car switched off. 'Home,' she said, removing the steering wheel. The doors of the car sprang open and, within five minutes, I'd extricated myself. Now that it was night I was beginning to see stars in the sky, when I looked to the west; the clouds were clearing off. In the direction of New York, the heavens were fiery-red. Eulie tapped in another code on a panel attached to the fence, and opened

179

the front door of her house. It was a little place, the equivalent of her car; there were four small rooms, but it felt comfortable. In her front room was a leather couch almost as long as the house, a low glass table; bookcases without books, a plant with blue and red leaves. On the wall facing the couch was what appeared to be a big grey mirror.

'I need changing,' she said. 'You've never seen TV?'

'What's that?'

'Television.'

I nodded, remembering her saying the word. 'I'm curious.'

She smiled. 'Catkiller.'

Once you got used to it, it was hard not to watch TV. Before heading into the shower Eulie showed me how the switcher worked and how to find the channels. She received four thousand and ninety-three; there were more, she said, but she didn't want to pay to bring in Asia, Africa, and Latin America. For the first few minutes, it was painful to watch; the programmes that came on the air were louder than any movie I'd ever seen, even after I turned down the volume; and the pictures came so fast and furious that I didn't see how anyone could make sense of what was shown. Then, suddenly, I got used to it. Watching TV was like watching a stew boil – you never knew what would suddenly come into view before sinking back down again. Eulie could have been in the shower for two weeks and I wouldn't have noticed. As I flipped through the channels, clicking them off, what I thought at first to be a black and white movie caught my eye, or rather my ear; I knew I'd heard the voices before. There were four people in a living room set, and as I listened I matched the voices to the faces I'd seen in radio guides. I was watching, stuck to the channel like glue, when Eulie strolled out of the shower, heavily towelled from top to bottom. '"I Love Lucy?"'

'I've heard this one before,' I said. 'Nothing looks like I pictured it.'

She pressed something on the table and a number appeared at the bottom of the screen. 'Livonia network. Show's almost a century old. How have you heard this?'

'It was on the radio,' I said. She turned it off. 'Hey, wait.'

Eulie unturbaned her head and shook her hair loose. 'You'll zone. You're already deadeyed.' Like her, I thought, but didn't say it. Once the set was off I heard the outer world again – beeping sounds that must have been sirens in the distance, whirling noises somewhere overhead, a low hum that never stopped. 'Quiet, finally. How are you?'

'Bearable,' I said. 'You?' She nodded. 'Why didn't you tell me you were from the future? It'd have been a hard sell, granted, but everything would have made a lot more sense a lot sooner –'

'It's more complicated than it seems,' she said. 'We're not from the future. Not your future, anyway.'

'Eulie, please –'

'If our world was yours, this might be your future, yes,' she said. 'But your world is different. Not just in look and feel. It's a different place, entirely.' She took something out of a pocket in one of her towels and ran it over her hair. As I looked, it dried. 'How explain that, simply?'

'I don't know. Give it a try, though –'

Even before she started I could have told her there wasn't any real point, but I liked the sound of her voice so much I just sat and listened. 'Our worlds coexist, separate but equal. You understand?'

'Which one gets the short end of the stick?'

'No, Walter, not like that. We don't exist in the same time. We're years ahead of you, or you're years behind. Depends on which side you're on.' She sat down on the couch next to me. 'There are different paths in the garden, and we're many paths later.'

There was nothing I could do but buy it. 'How do you get from one side to the other?'

'Holes in the fence, they've been called. Slip through, slip back.'

'Does Dryco have anything to do with it?' I asked, pretty much failing to get the idea, but giving her credit for trying.

'No, it tries to advantage the situation, but –'

'What does Dryco do, anyway?'

She looked at me as if I asked her why the sun was shiny. 'Everything.'

'If it's a company it must be a business,' I said. 'If it's a business it must make something. If it makes something, it must sell what it makes. So what does it do?'

'Dryco doesn't do. Dryco is.'

'Is *what?*'

'Lookabout,' Eulie said, and guided her hand in a wide circle, as if to take in the room, and everything that lay outside the house as well. 'All seen and unseen.'

'OK,' I said, trying a different tack. 'You said it runs itself, or did until recently. How?'

She took a deep breath, as if trying to remember. 'It replicates, organizes, controls, commodifies. Expands or impands as needed.'

'But how?'

'Until recent developments, under the guidance of Alice.'

'Is Alice the old lady?'

She shook her head. 'You know about computers?'

'You mean like Univac?' A second earlier, until I conjured up the deadeyes once again, she'd looked ten years earlier. 'Never mind. So Alice is the one wheeling, dealing, stealing –?'

'She was, until the manifestations began,' Eulie said. 'For forty years, communicating first through the Drydens, then Mister O'Malley, then through herself. Madam let her. Then,

182

four months ago, when the problems first evidenced, her systems began to negate. The day before yesterday, she blued.' She rested her head on my shoulder. 'That was when we came to get you.'

'Eulie,' I said, 'what's going on? What's happening?'

'Uncertain,' she said. 'Whatever it is, isn't good.'

'How so?'

'Indications specify that our worlds are starting to occupy the same time as well as the same space.' I'm sure she knew that some essential concepts eluded me, and so she tried to explain further, picking up what appeared to be a couple of small ceramic coasters from the table. 'Say each of these represent our respective worlds. Now say they are trying to be on the same place at the table at the same time.'

'One on top of the other,' I said.

She shook her head. 'Both touching the table in the same place.'

'How?' Again, she shook her head. 'It's not possible?'

'No.'

'What caused it?' I asked.

'Evidence of longtime disturbances in the field between. The initial breach between worlds, perhaps. The presence in the field of Jake, the person you've been seeing. Your ghost. He, and the woman he was with, were members of the second transitory group, following the first, thirty years ago. It's unclear why he continues to exist, or if his presence was the precipitory factor.'

She held her hands out in front of her, as if she herself didn't understand what she knew. 'He's not a ghost?' I asked.

'He is,' she said, 'but he isn't dead.'

Yellow lights flashed through the living room drapes, and for an instant I thought some kind of landing party was going to come crashing through the door and ask to see our passports. Nothing happened; I heard more beeping,

183

somewhere in the distance, and the sound of breaking glass. I picked up one of the coasters and looked at it. At first I'd thought it was ceramic; then, when I touched it, realized it was something else. 'What'll happen when both coasters touch the table at the same time?'

'Unforeseeable.'

'Will we still be here?'

'Something will,' she said. 'A third world, perhaps.'

'Will we be in it?'

'Unknowable.'

There wasn't much she had to add, and even little I could think of to ask. Maybe I was still under the influence of Pi; if so, I wasn't sure if this was a trip I wanted to come back from. All of a sudden I began to have a very hard time breathing. 'You got a back yard?' I asked. 'I need some fresh air.'

'There's interior recirculation.'

'Outside air,' I said. 'Please?'

'Of course,' Eulie said, standing. She walked down the hall towards what I gathered to be her bedroom, disappearing for a minute or two. While she was gone I spotted a few photos on the wall and gave them a look-see. Didn't spot anyone who might have been her father, or boyfriend; in one shot she stood on some kind of bridge with a dead-pale woman who looked her age. In another, Eulie didn't look older than ten or eleven – it was definitely her, the eyes gave her away. There was a different woman in that shot, one who looked maybe twenty or thirty years older. I turned away from them when Eulie reappeared; she'd put on a long white robe that closed in the front although it didn't have buttons or zippers.

'Your mother?' I asked, pointing at the photo. She nodded. 'Is she –'

Eulie looked at the picture as if trying to remember who either of them might have been. 'No. She sold herself.'

'Come again?'

'She sold herself,' Eulie repeated. 'For parts. Expenditure necessary if I was to college.'

'Parts?'

'Transplants. Back door's this way. Come, Walter.'

I nodded, and followed. The more questions I asked, the less I wanted to hear the answers. All I wanted for the moment was to stop long enough to let it all sink in. I'd forgotten any fears I'd had of what the Kennedys would do to me, or Bennett, or any of the other fools I'd been so preoccupied with, not two days earlier; and there was no need to worry about needing to get to Hawaii; I didn't think I could get any farther away from where I'd been than where I was now. Eulie unbolted three or four locks on the back door and we stepped outside into the dark. A cool breeze blew; helicopters flew over, shining searchlights down on the ground. I heard people shouting, on the next street over. A high board fence surrounded her tiny yard – her lot couldn't have been more than twenty feet wide, and not quite thirty feet long. The black silhouettes of surrounding houses poked up on all sides. I looked up; the stars I was able to make out looked to be in roughly the same place as the ones I was used to – not that I'd really seen any for a while, New York not being the optimum place to get into astronomy. The moon was there, and full. I saw the Gibson girl outlined in its surface facing left; just the way I'd have seen her back home. 'You have moon cities there?'

'Last man who walked on the moon died twenty years ago.' She looked at me, not the moon. 'Walter,' she said, 'Do you want to go back, or stay here?'

I smiled. 'What'd the first man on the moon say, once he got there?'

She looked blank for a moment; then giggled, trying to remember and realizing she couldn't. Then it came to her. I guessed it was something she'd been told back in second grade.

'"One step for man," she said. '"Two for mankind."'

Then, she kissed me. We held each other so tight that I think each of us was trying to blend into the other one, that we could somehow jump into each other's worlds and stay there. When at last I came up for air I looked at her, and she looked happier than I'd ever seen her; and I knew where I was going to be sleeping that night at least.

'I want to stay here,' I said. 'I'm getting used to it quicker than I thought I would.'

At that moment I think I was about as happy as I'd ever been. But then before I could kiss her again I saw her expression change; her eyes widened, as if she were seeing something that she'd always known she'd have to see one day, however much she didn't want to see it – the minister coming up the walk, the doctor with the chart, the angel at the gate. I stepped away from her, still holding onto her waist, just moving off far enough to turn around and see what she saw. In the western part of the sky (for all I knew, here, it might have been in the east) there was what appeared to be the thin white tail of a comet, stretching across the bowl of the sky, reaching unbroken from one side to the other. When I first saw it, the line seemed to be fixed, and steady; but as I kept my eyes on its narrow course, I saw it slowly beginning to widen.

'Walter,' she said, 'we may not have a choice.'

NINE

Throughout most of the rest of the night, while Eulie shook those little black boxes of hers out of her bag, diddled their absence of knobs, and made phone calls, I lay on her couch and found myself making my acquaintance with the dream world as I found it on her side of the aisle. Truth be told, and I'm truthing now, I've never been much ridden by nightmares, at least not of the sort that come during sleep, but that night I suffered a series that grew progressively worse. First I saw figures standing, covered in white sheets, no holes cut out for eyes; they were talking to me, but I didn't cop the plea they wanted to hear and they started piling on like blankets, suffocating me underneath. Then, nothing; then my father, sitting at the kitchen table back in our house on Queen Anne Hill, reading the newspaper. The headlines were large, but I couldn't read them. On the floor, near his feet, was our dog, a small mixed breed, like us; although it was disembowelled it was still alive, and tried to lick itself. Another pause; then I imagined that I lay on her couch, and tried to rise as a black form took shape inside my chest – first it was a square, then it became a circle, then a square again, increasing in size every time until I could see the points sticking out between my ribs. Relief; and then came the worst. I dreamed I was an island, my friends, an island at night, surrounded by ocean. Tiny Arabian pirates were trying to land on my shores, jabbing tiny iron hooks into my skin, jabbering and hollering and poking away. That was more than I could bear, and I shocked myself awake, drenched in cold sweat.

'Twelve nine seven four,' I heard Eulie saying. 'Five seven three three one –'

Reading aloud some list of numbers, I inferred, blinking myself into fuller consciousness; wondered why she was standing in the middle of the front room talking to herself until I remembered what she'd shown me last night, that this was how she made telephone calls. I supposed she was yammering on to superiors or inferiors somewhere else about the silver thread on high, seeing if they understood what it might signify. Every so often she'd pause and walk down the hall, or into the kitchen – she'd explained to me that there was so much titanium in the walls of her house that she had to shift around regularly, or else she'd lose the connection. Her phone apparatus was in her head, somehow; and all she had to do to get on the party line was to say the number and she'd be hooked up immediately. This seemed no more peculiar than anything else she'd told me; she said that the only time taking calls got tricky was when more than four came in at the same time. She didn't tell me how she put them on hold.

When I hauled myself off the couch I could tell that it was nearly dawn. Murky aquarium light seeped through the front room's bamboo shades. While Eulie carried on I wandered down the hall until I found the bathroom. The toilet told me where to aim – I could imagine that might be useful at times – and flushed itself, after I was finished; while I wouldn't have minded taking a shower, I didn't see anything inside the stall that looked like faucets, and it was only too easy to picture myself getting steamed like a lobster without even blinking. There were postcards stuck onto the wall of the bathroom

– photos of Italy, and of a painting by Modigliani, and a picture of kittens playing with yarn. Curious, I pulled back the corner of one to take a look at the postmark, but there wasn't any.

Eulie was in the kitchen, standing by the window and running her fingers over one of her boxes when I came back out. 'Blixamixa wooblegone,' she was saying, something like that; she'd returned to what I gathered must have been her native tongue, that impenetrable blend occasionally enlivened by recognizable words – 'badger,' or 'work,' or 'shit.' She stood by the kitchen window, running her fingers over one of the little boxes. She pointed to a round chrome ball with a black handle and stuck a small white package marked Kaftast in my hand. There was a cup nearby, and I made the necessary connections. Emptied the package into the cup, poured the hot water in after it. Nothing like good strong coffee, I thought; Nature's best amphetamine and brain clearer. I read the ingredients but wished I hadn't – one was soy powder, and nicotinamide another, and there was something just after the ingredient 'coffee enhancement' called Manipulated Fiberic. The stuff looked like coffee, smelled like coffee, even tasted like coffee – kind of – but it had a distinctly noticeable aftertaste, though it was hard to say exactly what – vitamins, pork, lime Jell-O; couldn't really tell.

'Walter,' Eulie said to me, 'televise if desired.'

I nodded, but before I went into the living room I took a peek out the window, looking up. The sky was overcast again, nothing but thick grey clouds except for where the white line ran; it was wider now, more of a hawser rope than a thread. As impossible to see where it began or ended as a rainbow. I glanced over at Eulie; she shook her head, and kept talking.

When I touched the TV screen it came on. Picking up the switcher I started running through the channels; it didn't take that long, as about three-quarters of them appeared to be on the blink – at least they were showing nothing but a screen as

189

grey as the sky, a burble of movement sometimes breaking up the stillness of the image. The stations that were on did seem to be keeping their eye on the sky. I turned on the volume and listened, but can't say I was much enlightened. The places that showed up, besides New York, were identified as London, Moscow, Shanghai, so forth, but every place looked so much alike that for all I could tell they just kept using the same backdrop to save money. In between the travelogues, on top of them sometimes, men and women would be coming on to blow hot and cold, and sounding no more understandable than Eulie did when she consulted with her own experts. I couldn't help but wonder if anyone understood them. The only thing I could be sure of was that they were all talking about the thing in the sky; every minute or so, there'd be another shot of it, and it always looked the same. Struck me as very odd that no matter where they were supposed to be broadcasting from, it was cloudy. The line seemed wider over some places – Rio, for one; Calcutta, for another – than it did where we were. Or maybe it had simply widened just in the time I'd spent watching. As said, once you park yourself in front of one of these things it's just about impossible to drag yourself away; but one by one, over the course of just a few minutes, all the stations took on that full-tilt grey tone, and went off the air. I heard Eulie saying a recognizable word, over and over again, in the kitchen.

'Hello? Hello?' A long pause. '*Hello?*'

'I'm here,' I piped up. She walked back into the living room, past me, and over to the front door. Throwing it open, she stepped outside into her small concrete front yard. I came up behind her, and slipped my arms around her waist. She didn't pull away. 'What's up?'

She didn't turn around to look at me; but kept her eyes focused on high, on that long, broadening stripe. It seemed to lie on top of the clouds, but I didn't see how that could be possible; as I squinted my eyes and gave it a closer onceover, though, I could see that the clouds were simply vanishing as the line touched them – that the line was, in fact, something that nearly seemed solid. 'All readings confirm theory,' she said, turning and stepping back inside.

'That means –'

'Spatial displacement, as I tried to detail last night.'

'It's happening now?' I asked. She nodded. 'So what's happening to us?'

'We're –'

Eulie stopped dead in the middle of her word as if she'd suddenly choked on something. She fisheyed the table and I looked over to scope what brought her up short. The coasters she'd been using, trying to explain what was happening; none of them were touching the table, contrary to her theory. All floated slightly above the surface of the glass, and I couldn't figure out what kind of magical trick was making them levitate.

'Godness,' Eulie said. 'Walter, we've got to go. Fast. You're ready?'

'Anytime,' I said, yawning. 'Go where?'

'Your place, if possibled.'

'No,' I said. 'No, why?'

'Come on,' she said, snatching up her bag and grabbing my arm, almost yanking it off as she pulled me out the front door. She had a grip like Chlojo's when she chose to use it, I could tell. Streetlights were going on and off as if somebody was playing with the switch, and it sounded like half the people in the neighbourhood had decided to start honking their horns. She pounded at the side of her car, but the doors refused to open.

'What's happening, Eule?' I asked, hearing the oddest sound behind me; as if someone was peeling labels off cardboard packages, lots of them. 'Eulie?' Turning to see what was making the racket, my brothers, I don't have to tell you what kind of notions went through my head when

I saw the paint on her little house literally stripping itself off the clapboards, and floating up into the air like ash, or dandelion fluff. *'Fuck –!!!'* I shouted, forgetting my manners; as I've never been one to use the vernacular around ladies.

'Follow, Walter,' she said, pushing open the front gate; at least it didn't seem to lock from the inside. 'We have to position ourselves if we can chance. Come on.'

When I touched the metal I felt an electric shock, but nothing too severe. Once we were out on the sidewalk she fumbled through her bag until she found a long flat blue rectangle, not much thicker than a chequebook. Flipping it open she looked at the inside top while running her hand over the inside bottom. If I shifted my head into the right angle I could just catch what she was looking at – some kind of map, with green lines, I thought – but couldn't tell what she did with her fingers. 'Five blocks that way, Walter. There's a park. Run.'

'What are we running to?' I asked as I started to let my feet do their stuff. 'What's happening? Eulie –?'

'Run, Walter,' she shouted, taking the lead, 'life depends. Our life.'

I didn't have to look up anymore to see the white line; it was directly in front of us, somewhere between ten and a thousand miles away. It was really starting to open up now; what was apparent in daylight was that it didn't quite reach the horizon – it stopped just short of the treeline, so I couldn't exactly see where it came to a halt. Thing was, I could tell that it wasn't just widening, but lengthening as well, getting closer to the tops of the trees and the houses. Every horn in New Jersey sounded as if it were going off, every air-raid siren, every civil defence signal, every ambulance bell. Eulie's neighbours poured out of their houses, trying to get their own cars started; I saw that some were trying to cut their way through their fences, or climb over – those were the ones whose gates must have kept them locked in. The air felt heavy, and full of electricity. The clouds were starting to swirl now, as if they were being mixed from above. A tornado, I thought, but there was no wind. I didn't hear any birds, but when I thought about it, as I raced on, feeling my heart pound as I kept up with my little one, I remembered that I hadn't heard any real birds since getting here; it occurred to me that they probably didn't have any.

'Walter,' Eulie shouted back, slowing enough to let me catch up with her and then taking my hand so she could help me move at her pace. 'Left here. That park, over there. It's windowed. Hurry.'

'Eule,' I panted, 'what's happening?'

'When the breach underhorizons,' she said, nodding at the white gash in the sky, 'that times it. Walter, hurry.'

A few minutes more and we reached the park, a small strip of green running through the middle of Maplewood, at the bottom of the hill that led up to her house. We were surrounded on all sides now by people running, shouting; where they were heading, nobody knew, but I guessed that was as good a way to spend the time they had left as any. The screams in the air made me think of the last game in the Series the year before, Dodgers versus Yankees. Brooklyn won. No time for hot dogs here, though. Breaking loose of the crowd Eulie and I dashed into the park, stumbling through bushes, nearly running into a bench. A stream ran through the centre of the green; the water looked as if it were starting to boil.

'Here!' Eulie said, coming to a dead stop in the midst of a sloping meadow. She knelt down, throwing her green thing back into her bag and starting to look for something else. I heard thunder, but saw no lightning. I watched this part of the town of Maplewood running toward Milburn. Eulie took out a small metal box the size of a cigarette pack. This one had a visible button, round and blue and located dead centre at the top. A thin red bar was inset along the side of the box. 'Your world evidences no changes. We're safe there, momento.'

'What if this happens over there, later?' She shook her head. 'Dryco can't do anything?'

'Nada,' she said. 'Not anymore. Dryco's going. Gone.'

My head began to sting, as if someone were plucking at it with needles; as I watched Eulie slide a small red bar along the side of the little box, I understood where the pain was coming from. Our electrified hair was being pulled out, one at a time; I saw Eulie's wriggling like thin worms as they drifted skyward.

'Walter,' she said. 'I'm uncertain if transience remains workable. If not –'

'We won't be worse off than we are.'

'Ready yourself,' she said, looking off toward the west. As the white line drew closer to the earth its colour, nearest the ground, began to change. From white it darkened into something of a lemony yellow; then deepened further into Halloween orange. As the line dropped, the orange turned into firetruck red, and then into a deep predawn purple. The orgone in the sky shimmered, waved, seemed ready to catch fire; red halos flared up around everything in sight – trees, people, cars. There came a roar as if from underneath the earth, far below; as it grew louder and louder I saw blades of grass pulling out of the ground, sailing into the air; leaves fell upward from the trees, and then the trees themselves began to rise, their roots churning and tearing the earth apart into great clumps as they heaved loose of their footing. Nails pulled out of the boards in the park benches, and both flew into the air. The bricks of chimneys came apart, the roofs of cars, the laundry on lines. The sky was filling up fast with all the pieces of the world – kitchen utensils, shingles, bicycles, clothing, slices of bread, trash cans, twigs, frogs, dogs, children. Everything floated up more slowly than you'd have expected, as if being drawn towards the now rainbowed split. Just as we found ourselves beginning to lift off from her world, just before the split came up against it, Eulie pressed the button.

'Godness, enshield –'

'Valentine –!!'

We both saw the flash, but neither felt nor heard it; we shut out eyes, and when I opened them again we were back in that place between, where all was flat and white and silent. This time I knew that what I felt or didn't feel, was genuine, and not merely Pi-induced tactile sensation, and marvelled at how still everything had become, so suddenly. I was still holding onto Eulie's hand, but wouldn't have known that I was, had I not been looking at her. She looked back at me; smiled. For several moments we floated there, silent, at peace. I wondered why my ghost, that poor fellow trapped within, had never come to like it. Honestly, it seemed more like being on the ultimate horse trip than anything else – this gizmo of hers was definitely something to keep out of the paws of junkies. All at once it seemed to me that we were coming in for a landing. Eulie's mouth began to move, and though I couldn't hear her yet, I knew it'd be only a matter of seconds.

'Walter!!' she shouted as we came through. 'Hold!!'

'Holding!!!'

This being the second time I'd taken this particular train, I thought I knew what to expect when we came out on the other side; but actually I wasn't surprised when I felt myself rolling, with Eulie, down a long hill towards what looked like an expressway. We came to a stop long before reaching the shoulder, however, and for several minutes lay there catching our breath. Something fell on us and I looked to see what; tiny silver fish, sardines or minnows or sand dabs. Their rain didn't last long, and they flopped around in the grass, lips gasping, before saying uncle. While I didn't feel as if I were going to upchuck, this time around, most every part of my body felt as if someone had gone over it with a sharp rock.

Staring up, I saw red brick apartment buildings lining the top of the hill; rolling over, I saw that it was an expressway, the Jimmy Walker. We'd come out in the Bronx. Best of all, when I looked straight up, into the sky, I saw nothing but bright blue – safe again, I thought; thought it until I remembered why we'd had to leave so quickly in the first place, and why I was getting ready to leave, even before that. First things first, though. I reached over, and touched Eulie's hand. She lifted her head, shook the dust off, and stared first at the expressway and then at me.

'OK?' I asked.

'AO.'

After some small struggle we made our way back up to the top of the hill, and climbed over the fence onto the sidewalk. We were both still dizzy; going from her place to mine seemed to produce some semblance of a hangover. Just when I started to think that I hoped I'd never have to go through transfer like that again, I realized that that possibility had been pretty much ruled out. We walked down to 178th Street and headed toward the Concourse, to catch the IND downtown. Neither of us said much for the first few blocks. As we walked past multitudes of Bronxers – young women with strollers, kids tossing balls back and forth, old men with small dogs; firemen, plumbers, beauticians, deli clerks – I tried to figure out what, exactly, had happened; Eulie seemed lost in her own thoughts, as you'd expect, and I didn't want to interrupt her with foolish questions on my part until she gave me some indication she was ready to hear.

A short distance from the subway entrance, Eulie left her world, and returned to mine. 'Walter, are you still capable?'

'Of anything,' I said. 'What happened?'

She gave me the old thousand yard stare, and pulled at her lower lip with her fingers; she'd bitten it, though the cut had closed over. 'We couldn't theorize which world would remain,' she said. 'Yours, it seems.'

'I'm sorry,' I said. 'Yours –?'

'Nada,' she said. 'Remarkable experience of spatial displacement. Any number of theories–' Although for a second or two she'd brightened, maybe with the thought of scientific papers to be written, she appeared to realize that she might have a hard time peddling them over here. She started to cry, and I guided her to a bench at a bus stop. An old lady taking up half the seat scooted over enough to let us sit down. 'Walter, excuse –'

'I know,' I said, although in fact I hadn't the foggiest idea of how you'd feel, being the only survivor of your entire world. It was a feeling she didn't seem to be getting used to very quick.

'Walter –'

'Yes?'

'Because it hasn't happened here yet doesn't mean it won't,' she said. 'Fluxation continues. If anything the situation's instability is heightened. I've no way of telling, however.' She reached into her bag and took out one of her little black boxes. 'The connection's gone. Worthless, all. There's no way of telling, Walter –'

'We'll burn that bridge when we come to it.' I said, realizing that every minute or so I was still looking up, hoping that I wouldn't see that tell-tale crack starting to take shape. As before, all above us was bright and clear. 'Are you really all right? I mean physically. That was a pretty rough landing –'

'Chlo and I always came through in Central Park,' she said. 'But our departure site was fixed. It could have been rougher.' I gave her a kleenex I found in my jacket pocket; she dabbed her eyes dry. 'Are you all right?'

'Dizzy. Feel like I've broken half my bones. Worn out. Otherwise, perfect.' I stood, and offered my arm. 'I've got

197

to lie down somewhere. Both of us do. I think we'll be safe, heading down to my place.'

'You're sure?'

'I think the only person anybody'd remember from the Astor would be Chlo,' I said, 'and I guess they won't be taking her in.'

'What about your superior?'

'Inferior, more like it,' I said, thinking of how Bennett had managed to land feet first; wondering what kind of tricks he'd managed to play in my absence – it came to me that I didn't even know how long I'd actually been gone; it seemed no more than a day and a half, but the weather in the Bronx, at least, seemed a vast improvement over what it'd been when we fled the coop. 'Maybe I'd better check in with Martin. Get a line on what's what.'

There was a newstand next to the subway entrance, and I sidled over to see if I could read the date below the mastheads. Must have been nothing but a warm spell; the date was as I figured it to be. But what I hadn't expected to see were the particular headlines plastered across the front of the *News*, the *Trib*, the *Mirror*, the *Times*.

BLAME BOOZE, CLAIMS BOBBY

'Walter,' Eulie asked as I laid down fifty cents and gathered up a copy of each. 'What troubles?'

KENNEDY VICTIM STILL IN COMA
Recovery Uncertain
Insanity Plea Believed Likely

Robert Kennedy Rules Out Run This Year
'FAMILY FIRST' EX-CANDIDATE STATES

JIM SLEEPS
Mirror Foto Exclusive
REAGAN: LIKE FATHER, LIKE SON

'*Kennedys*,' I shouted, pounding my fists against the nearest streetlamp post. People slowed down to see if I was going to completely wig out, but when I didn't, they continued on their way. 'Damned Kennedys. Every last damned one of them –'

'Walter –'

'I hear you, brother,' some cheerful Republican shouted over to me, not breaking stride. 'This fixes Bobby's wagon but good.'

Before heading into the subway I made two calls – there was no need to call Jim; he wouldn't be at home. Biting the bullet, I dropped my dime and told the operator to place a collect call, person to person, to Martin. After a moment or so a voice I didn't recognize came on the line.

'Walter Smith?'

'Speaking,' I said. 'Is Martin there –?'

'We've been waiting to hear from you,' the stranger said.

'Is he there?'

A pause; for some reason, I thought that he was trying to stifle a laugh. 'He's in the field. He expected your call, though, and left word to notify –'

'I need to talk to him, sooner the better.'

'Yes, certainly. Your directions are to go to your usual contact point, and wait there.'

Go home, in other words. That was fine with me. I made one last call, to Trish. As I feared, she wasn't around either. When I hung up I looked around, quickly, to be sure no one was paying too close attention to me. No; everyone in sight looked as innocent, or as guilty, as anyone in New York ever does.

'Let's go,' I told Eulie, and we headed downstairs to catch the train to Manhattan.

When we got off the train and came up the stairs I couldn't help but check the sky again; not a thing. We walked over from Sixth Avenue, making for my crib. As it had been my turn to clam, I hadn't said a word to Eulie the whole trip down. The events of the past two – three? – days burned in my mind. There was really only one thing I wanted to do, after talking to Martin and trying to find out what hospital Trish was in, and that was dig out that perma-bud Chlo had left me – willed me, as it turned out – and send myself (and Eulie, if she wanted to join in) into a four-day spin. I'd had enough of both worlds; had enough of people. My ire thickened in my throat; I might have finally let go all the way, had Eulie and I not seen what we saw, moments after walking underneath the El and stepping onto my block.

There was an old sportster wearing a seersucker suit walking toward us, leading his wirehaired terrier on a long black leash. I'd seen him around before – thought he lived on 19th, in one of the old townhouses – and would have at least nodded, out of habit, but he was gone before we reached him. One second he was there, and then in the next second he was gone; he'd been replaced. He turned into a young woman in her twenties, wearing a Yankees cap, her blonde hair pulled through the opening in the back and tied in a ponytail. She wore a sleeveless guinea T and dancer's black tights. On her feet she wore the fanciest-looking sneakers I ever saw. The wires for her hearing aid ran from her ears down to her waist. She trotted past us, looking neither right nor left; if I hadn't stepped out of her way, I think she'd have run right into me.

'Eulie –'

'Seen.'

We stood there for a minute or so, frozen in place as

200

we watched her turn the corner at Third and head south. 'What happened? Eulie, who was that? What happened to the old coot?'

'Unknown,' she said, wide-eyed. Both of us glanced upward; nothing, still, but blue sky. When we returned our gaze to the sidewalk ahead of us, we watched three dented metal garbage cans turn into a pile of black plastic bags filled with something that didn't seem to be sand; they barricaded the sidewalk, safeguarding it from Eighteenth Street traffic. A pair of pigeons poked along the curb, filling up on seed some kind soul had dumped for them. One turned into a sparrow, and flew away.

'Let's get inside,' I said, hurrying her along to my building's stoop. 'Quick.'

'Walter, something's happening –'

'I know. I don't want to know what, yet.'

We made it up the stairs much quicker than I figured we would; nothing within my building changed – the dark wainscotting still lined the walls up to where the painted tin began, there were still white tile swastikas embedded in the scuffed red of the ground floor hall – but somehow the look of everything seemed just as frightening as it had started to seem, outside. We didn't pass any of my neighbours on our way up; whether they were inside their apartments, or somewhere around the corner, I wondered if they were still themselves. The humidity was terrible, that afternoon; we were sweating buckets by the time we got to my floor. I had my keys out and ready, and was about to shove them into the locks when someone opened the door for us.

'Well, well, well,' Bennett said, sitting in my chair, at my kitchen table, one foot propped up on the stove as if he owned the place. 'Here's our wandering boy now.'

Before we could step back out the doorman, a fairly hulking bruiser wearing Secret Service glasses and with the look of Agency muscle about him seized both Eulie and myself, dragging us inside. Bennett was looking up at a sign I'd nailed up over the door leading to the music room, one I'd found hung on the fence at Tompkins Square the year before. NO LEFT TURNS UNSTONED.

'You're a card, Walter,' he said, evidencing a fine case of the smirks. 'A regular card.'

'Can't say I'm as pleased to see you as you are to see me, my brother,' I said. 'Any special occasion for this break-in?'

'Where were you, anyway? We looked high and low.'

'You'd never look high enough.'

Another big grin flashed in our direction. Off in the music room I heard the sound of crunching, as if someone were eating celery. Sartorius stepped out of the room, one of my discs in his Nazi mitt. From ten feet away I could see the Paramount label. Holding it out in front of him – farsighted, no doubt, but to admit the need for glasses would have been a sign of inferiority – he read aloud the pertinent information. '*Sugar Tin Blues*. Charles Patton. This is your American Negro music?'

'Yes. Put it down.'

He lobbed it discus-like across the room; when it struck the wall just above the sink, that was the end of Charlie.

'When the performers are gone,' he said, 'why should there be music?'

'And I figured you spent all your money on drugs,' Bennett said.

I craned my neck and managed to glimpse what remained in the music room. Every shelf was emptied; the floor was several inches deep in shattered shellac and black wax. Sartorius's footsteps crunched as if on fresh-fallen snow.

'So Walter, have you seen the papers?' Bennett asked. 'I know you don't usually pay much attention but I thought this morning's headlines might have caught your eye.'

'Get out of my house,' I said. 'I told you I quit. I –'

'Oh, shut up,' he said. 'I have to hand it to you, though. Mission accomplished with a minimum of bloodshed.' Clearly he didn't know about the Astor; not that it mattered, at this point. 'Bobby out of the running, thanks to his poor little brother. Didn't come off quite the way Hamilton had planned, but effective enough in its own way. Congratulations.'

'He hurt Trish, didn't he?' I asked. 'My friend. What did he do to her?'

Sartorius smiled. Another one of their attendants wandered through the music room from the front, stopping directly behind Sartorius. 'That's the one sad aspect of the whole situation,' Bennett said. 'But when Kennedys are involved, the innocent always suffer. Although from what we know about your friend, we feel fairly sure she led him on. Certainly she was the one who convinced him to fall off the wagon.' Bennett put his foot back down on the floor. 'Fell pretty hard, I'd have to say.'

'Where is she?'

'Lenox Hill,' he said. 'Don't know if she'll come out of it, though. The other one never did. This time around there was a little more press, of course. We made sure of that.'

'Where's Martin?' The bruiser had such a grip on Eulie that I thought he was going to break her arm; she stayed remarkably calm, considering. For the first time since I'd seen her, I'd have been very happy if Chlo had been able to come along for this ride.

'Oh, him,' Bennett said. 'Martin chose to resign his position. The department requested that he resign, I should say. Certain records turned up.' He made with the tut-tuts. 'Very disconcerting. You just never know who's who if you're not careful. Don't worry about him, Walter. As far as I know, he's probably getting used to his new home.'

'Bennett –'

'He played a little fast and loose when he hired freelancers, after all. Now that I've taken over his responsibilities, there'll have to be some changes made.'

'What kind of changes?'

'You've covered your tracks very well, Walter,' he said. 'Nothing, nowhere. But we just have that feeling. You know how

203

it is.' He looked at Eulie, whose face remained expressionless. 'As for your friend here, her status is clear as the nose on her face.'

Sartorius and the two thugs accompanying them laughed.

'You know a little more than we'd like you to know,' Bennett said. 'So –'

He reached into his jacket pocket and extracted a small bottle and a plastic case; when he opened the case, a hypodermic lay gleaming in the slot. 'You've never been much of one for narcotics in the pure sense, have you?' he asked, slipping the needle into the apparatus. 'This is about as pure as heroin gets. Medical quality. This should do both of you fine. When your bodies are found, I doubt that anyone will be surprised. Walter, don't look at me like that. I'd think you'd appreciate my thoughtfulness in selecting a style of exit that fits you best.'

'I'm not looking at you like that,' I said.

'What then?' he asked, stabbing the needle into the top of the bottle's cap. I gestured, slightly, towards the wall behind him. Where it had been covered completely with chipped and cracked yellow plaster, it had now been stripped down to the bare brick. I'd also gotten a new refrigerator during the previous second or two; this one was four times as large as the one I'd had, made of what looked to be burnished chrome. When he glanced behind him he looked as bumfuzzled as Sartorius and the thug standing behind him. I felt the one holding us loosen his grip, slightly, but not enough to allow us to get away. For the first time in his life, Bennett seemed at a loss for words.

'Walter,' Eulie said, shaking her head at the music room. Looking over, I spotted my ghost, still on his own. At the first moment I saw him he appeared as crystalline as he always had, floating some few inches above my broken records. Though Eulie was seeing him, I couldn't tell if the others had spotted old see-through yet. That would happen soon enough, I knew. As we watched he began to fill with colour. His jacket and pants took on the dirty-white look I'd seen when I'm glimpsed him

204

between worlds; his hair turned brown, his skin took on a pinkish tone. At last I saw his shoes; they were black as a 78. It didn't take him more than ten seconds to solidify; the moment he did, they all saw him. I felt the bruiser behind us let go as he thrust his hand into his jacket. Bennett dropped both bottle and needle as he backed up against the sink. Sartorius blinked, once; his associate wasn't able to do that much before Jake, back in a world he knew, if not his own, made his move.

'*Scheiss –!!*'

It quickly became clear to me where Chlo had learned her stuff. Even as the man behind us fired, striking him in the shoulder, Jake lifted his right foot above his head and swung his left arm out toward Sartorius. The thug in the music room fell backwards, a huge red blot in the centre of his face where his nose had been – it appeared – kicked directly into his brain. Sartorius sank toward the floor, clutching his crushed throat; Jake's fingers must have caught him right on the adam's apple. I started to think Jake was upholstered in the same coating Chlo wore until I saw his jacket's shoulder turn red. As he grabbed Sartorius by the forelock, slamming his German noggin against the new refrigerator, cracking it like an egg, Jake picked up the unbroken half of one of my records and winged it past my head. I felt something warm on the back of my neck as the thug behind me relaxed his grip, and as I turned I saw him trying to pull the record out from beneath his chin; it was slippery, and he couldn't get a solid grip. It was fascinating, watching my ex-ghost do what he was clearly best at; everything seemed as slow-moving as it had been under the influence of Pi, and I couldn't help but think I was having some kind of breathtaking flashback. The one behind us managed to get off another shot as he collapsed, striking Jake directly in the stomach; he leapt into the air towards Bennett, trailing streams of red and yellow. He caught my would-be druggist by the collar with one hand, picked up my cheese grater with the other; raked it across Bennett's face, slowing him down long enough until Jake could take my corkscrew and

205

plunge it directly into B-boy's temple. He twisted, as if seeing what might come out.

I huddled with Eulie, crouching in the corner. Jake stood in front of us for a second or two as if admiring his handiwork, holding his stomach. Bright and dark red blood oozed between his trembling fingers. When he looked at us he smiled; terrible teeth, but they didn't seem to bother him.

'Thank you,' he whispered; paused there for a second, and then fell backwards, landing heavily upon the floor.

'Eule,' I said, wondering if anyone could hear me. 'You there?'

She nodded, and squeezed my hand in hers. As thrilling as it had been to watch, the moment it was over I began feeling as if I was going to shoot every cookie I had. Both of us stared at the five bodies on the floor. I heard doors opening elsewhere in my building, and footsteps. As we looked on, the corkscrew in Bennett's temple vanished, replaced by what appeared to be a professional chef's meat thermometer.

'Let's go,' both of us said. Stepping over Jake's leavings, we made it out into the hall, pushing past the old lady who lived upstairs from me. We'd made the third floor landing before she began to scream. We ran into no one else before we got outside; and the moment we hit the sidewalk we took off toward Third Avenue, toward the El. I didn't hear any sirens yet, but they'd be starting up soon enough. I was amazed by how much wind power I had left, considering. As we got close to Third I heard a train's brakes grinding against the rails as it slowed, pulling into the 18th Street station. With luck, I thought, we'd be able to barrel upstairs and get on, whichever direction it was heading. That didn't happen, however; for just before we reached the stairs leading up to the station, they disappeared – the stairs, the train, the El itself; all gone, just like that.

'Walter –'

'I know.'

We both looked up, and saw the same benign blue sky. As

206

we lowered our heads we watched the tenements at the corner, fully visible for the first and only time, vanish; at once it was supplanted by some white-brick thing with sashless windows, fifteen storeys taller. I glimpsed the light changing from orange to blue, and then to red; and then to green.

'It's happening here, too,' I said. 'But it's different –'

'Walter,' she said, 'walk. Don't run.'

'Shouldn't we –?'

'As you note, it's different.' She took my hand, and deliberately slowed our pace to a gentle amble. 'I'm tired of running.'

So was I; we stopped long enough to catch our breath, and watch what ensued. No one appeared to notice, or mind, anything that was happening – and there were considerable transformations in progress. We continued on, towards Park Avenue. The long *whirrr* of a siren turned, as we listened, into a *whoop whoop whoop*. Two little girls played hopscotch in front of a small, basement-level dry cleaner's. The little girls disappeared, as did the dry cleaner's, replaced by what appeared to be some kind of restaurant; Vietnamese, of all things. As we crossed Park, heading toward Broadway, I remembered the vision I'd had months earlier, of a New York that looked neither like mine nor like Eulie's, and began to think that I'd caught a premonition of what was to be: Fortean phenomena, once more working its wiles upon the unexpecting. She put her arm around my waist as we walked, and I returned the favour. This was about the most remarkable high I'd ever enjoyed. At Broadway there was still a newsstand; now it was freestanding, at the curb, and not attached to the side of the cafeteria. There was no *Sun*, or *Mirror*, or *Trib*; the *Times* and *News* and *Post* remained. A red and blue mailbox attached to a streetlight post at the corner disappeared; the post itself changed from green metal to matte aluminium. The cars in the street changed, turning into the small coupes and oversized station wagons I'd seen so briefly earlier. A piece of paper blew across the curb, coming to rest at my feet. *Hot dog stand*, it read.

Just before we reached Fifth Avenue, we both came to a stop; while I remained the same inside, I could feel something beginning to happen on the exterior. I'd never seen Eulie look as calm as she now did. 'Where are we going?' I asked.

'I don't know,' she said. 'We'll be there, wherever it is.'

She began to fade from the sidewalk up. Although I didn't feel myself disappearing, I knew without looking that the same was happening to me. She looked no more scared than I felt. I can't remember, precisely, what was going through my mind; it was as if my memories were being replaced as well, although the new ones were mine all the same as my old ones. I remembered different teachers, back in Seattle; different friends, different houses. No one noticed our transformations; they were changing as well, into a third world, one we always seemed to have known, even as we discovered it. I'm not sure what there was left to see of us after a few moments more; at that point, my brothers, with smiles on our faces, we were going, going, go

When I opened my eyes she was there, lying next to me.

Rain drummed against the window with child's fingers, and as I lay in bed I listened to the soothing *swuussbbb* of cars as they slowly swung down Southern Street's hill. Tankers' foghorns echoed through the air across Puget Sound.

Then I heard Eulie say, 'Love you.' She slid her arm under my neck, and shifted her weight until she pressed directly against me, pulling up the covers until we were buried wholly beneath them. We kissed. After a few minutes of kissing, we made love.

'It's Saturday,' she said as I stood up, stretching out a hand, letting it drop back down on the bed. 'Where're you going?'

'Got to write,' I said. 'Woke up with something in my head.'

'Jeez Louise,' she said, closing her eyes and smiling as she repositioned herself into her pillow. 'Get it out, for God's sake. You know what happens when you don't.'

I made myself coffee, good and strong. Then I walked into

the front room, sat down at my computer, turned it on and for a minute or two looked at the screen, thinking of what should be there; of what would be there, when I was done. Once a very good friend of mine – another writer, needless to say – talked about how he thought we went about writing the things we wrote. It was, he said, like finding a magic place in childhood, somewhere in dark woods. But there is no map, and no sure way of reaching it the same way the next time, or of reaching it at all. The path is always there, no question about that; but until you come to it again you won't know for certain if you'll find your way in, much less find your way out. All you could do was head out every morning and see what turns up.

That morning I closed my eyes as I sat in my chair, and evoked anew what I had seen. The woods, the path, and what lay on the other side, were all there in front of me. Having seen this time what I needed to see, I started writing; and in time, wrote all that you have read.

IN THE NEW WORLD

James Fitzgerald Kennedy, an egg well left unseeded. Expelled, unnoticed, in September, 1932.

Chloe Josefyn Kugelberg, whose spikes at the net are wonders to behold, guarantees without bragging that the Swedish beach volleyball team will head home with Olympic gold. Her favourite things are horsemeat sausage, salt licorice, cloudberry pie, the songs of Lee Hazlewood (especially *Some Velvet Morning*, as sung with Nancy Sinatra), and the buttocks of Agnetha Falkstog, *circa* 1975.

Judetha TaShawn Williams, a.k.a Judy, Jude, Avalon, aced her finals at Stuyvesant, where she had since eighth grade controlled the in-house drug circulation network. While attending Yale on scholarship, majoring in business, controlled the 'White Triangle,' i.e., that portion of New England angled by New Haven, Boston and Manchester Center, Vermont through which (thanks to her far-sighted conceptualization) travelled an estimated one-third of all heroin entering the United States. After being graduated from Wharton oversaw the development of her new web site, through which any drug could be effectively bought and delivered anywhere in the world within twenty-four hours. A year later, shortly before announcing the date of her company's IPO, she was killed by a Portuguese Water Dog as she prepared to cross Third Avenue at 86th Street. Chasing a ball, it leapt off a 38th-floor balcony. ARFUL! read the *Post* headline. The web site still exists, though no search engine will find it.

John Bonney felt much more capable of handling difficult life situations once he ramped up to a 300-milligram daily dose of Wellbutrin.

Leverett Saltonstall Gladstone was the male fatality in the sole recorded instance of mutual autoerotic asphyxiation. 'We know very little about some aspects of human behaviour,' as J. C. Rupp, M.D. notes in his classic essay regarding a less elaborate case, *The Love Bug* (*Journal of Forensic Sciences*, Vol. 18, No. 3, July 1973).

Gogmagog St. John Bramhall Malloy lives with his lovely wife Allison and two children in the East End of London. As he rides the Jubilee Line into work each morning he thinks long and hard on how the neighbourhood used to be a halfway decent place until bloody fat bastard yuppies with their bloody mobiles started pouring in like cockroaches, making it fucking well difficult for sensible people to be able to get a bloody pint without having to hack a path through a wall of fat bastards who bloody well should have stayed in Cockfosters with their bloody assurance policies and Range Rovers where they bloody well belong instead of lowering the tone of Spitalfields and Hackney, and we won't even talk about the Isle of Dogs. Works in the garden on weekends, knows his delphiniums. In low moments, fantasizes taking a torch to the Millennium Dome. He hacks into his blancmange instead, and is right as rain once more.

Elvis Presley, doornailed in body for lo these twenty-four years, enters no Kalamazoo 7-11s, drives no Chevy SUVs, shoots no TVs, eats no cheeseburgers, waits in no bank lines in Lincoln, Nebraska, pumps no gas outside Bellingham, Washington; he blesses no magdalenes, heals no lepers, embraces no cripples, rips not asunder the curtain of the temple and darkens therefore no firmament. Nine hundred and seventeen restaurants around the world include on their menus dishes named after him. Some include bacon.

Isabel Bonney tested positive for tuberculosis on March 15, 1997. Six weeks later received diagnosis of multiple-drug-resistant form, type W. Treatment initiated immediately. Was isolated at Roosevelt-St. Luke's, in a room that looked as if it had been designed as the ultimate Phillipe Starck environment. Although AFB tests were foreseen to remain positive for eight months to forever – depending – she converted to negative in four and a half weeks. Her doctor okayed release on May 23. Went to St. Luke's-Roosevelt every day for eighteen months afterwards for directly-observed therapy; there took 1200 mg ciprofloaxin, 750 mg ethionamide, 750 mg cycloserin, 100 mg capreomycin injected into alternating hips, 900 mg isoniazid and 1200 mg myambutal daily. Developed arthritis of the knee brought on by ciprofloaxin, developed profound depression partially brought on by cycloserin (a.k.a. *psychoserin*, within the medical community), developed stomach trouble, lassitude, narcolepsy and numerous other symptoms that may or may not have been psychosomatic. Recovered, slowly. Finished chemotherapy after eighteen months, November 30 1998. Doctor proclaimed her to be well as she'd ever be. A year and a half later, she awoke one morning and at last felt returned to the world; no longer imagined she felt the rubber beneath the sheet, the dryness of constantly recirculated air; no longer saw the eyes of those who mattered above the masks; felt the uncontrollable coughing up blood, the 104-degree fever day in day out. No longer had the dreams. These terrible scenes were no longer any clearer than a tenth-generation videotape. They were only in her memory; she forgot them, deactivated them, she let them go; she removed them. She had the power, and she did it.

Vladimir Bulgarin, a.k.a Maliuta Skuratov, lives in Moscow and uses his 1974 Zhiguili to pick up those in need of rides. His standard rate is one ruble per kilometre. A drunken man from Trenton, New Jersey, once gave him a fifty-dollar bill over the protests of equally drunken Russian friends, but it was one of the new fifties and banks refused to accept it. He has lost nineteen teeth, his wife refuses to sleep with him. On days when he tires of driving he sometimes goes to the new underground mall in Manezh Square, listens to the instrumental music half-heard over speakers in the ceiling, and gazes at ceramic statues of Mafia thugs hollering into mobiles. Although he is loathe to admit it, he liked it better when you could call strangers *comrade*.

Oktobriana Osipova, with her mother, emigrated at age 15 to the United States. Worked, briefly, as a flashdancer in Kearney, New Jersey, employing the professional name Platynym Card. Quit after refusing to have breast implants, telling her boss she had no desire to be a *broiler chick*, i.e., factory-enhanced. She had no greater desire to work as a cosmetologist, fast-food employee, court interpreter, or waitress. With good old Russian know-how borrowed a Powerbook 145 and successfully hacked into Chase, NatWest, FirstUnion and Citibank N.A., deducted five cents from each account at every bank. FBI team arriving at

213

her Brighton Beach studio found the remnants of a charred female corpse, not hers. Spontaneous human combustion ruled out as cause of death. The suspect's present whereabouts, the institution or institutions to which she made electronic transferrals, and the total amount transferred from all banks remain unknown. Those who have studied the case believe that wherever she is, she is content with her lot.

Dr Alexander Arnoldovitch Alekhine, after the fall of the Soviet Union, moved from the field of ferrous metals to that of bartending. You may find him working the 6 to 2 shift at a bar called Pizdyetz, on Clinton Street between Rivington and Delancey in 'happenin'' LoEaSi (as some in the neighbourhood have taken to calling it, although none who have lived there longer than six months). His claim to fame is a brutal mixture of three parts Ketel One vodka, one part Chambord liqueur, one part Everclear grain alcohol, topped off with Ocean Spray cran-raspberry juice, stirred (not shaken) and served over finely-crushed ice. (A similar drink is served at finer Moscow establishments, Hermes men's cologne substituting in some cases for the grain alcohol.) He calls it a Red Mercury.

Norman Quarles, who during his Army days played bass clarinet in James Reese Europe's famed marching band, returned to the U.S. in time to die of the flu during the great pandemic of 1918–1919 that killed, among others, Randolph Bourne, Gustav Klimt, Egon Schiele, and two of the three children who'd witnessed the sun stand still at Fatima. Norman's father had wanted him to be a Pullman porter, but Norman had other ideas. His father never found out what they were.

Wanda Carroll [Quarles, in some pasts] applied for a job as a charwoman at the Empire State Building. The hiring

214

agency chose not to hire a Negro, and she was, happenstance, not killed when a twin-engine B-25 Army bomber crashed into the 78th floor of the structure on July 28, 1945. She found employment instead as a charwoman at 44 Broadway, had three children, and outlived them all.

Luther Biggerstaff, never married, served as a quartermaster in the New York National Guard, bought a house in Staten Island, had a heart attack in his driveway in 1998, died while his dog, a Toy Manchester Terrier, licked at his ears.

Avi Schwartz wasn't.

Bernard Pearlstein, a dentist, specializes in preparing multiple crowns and fixed bridges. Lives with his wife and two children in Upper Montclair, New Jersey. Used Nair on the backs of his hands until the use of rubber gloves became mandatory. He loves the smell of novocaine.

Gus Gleason, for a number of years, could have been working in an unofficial capacity for Gus Bevona, one-time head of Local 32B-32G. Knows all the words to 'Stickin' With the Union.' A good man to have around when an iron pipe needed to be swung in the dark. Presently serving twenty to thirty-five upstate, he could be out in three.

Lester Macaffrey would liked to have been a doctor but became a mortician instead, finding employment at W.H. Milward in Lexington, Kentucky. Loves to pore over old issues of *Casket and Sunnyside,* and perceives in the names of preparation dyes an almost epiphanic euphony. Sometimes, lying in his bed at night, in the small apartment off Newtown Road where he lives, he lets them roll over the tongue in his mind: *eosin, erythrosine, ponceau, fluorescein, amaranth, carmine.* Sometimes he thinks he hears voices, but chalks it up to the stress of living in interesting times.

Joanna, who never uses her last name among friends, lives on the Vermont side of Lake Champlain. She worked as a senior manager at Chemical Bank for twenty years until it merged with Chase Manhattan and she was laid off. Having invested wisely, she was prepared. Soon after moving she believed, one morning, she saw the legendary lake monster known as 'Champ' (thought, by cryptozoologists, to be a surviving representative of *Zeuglodon*) but everybody she told smiled, when she told them. She has twenty-seven cats. At night, in dreams, she flies.

Elmer Thatcher Dryden, Sr. Lived, briefly, in Nicholasville, Kentucky. In 1964, age 18, he decided to see how high he could get if he mixed bourbon and phenobarbital and then huffed two tubes of Testor's Airplane Glue. He found out. At the service the minister, trying to assuage the mourners, assured them that sometimes God's plans are not for us to know. 'Well,' his mother said, after the service, passing everyone thick slices of transparent pie once the chicken was gone, 'Surprised he lasted this long.' His father might have cried, had he still been alive, but he wasn't. His third wife shot him in 1959. Alcohol might have been involved.

Susie North (Dryden), married a fellow worker at the 53rd Street Doubleday in 1980, having initially gained his attention by climbing the store's spiral staircase, wearing a short dress, while he was stationed directly below. A year after their marriage she assured her husband that Thorazine was 'sort of like Valium.' After she left him, two years after that, he was sorting through her belongings when he found, secreted throughout their apartment, thirty-seven spiral-bound school notebooks. In each notebook she had written and rewritten, on every page, the same sexual fantasy: one involving herself, a 103 degree fever, a rectal thermometer, five jars of Fox's U-Bet Syrup, a jumping

216

rope in which seven granny knots had been tied, Sylvia Plath's poem *Elm*, a baby-doll nightgown (peach) with open-crotched panties (mauve), a porthole in a luxury cabin on a cruise ship, Spanish extra virgin olive oil, and long-time Boston cult sensation Jonathan Richman. Years later, he found himself unable to think 'all work and no play makes Jack a dull boy' without feeling heartfelt memories of his ex-wife.

E. Thatcher Dryden, Jr see Senior.

E. Thatcher Dryden III, see Junior.

ALICE is a gleam in the eye of a C+ + programmer who lives, in his car, in Menlo Park; and who has read *Neuromancer* far, far too many times.

Margot Lorenzo Padilla tires of explaining to her fellow sophomores at Hunter College that she is a physically challenged little person: not a dwarf, or a midget, or a freak; and that her name is neither Shorty, Tiny, Teeny, Peewee, Thumbelina, Tater Tot, El Loco Petito, or Fabulutmost Shrimpmeister. In chat rooms, in the evening, she is blonde, and five-foot six.

Enid O'Malley, twenty-one, lives with her mother in Ridgewood, Queens, and has twenty-four different piercings (lip, underlip, left nostril, right nostril, four in left ear, seven in right ear, left eyebrow, right eyebrow, left nipple, right nipple, navel, hood of clitoris, left labia majora, right labia majora, tongue). Misses the Duchess Club, but remains popular with the ladies. She favours steel-toed boots and her favorite novel is Bernard Wolfe's *Limbo*. She plans to switch her major from English to Business, in case.

Seamus O'Malley, a confirmed bachelor, walks yet never stops on Christopher Street. He avoids seeing his sister, Enid, whose lifestyle he frowns upon. He believes he would do reasonably well in the world of his favourite movie, *The Road Warrior*, and thinks he would look more like Mel Gibson if his eyes weren't so beady and his ears so big, although he wouldn't. In his workaday life he happily ascends the ranks at Big Apple Demolition, and has also developed a thriving sideline trade selling, on eBay stained glass, gold and copper fixtures, marble sinks and tubs, teak and mahogany woodwork, plaster mouldings rescued *in situ*, chandeliers, sconces, iron gates, lengths of tin cornice, stone gargoyles and grotesques and (when lucky) cast-iron storefront. Like most New Yorkers, though perhaps for different reasons, he never passes the Chrysler Building without heaving a sigh.

Jake, like Isabel, persists.

Walter Bullitt is a novelist whose seven books are generally considered to be science fiction (which may be so), and popularly believed to be written with the assistance of chemicals (perhaps self-generated). Deeply appreciated by a cult audience, most of whom he believes he personally knows. Five of his titles have been much read in Slovakia.

Eulalia Bax married Walter. They live happily in West Seattle, on S.W. Southern St., where Walter has easy access to the ferry to Vachon Island, and its mushrooms.

Lola Hart still thinks *Titanic* was the best movie she ever saw. Her girlfriend (who attends Nightingale, not Brearley, but these things can't be helped) is more of a Kate than a Leo.